"I HAVE A TRADITION INVOLVING WISHES."

"And what's that tradition?" Parker asked the question in a low murmur. By this time, he'd moved too close for comfort. What she ought to do was wish him away.

"I call it pillow talk," she said softly.

"And it has to do with wishes?"

She nodded.

"And can I make more than one wish?" Parker asked, stroking the bottomside of Meg's pinky finger.

"One or two," she said, her gaze fastened on his hand. He skimmed her forehand with his palm.

Before she could consider objecting to his caress, he tucked her long hair away from her cheek, and leaned close to kiss her. His seductive lips hovering over her mouth, he whispered, "And could I wish to spend more time with you?"

Other Avon Contemporary Romances by
Hailey North

BEDROOM EYES

Hailey North

Pillow Talk

AVON BOOKS ◆ NEW YORK

AVON BOOKS, INC.
1350 Avenue of the Americas
New York, New York 10019

Copyright © 1999 by Hailey North
Inside cover author photo by Don Cooper
Published by arrangement with the author
Library of Congress Catalog Card Number: 98-94823
ISBN: 0-380-80519-7
www.avonbooks.com/romance

First Avon Books Printing: July 1999

AVON TRADEMARK REG. U.S. PAT. OFF. AND IN OTHER COUNTRIES, MARCA REGISTRADA, HECHO EN U.S.A.

Printed in the U.S.A.

WCD 10 9 8 7 6 5 4 3 2 1

For the Man Who Broke the Mold

With a heartfelt thank-you to some very
special friends who helped keep me sane
during the writing of this one:

Deborah Harmse
Metsy Hingle
M. L. Christovich
Marie Goodwin
Betsy Stout
Keith Wagner

And a grateful acknowledgment to
Chris Dunham of ICD and
Sue Pulliam of ETD/Bayou Periodicals.
Thanks!

One

"D-dead?" Margaret "Call me Meg, please!" McKenzie Cooper Ponthier heard her voice rise. The wool suit she'd grabbed to cover her camisole dropped to her lap as she stared open-mouthed at the dark-eyed stranger who had entered her hotel room, key in hand. "Jules is dead?"

The man nodded, a grim turn to his lips.

Meg fumbled for the hotel robe she'd dropped beside the bed when she'd started trying on the outfits Jules had insisted on having sent over from Saks. She knotted the sash firmly, then stepped from where she'd been sitting on the king-size bed in which she'd slept alone after Jules had settled her in the room the previous night, before he had disappeared.

"Tell me two things," she said, drawing herself up to her full five feet four inches. "Who are you and how do you know he's dead?"

A dark shadow passed over the man's face. He clenched his fists and Meg knew there was no sense in protesting. This man had seen the

1

mask of death. She swallowed and tugged at the knot of her robe.

He stepped forward. His dark eyes had a storm brewing in them. He took in the rumpled covers of the bed, the dress boxes from Saks, then raked her with his gaze. The piercing survey began at her bare toes, ran her up calves, swept over the white terry robe, noted the curly jumble of her long brown hair and fastened on her mouth.

Meg felt as if he could see beneath her robe to the skimpy camisole and tap pants she'd tried on right before he'd opened the door. She opened her mouth to order him from her room, when he said, "Jules always did get his money's worth."

"And just what do you mean by that?" Meg's reaction was more alarm than indignation. Had Jules told someone why he'd hired Meg? "I'm asking you again, who are you?"

"Why? You always get your customer's identification before you take their cash?"

"Excuse me?"

The man shrugged and produced a smooth leather wallet. "Knowing Jules, he didn't pay you before he left. What's he owe you?" He fingered a hundred-dollar bill. "Two? Three?"

Meg stared at the cash. This man thought she was a hooker! She started to laugh at the preposterous notion, an urge that grew as she thought about what his reaction would be if she answered, "Twenty thousand dollars."

Instead of responding, she grabbed the phone. "If you don't leave this room in the next two seconds, I'm calling security."

"Look, honey, the jig's up. Money train's gone bye-bye." Several bills fluttered from his hand and landed on the bed. "Put your clothes on and get out. Take the new ones with you for all I care." The man's shoulders slumped and sorrow softened his expression. "Sugar daddy is never coming back."

Noting the sense of loss, Meg said once more but in a less demanding voice, "Who are you?"

He had crossed to the sofa on the other side of the large room. Over his shoulder, he said, "If you must know, I am Jules's brother."

His brother. Meg clasped a hand over her mouth to keep from responding. She wouldn't have reacted more strongly if he'd said the devil himself. Yet the resemblance was there. While Jules had been slimmer, almost effete, this man was solid, strength evident in his broad shoulders and a sense of purpose signaled by his bearing. Jules had worn polo shirts and slacks under his blazer; this man wore a white dress shirt and dark tie with his expensive suit.

A knock sounded at the door and both Meg and the man called, "Come in."

A uniformed hotel employee weighed down by a huge basket wrapped in purple and green cellophane walked in. "Excuse me, Miz Ponthier," the man said, "but the manager wanted to send these to you and Mr. Jules with his compliments."

Meg stared at the basket, admiring the magnum of champagne nestled among chocolates and beautifully polished fruits. Compliments? For a marriage for hire entered into out of desperation on her part, desperation born out of trying to hold her family together after her husband's untimely death a year ago and the resulting discovery that his legacy to her had been a financial quagmire that threatened to overwhelm the lives of her three children and herself.

He carried the basket in and settled it reverently on the low table in front of the sofa. As he lifted his head, he said, "Oh, Mr. Parker, sir, I didn't see you, what with the basket and all."

"Clinton, isn't it?"

The employee nodded.

"How's your mother?"

The man dropped his head and rubbed the raised seam along the outer leg of his uniform pants. "She's good some days, Mr. Parker, and not so good other days."

Meg stared as the man produced his wallet a second time and pressed a bill into the employee's hand. Jules had described his brother as the most tight-fisted man in the world, yet here he was opening his own purse for the second time to cover expenses that properly belonged to Jules.

When Jules had tried to persuade her to assist him in his plans, he had described his brother as ruthless, selfish, and utterly bent on having his own way in the management of the family's corporation, despite what was good for the family and the hundreds of employees. And that meant refusing to accept a buyout offer Jules had wooed from a multinational corporation, an offer that would leave everyone in the Ponthier family on easy street for the next several generations.

The brother knew Jules was dead. Was he responsible?

Meg shivered. The hotel employee was smiling and saying something in a low voice to Parker. She'd lost the thread of the conversation.

". . . the manager had it from the nighttime bartender who had it from Mr. Jules."

The man called Parker said, "Thank you, Clinton, and thank Mr. Stibbs for the basket."

Clearly dismissed, Clinton headed for the door.

"Wait!" Meg hated to be outdone. This man had delivered the gift to her and her—well, her husband. Jules had drilled into her during their flight from Las Vegas that she had to convince the family she was well-bred and dignified enough for Jules to have married.

She lifted one of the hundred-dollar bills Parker had tossed on the bed and pressed it into Clinton's hand. "My best to your mother," she said.

"Bless you," he said. "I hope Mr. Jules appreciates what a nice lady you are."

Meg glanced at Parker, who had one eye-brow raised in a cynical manner that really got her back up.

Clinton left the room, shutting the door behind him.

Meg and Parker faced one another from opposite sides of the celebratory basket.

She waited for him to speak. What the heck. He had to be just as surprised to meet his new sister-in-law as she was to meet her brother-in-law.

There was only one thing she really wanted him to say. She wanted to hear that Jules wasn't really dead.

"Overdoing it a bit, aren't you?" His voice was rough-edged and drawled just a bit too much for Meg's comfort. The slow winding of his question made her think of one of the many rattlers that loved to sun in the rocks outside Las Vegas, in the wild of the desert the city hadn't etched its name on.

"What do you mean?" She tried not to sound hostile; her situation was far from good right at this moment. She thought she'd been thrown for a loop when Ted died. But this!

The difference was Ted had been her husband for eleven years.

He gestured to the basket. "You and Jules. He told the bartender downstairs he'd decided to settle down. He never gave a thought about the reputation of the women he brought to this suite before. Certainly not enough to make up some bogus tale." Parker stroked his chin, eyes narrowing. "What's different about you?"

Meg wanted to slap him for his arrogance, for his refusal to give credit to the story. Then she realized he was running a critical eye over her body, cataloguing her as she stood there in the white terrycloth robe with its Hotel Maurepas insignia her only accessory. Even her feet were bare. She thrust her chin in the air and dared him to comment.

Which he did, being the arrogant jerk he was proving himself to be.

"I can see why he tried for a degree of respectability," Parker said, reaching down and undoing the bow that held the cellophane covering the gift basket. "You're certainly a step above his usual floozies."

"What did you say?" Meg heard the frost in her voice. No one talked to her this way. Back in the old days of her youth when she'd had to fend for herself in the girls' home, then been bounced from foster home to foster home, she'd learned the value of toughness, of defending herself.

"I said—" He looked up from the ribbon that he'd worked loose. "Look, whoever you are, there's no point in sparring. My brother is dead. I just identified him to the satisfaction of the New Orleans Police Department." His shoulders slumped and he let go of the ribbon. "I came here, to Jules's favorite place to hide from the world, for a few moments of peace to say good-bye to my brother, so why don't you get your things and run along and leave me in that peace?"

Meg stepped forward and with one swift jerk unfastened the ribbon. The cellophane fell open. She'd been of a mind to do just what Parker had suggested—get out of that room as fast as she could and find her way back to Las Vegas. With the several hundred dollars the s.o.b had flung onto the bed, she could have done just that.

But then she'd given Clinton a hundred dollars.

Besides, taking that money would mean accepting the implication she'd earned it from spending the night with Jules.

But this man needed to learn a lesson.

And she, Margaret "Call me Meg, please!" McKenzie Cooper Ponthier, was going to give it to him.

He sank onto the sofa and reached for the magnum of champagne. He turned it in his hands, hands that Meg saw held the heavy bottle without any show of effort. "He did like champagne," he said, rubbing a finger over the label.

"Yes, he did," she murmured, knowing full well Jules preferred bourbon and water. At least that's what he'd consumed at the Pinnacle Casino the night he'd asked her to marry him.

"And chocolate," Parker said, pulling out an

orange-foil-covered chocolate delicacy.

Meg murmured something that sounded like agreement. She had no idea what Jules liked. The only thing she'd seen him consume were the bourbon and waters she'd served him during her shifts at the Pinnacle's lobby bar. He'd skipped the peanuts offered on the flight to New Orleans, ordered dinner for her from room service and prowled about the room while she'd attempted to eat.

Then he'd disappeared on that mysterious errand and she'd not seen him again.

"And hazelnuts," Parker said, reaching for a handful of nuts in the basket. "I've got to hand it to Stibbs, he's got a great memory."

Meg nodded, surprised to hear something that sounded like a choked-back sob coming from the man seated on the sofa. Perhaps he really had come here to mourn his brother. But everything Jules had told her warned her otherwise.

"Nice show of sympathy," Meg said, thinking to feel him out.

He raised his head and his eyes bored into hers. "Only a fool talks of what they do not know," he said, his voice so low she had to lean forward to catch his words.

She felt as if he'd slapped her; then she realized the folly of him speaking those words.

"Now ain't that the truth," she said, mimicking his own drawling speech.

He cocked his brows.

She smiled.

"I'd like to be left alone," she said, walking to the door and holding it open. "With my memories of my husband."

He didn't even budge. "Hus-band?" He fingered several of the hazelnuts and gazed at her beneath lowered lids. "Look, I went along with that story when Clinton was here to salvage whatever is left of the family's reputation. But if you think I believe my brother married you, you're nuts. Jules was a snob and even though he messed up both his marriages, he always married his own kind."

This man was a snob, pure and simple. Meg bristled, forgetting that a stranger's opinion didn't matter a hill of beans to her. So what if he thought she was an expensive hooker. She should go home to Las Vegas and use the ten thousand dollars Jules had paid her in advance to bail out her family's finances.

Yet she couldn't stand to let this man judge her as a one-night stand who'd meant nothing to his brother. In an icy tone, she said, "Perhaps you didn't know your brother as well as you think. Because we did marry and I have the papers to prove it."

He rose from the sofa, his body uncoiling like a rattler changing position in the desert sun.

Meg started to retreat, then curled her bare toes into the lush carpet to steady herself. She did have the documents that showed she was

Mrs. Jules Ponthier III. Just let him dispute it.

She had no clue what would happen to Jules's plans for his family's company now that he was dead. He'd gone into a lengthy explanation of the complicated setup of the family corporation, but all Meg knew for sure was that by being married, Jules's voting power doubled. Whether she inherited that with his death, she had no idea.

Should she remain in New Orleans and do what she could for him? Meg was too stunned by the news of his death to process her decision. For the ten thousand dollars Jules had already paid her, did she owe him loyalty? He'd been kind to her, too, and kept his word about not jumping her body.

For that alone, Meg would carry out her end of the bargain. She held out her hand, every inch the grand lady Jules had wanted her to play. "Forgive me," she said, letting her words catch in her throat, "my distress over the news of Jules's death has kept me from remembering my manners. I'm Margaret Cooper—er, Ponthier. But call me Meg, please."

"Well, I'll be damned." The drawl had disappeared. Parker towered over her, his hands on the hips of his expensive wool suit pants. "I do believe you're serious."

Meg gave him what she hoped was an imperious stare. Hard to do garbed in a bathrobe, but determination helped. A lot.

Ever so slowly, he extended his right hand.

"Parker Ponthier," he said, staring at her hand as she accepted his overture.

She nodded. "The—er, younger—brother." Darn, but she'd almost said the words "evil." She flushed and observed that he seemed to notice. He retained her hand in his.

Without saying anything, he just kept holding her hand, his dark eyes studying, assessing, then he released his hold.

For a second, she wished he hadn't let go. She'd sensed in his touch a gentleness his words and his body language hadn't even hinted at. She'd felt, too, a connection with another person—face it, Meg—a man, she hadn't experienced in a long, long time.

"I see you were already busy spending his money," he said, jarring her with a scathing glance at the Saks boxes scattered across the bed. "At least you won't need to shop for the funeral."

Funeral. That word rang in Meg's mind. She still found it impossible to conceive of Jules as dead. She also didn't know how he'd met his end. As the grieving widow, she'd certainly be expected to ask. And as a caring human being who'd known the man only for a short time, she sincerely wanted to know. "How did Jules—die?"

Parker's response was a strangled sound that ended in a harsh laugh. He shook his head, then studied her with his head tilted to one side. "Just how well did you know your late husband, *Miz* Ponthier?"

He drew out the Miz so that it sounded about eight syllables long. Meg tried not to squirm and said, "Well enough. Why?"

"Then you should know he didn't go out fighting the worst demon of his life."

She licked her lips and wondered what in the world he meant. Having known Jules for less than three days, she was definitely at a disadvantage in this conversational parrying. So she waited, fingering the lapels on the bathrobe as she observed Parker warily, waiting for him to reveal enough information for her to form a response.

As she watched, Meg noticed the curve of his lips, the restrained power of his broad shoulders. She followed the line of his arm, admiring the graceful strength that Jules had lacked. Her eyes rested on his hand that had touched her own and she felt again the warmth of his skin.

Meg, Meg, you're in enough trouble! She hastily tucked her hand into the pocket of her robe. After what she'd done, she had no business responding to Parker Ponthier as a woman to a man, no matter how compelling she might find him.

Even though she'd sent Jules Ponthier packing when he'd first proposed what he termed a cut-and-dried business proposition, Meg had acquiesced when he persisted. It seemed to her to be an answer to her prayers on salvaging her family from financial ruin and she'd never been one to turn away from an opportunity.

But now, with Jules dead, this masquerade had reached a whole different level of complications than she'd imagined when she'd leapt feet first into the role of Miz Jules Ponthier the Third.

"Since you're obviously going to pretend you don't know what I'm talking about, I'll get to the point." He slammed one fist against the palm of the other hand. "He died trying to buy a few lousy grains of cocaine. But you wouldn't know anything about that demon or any other one, for that matter, would you?" He was practically shouting and Meg kept from flinching by telling herself he was understandably upset. He'd just lost his brother.

She licked her lips and let him rave on.

"He'd been clean for almost a year. Then—" he pointed to her "—off to Las Vegas for the weekend and he's hooked again."

Jules hadn't seemed high to her, not that she knew much about drugs. Mulling over the question, she let the implied accusation slide. Naturally she hadn't had anything to do with Jules's decision to purchase cocaine. Meg hardly even drank alcohol, had never smoked marijuana, and certainly had no knowledge of cocaine. Jules had been jittery, she admitted, and he hadn't eaten much of anything. "Where did it happen?"

"Three blocks behind the hotel."

"How—how do you know for sure he was buying drugs?"

He threw her a look that said she would be a fool to think he ever spoke from less than a position of knowledge. "He bought it from an undercover cop and when she tried to arrest him they fought over her gun."

"The police killed him?" Meg heard the shock in her voice. Poor Jules. What a way to die. And with all he'd said about how his family had such social position and cared so much about what society thought of them!

Parker shook his head, then dropped to the sofa. From behind his hands, he said, "He shot himself with the officer's gun."

"Oh, no. Why would he do that?"

Parker lowered his hands to his knees. Speaking almost to himself, he said, "Perhaps he couldn't take the disgrace."

"That's the stupidest thing I've ever heard." Meg paced to the sofa then back towards the door. "Being arrested isn't the end of the world. You're innocent until proven guilty, even—" She stopped. She'd heard from visitors to Las Vegas that in many ways New Orleans was like a third-world country.

"Even in New Orleans? Even when you tussle with the NOPD?" Parker shook his head. "He couldn't have taken people knowing he was back on drugs again." He clenched his fists and beat on his thighs. "He could have been so much more. His entire life he fucked up in the stupidest, most senseless ways, but he didn't have to end that way."

He stared across the sitting area towards the fireplace as if seeing images of his brother playing there. Quietly, Meg crossed back to the sofa and sat gingerly on the edge. A rush of sympathy guided her hand. She touched his arm but did not speak. She knew only too well how little words helped with the loss of a loved one.

She stroked the sleeve of his wool suit, soothing him the way she caressed Samantha's soft curls when she awoke frightened from a bad dream.

Slowly he pulled his focus from across the room, shifting to stare down at her hand. His jaw worked, then he flung her hand off. "Don't try to get sweet with me. For whatever reason, he was using again and you're the only new factor in the equation."

Meg cradled her hand as if it had been burned. "Any idiot knows no one but an addict is responsible for his behavior. Or didn't you take Psychology 101?"

He gestured toward the boxes overflowing with expensive clothing. "It doesn't take a psychologist to figure out your interest in my brother was monetary, so don't try to sound so sweet and caring."

"I hope you don't think—"

He threw her a look of mock horror. "Oh, no, marry for money? Not little Miss Innocence. Come on baby, what were you? A Vegas call girl who trapped my brother in a moment of weakness?"

Meg opened her mouth to protest then snapped her lips shut. His words rankled, but he'd gotten a little too close to the truth.

"Hit home, did I?" He rose and hands on his hips, looked down at her. "Everyone in town knew he had a steady girlfriend. So why would he fly off for the weekend and come back married?"

"He what?" Meg couldn't believe what Parker had just said. Why had Jules needed a wife if that was true? Then she narrowed her eyes, remembering Jules's words of warning about his brother. *Parker will do anything to win.*

"You heard me. If you don't have any legal proof you were married, you're going to be in quite an awkward spot."

Any thoughts Meg had of turning tail and hitchhiking home to Vegas, leaving the Ponthiers to their own mess, disappeared as her temper flared. "You are one arrogant son of a—" Meg caught herself just in time. Swearing like a sailor was just what Jules would not have wanted her to do. He'd been most particular about the type of woman she had to portray and after hearing what a snob his brother was, she could understand why.

His right brow quirked.

She leapt up, then gathering her dignity, pulled the lapels of her robe tightly against her neck. She took her time strolling to the armoire where Jules had stored his buttery soft leather portfolio, an item she guessed cost more than all the pairs of shoes she owned combined. Reaching inside, she pulled out the marriage license bearing her and Jules's names.

She turned around.

He'd followed her.

The document slapped against his chest. Watching her expression a little too closely for Meg's comfort, he lifted it from her hands and read it without stepping back. Her breath came too quickly and she fought the urge to push him away.

He scowled as he scanned it, then fingered the raised seal. "Yesterday?"

Meg nodded, still trying to breathe properly. Her chin was level with the knot of his tie.

His brows rose. She was so close she could see the front of his shirt rustling slightly from the rise and fall of his lungs and the pounding of his heart. She inched backwards to the armoire.

He said again, "Yesterday." This time the question had left his voice.

"Yes."

He handed the certificate back to her. Eyes dark and unreadable, he said the words that stopped her breath completely.

"The family will expect you at the house within the hour."

Two

"The—house?"

Parker looked at her as if she'd said something extraordinarily stupid. "Even though Jules preferred hiding away in this suite, he did have rooms both at Sugar Bridge and Ponthier Place."

Meg furrowed her forehead at the lofty-sounding names. What kind of life had she stumbled into? Then she caught herself. Forcing a smile, she said, "Of course I knew that. I was just . . ." She trailed off, then glanced over at the bed, anywhere other than at this man who seemed to be able to see through her and certainly stood far too close to her.

"Wondering what to wear?" Parker, at last, stepped back and Meg inched away from the armoire. When he stood there staring at her, she wished she'd backed into the safety of the clothes closet and slammed the doors shut. "You look better in a bathrobe than any other woman I've ever seen, so I think you'll be able to pass muster."

"Oh." Meg digested that statement, figuring he must not have seen too many females in bathrobes, then said, "Thank you."

Parker laughed, that dry, not-funny sound again. "Don't thank me and don't think I'm going to accept that marriage license you waved in front of my face without verifying it myself."

He'd closed the space between them as he spoke, and Meg found herself having that problem breathing again as he reached with one hand and tipped her chin upwards. For the wildest moment, she thought he was going to kiss her. And God help her, she knew she'd like it.

Instead he said slowly, as if weighing his observation, "Jules did have a soft spot for a pretty face, and you are one gorgeous woman." He dropped his hand and said, "Welcome to New Orleans, Mrs. Ponthier. I'll be back for you in an hour."

Then, before she could figure out just what he'd been trying to prove, he was gone.

The man was not only arrogant, he was ridiculing her and his brother too. Because she most definitely was not a gorgeous woman. Meg hugged her arms to her chest and did the most comforting thing she could think to do.

She called home.

Seated crosslegged on the sprawling bed, she

dialed Mrs. Fenniston's number. The cost for calling from the hotel had to be exorbitant, but Meg squeezed her eyes shut tight as she waited for someone to answer on the other end.

Jules was dead, but Meg knew the bill would be paid.

She'd already called twice, and each time gotten only Mrs. Fenniston's dignified voice on the answering machine, with the message that the children were fine and keeping busy. But Meg wanted to talk to them, to hear their voices and hug them long-distance.

Or maybe she was the one who needed the hugs. Here she was alone in a strange city, the man she'd traveled with shot to death in a sordid and unnecessary encounter. The crusader in her bristled as she thought of the policewoman involved in Jules's death; but the mother in her couldn't blame the authorities. Drugs were a scourge and if Jules had been trying to buy, well, he shouldn't have been.

Still . . . to die for such a senseless reason.

Meg sighed and wondered why no one answered the phone. Then she checked her watch. Almost noon in New Orleans was ten in Las Vegas. Perhaps they'd gone to breakfast. Or church. Mrs. Fenniston was very big on church. She could've turned on the answering machine, though.

An electronic voice broke into her call and reminded her none-too-gently that her party wasn't answering and that she should try the call again later.

Meg slammed the receiver down, then lifted it and returned it much more nicely to its resting place. She wouldn't have let Teddy or Ellen get away with such behavior and there was no reason for her to display such temper.

No reason at all.

Hah!

She leapt from the bed and began to pace the room, the skirt of her bathrobe billowing behind her as she worked herself into a frenzied tempo. From the bed to the fireplace over to the armoire, where Parker Ponthier had practically held her captive. From the armoire to the couch, where he'd sat, staring at her, his gaze measuring, judging, condemning.

How dare he.

Meg walked faster. She shrugged out of the robe, changed from the satin camisole that she'd found in the Saks packages back into her UNLV t-shirt she'd slept in, one of the few pieces of her meager traveling wardrobe. Not exactly what your traditional bride packed for her honeymoon, but then, she wasn't your typical bride.

That thought sent her to the sofa. She dropped her head in her hands, much the same gesture Parker had made earlier.

What was she supposed to do now? Show up at the family home playing the grieving widow?

What else could she do?

Confess. Hand back the ten thousand dollars minus plane fare back to Las Vegas and resume her job at the Pinnacle. Return the wardrobe. Give Mr. Parker Ponthier the satisfaction of proving her a phony. Hard as it all would be—this last would be the worst.

Meg dropped back on the bed and hugged one of the pillows to her chest. Laying her cheek against the fine cotton cover, she closed her eyes and asked herself what she'd want one of her children to do. She tried so hard to teach them to make choices that added up to the right decision.

She'd done the wrong thing by letting herself be tempted into Jules's plan. Even though she'd done it to pull her family out of turmoil, she'd closed her eyes to the consequences. And now she was paying the price.

But she'd been tired of watching her children pay the price for their father's shocking financial mismanagement. Since his death, Meg had been confronted by the ruin of his company, the loss of their home, and the realization that he'd cashed in his life insurance policy without ever telling her.

Three days work for thirty thousand dollars had seemed like manna from heaven. She could finish college, get a better job, and pay off the nastiest of the creditors.

Now Jules was dead.

As embarrassing as it was, she really should tell the Ponthier family the truth.

She stroked the pillowcase, opened her eyes and reached for the phone to call home again. As she touched the receiver, the bell rang.

She jumped and clutched the pillow.

"Silly," she said aloud, "it's either for Jules or Mrs. Fenniston's finally home."

The phone pealed again.

Yet she hesitated. If it were for Jules, she'd have to make some explanation; she couldn't chicken out by just taking a message. Truth had to be faced. But if it was Mrs. Fenniston, why then she could talk to Ellen and Teddy, and Samantha.

The ringing continued, and to Meg's agitated imagination, the volume seemed to increase.

"Okay, okay!" She snatched it up. "Hello!"

"Mrs. Ponthier, please," an authoritative baritone voice ordered.

"Mrs. P-onthier?"

"Yes, this is Dr. Prejean calling."

"Y-yes?"

"Am I speaking with Mrs. Jules Ponthier?" A note of impatience sounded clearly on the line.

"May I ask why you're calling?"

"Only if you're Mrs. Jules Ponthier." The voice was dryer this time, but still impatient.

"Well, when you put it like that, then, yes I am." Like it or not, the statement was true.

"Mrs. Ponthier," he said, stretching the three

syllables of the name out longer than Meg really cared to hear it, "I have just left Teensy's bedside. She is taking this tragic loss as hard as you might expect, and by the way, may I offer my condolences also"—he kept right on, not even pausing and Meg just knew he disapproved of her very existence and more specifically of her hasty marriage to the deceased—"but it is my considered opinion that your presence may be the only comfort Teensy will have to support her through this grievous loss."

Ever mindful of her manners, Meg mumbled a thank you over the caller's barrage of words. But who in the world was Teensy? Better yet— "Excuse me," Meg finally managed, "but how did you get my number?"

"It's Jules's suite," he said, as if that explained everything.

"But how did you know *I* was here?"

"Am I or am I not speaking to Mrs. Jules Ponthier?" The impatience had bloomed far beyond a tinge.

"Yes, but how did you know about me?"

Silence ruled the line.

Finally, the man said, "You're not from here, are you?"

She shook her head, then said, "No." What a silly question. Why would she be in a hotel if she were from New Orleans? Then again, Jules had lived in a hotel. Meg shook her head, wondering if the ring-a-ding-buzzing in her head was what a boxer who'd spent too many rounds in the ring experienced.

"You'll come to learn what a small town this is, my dear," he said, a trifle more kindly, and in almost a paternal way. "The point of my call is to warn you that only your presence makes Teensy's grief bearable. She is greatly comforted by the knowledge that her son found love in the last days of his—uh—" He hesitated, then continued with "—somewhat troubled life. With you here to stand beside Teensy she may just make it."

Meg swallowed and stared at the telephone. *Jules's mother!* Oh, what had she done? She pictured an older woman prostrate with grief from her son's death reeling from Meg's revelation that her son had hired a wife to undo his brother. "What would happen to Teensy if I for some reason weren't able to stay by her side?"

"Where else would you be? She's your mother-in-law."

"It's only a hypothetical question."

"Leave those to the lawyers." He cleared his throat. "I shouldn't be discussing her case with you, but you are family now. My prognosis would be complete breakdown. As it is she's fragile, extremely fragile. Like an impatiens planted in full sun." He sighed. "But I'll be at the house around the clock, just in case."

Meg almost would have guessed the doctor had a severe crush on Jules's mom. Jules's frail and dotty mom. Meg shook her head. She'd only read the Cliff Notes of the Tennessee Williams books she'd been assigned in freshman English, but somehow she recognized some pretty stock southern characters on stage here.

She also recognized a cry for help when she heard it.

"*Complete* breakdown?" she asked.

"She was sobbing her heart out before I gave her a sedative. But she kept saying, at least he found love."

Meg gripped the phone, wondering if her guilt came through in her voice. Ever-so-slowly, she said, "I'll be at the house within the hour. Will she be able to see me then?"

Parker Ponthier thrust his Porsche into fourth gear and glared at the cell phone he'd tossed onto the passenger seat soon after roaring away from the Hotel Maurepas. What had possessed him to tell that meddling quack Prejean that Jules had a wife stashed at the hotel?

If her existence remained his secret, he might have reasoned with her. Even though he'd promised to return for her in an hour's time, he might have thought of some way to worm the truth of her marriage from her. He could have paid her off, if necessary, to save the family any further embarrassment.

His business instincts, naturally savvy and sharpened over the years he'd run Ponthier Enterprises, told him she was up to no good. Or maybe it was the combination of this unknown woman thrust upon them by Jules, who had always been up to no good in one way or another.

His survival instincts shouted the same thing.

What a woman, though.

When he'd entered Jules's suite, he'd stopped short at the sight of her. She'd looked almost childlike, sitting crosslegged on that massive bed. Her hair tumbled down over her shoulders, dark and slightly curly and tousled in the way beautiful women looked after making love for hour after passionate hour.

His gut had tightened at that thought.

This beauty in a bathrobe had to be up to no good.

"So you tossed her a couple of hundreds, insulted her thoroughly, and only then paused to get the facts." He heard the derision in his voice as he spoke aloud. But how was he to know? Jules used to brag that he kept his suite year-round for entertaining whores and mistresses.

Great way to get to know his sister-in-law.

Sister-in-law.

Parker had to repeat that title to himself. Here he was thinking of the woman in Jules's suite as room service for a starving man's appetites.

What if she turned out to be Jules's legitimate wife? Parker sensed something awry, but out of respect for his dead brother, he reined in his hungry thoughts. It wasn't that woman's fault Parker hadn't been with a female for more than a month.

With Jules dead, there'd be pressure on Parker to settle down. In the flash of the gun that had killed Jules, Parker had become the elder son.

Parker tightened his mouth. A harsh heat tugged at the corners of his eyes. Jules had been the first born but Parker had always played the role of the elder brother. Perhaps if he hadn't, perhaps if he'd abdicated the responsibility, or refused to cover for Jules time after time the way he had, Jules wouldn't be lying in the morgue.

The traffic edged ahead, then sped up as a tour bus pulled over to let the jam clear itself. Parker didn't want to think of his brother dead. He wanted to think of him at his best before he'd bowed out on his responsibilities and let drugs and booze and all the wrong women dull his pain.

It was easier to think of this woman Jules had left behind and focus his anger on her than it was to accept that for Jules there were no more chances.

Poor Jules.

Parker knew two things for sure. One, his brother was dead. And two, when Jules had left for Las Vegas three days ago, it had been within hours of a stormy meeting between the two of them, an encounter during which Jules

had threatened to do whatever it took to get
Parker to agree to the buyout offer for Ponthier
Enterprises.

Whatever it took. Parker mulled over that
phrase and wondered what it had taken for
Margaret "call me Meg, please" to marry a
man she scarcely knew.

Money? A chance to better herself? The
promise of luxury? A fancy wedding ring?

He frowned. He played the image of her
hand over in his mind. Surely she'd worn only
a thin gold band, a ring that looked lost on the
tapered fingers of her hand, and not at all the
type of ring Jules had given to either one of his
previous wives.

Of course, most of the women Parker dated
wanted a ring on their fingers at any cost. But
none of the ones in his circle—or Jules's—
would have settled for such an inexpensive se-
lection.

Perhaps Jules had promised her the family
diamond and emerald ring both his first and
second ex-wives had graciously returned. No
doubt that explained the temporary gold band.
Parker remembered his ex-fiancee's curiosity
over the Ponthier heirloom. Jules had divorced
and sworn never to remarry at the time Parker
had found himself engaged to Renee DuMont.
That knowledge must have prompted Renee to
inquire whether the famous ring would be offered to her.

Parker grimaced and settled into a crawl behind yet another tour bus that had positioned itself in the middle of the avenue. He hated to remember how foolishly he'd behaved over Renee. His engagement to her was the only thing he'd ever done that pleased his mother, a fact that should have tipped him off much earlier to the mistake he was making.

Renee and the other women of her class—Parker's class, to be sure—held college degrees and reasonably responsible jobs. But given the chance, and the ring on their finger, they exchanged their business suits for designer dresses, white gloves and round-the-clock nannies.

But Parker didn't want to spend his life with a woman who played at the job of wife and mother. He wanted someone who tackled it from the heart. Having grown up with a socialite mother who cared more about who painted the family portrait than whether her children felt loved, Parker had promised himself he'd remain single his entire life rather than enter into a marriage that was for show only.

Recently Parker had taken to dating professional women his age or older. Trouble was, with those women, he came in last in terms of their time and attention.

"You're a greedy sort, you know." He said the words aloud and smiled at himself. It was true. He did want it all—a woman who wanted to love him and only him, put him first in her sphere, and not insist he settle down to creating a nest full of children and so many demands he couldn't work late if and when he needed or wanted to. In turn, he knew himself capable of worshipping the right woman. The intensity he brought to work he would bring to the woman he loved.

Renee hadn't understood why he couldn't put business pressures aside to attend all the social functions she insisted were equally as important to a man of his position. Their final fight had occurred when he'd forgotten he was escorting her to a Carnival ball and driven hours southwest of the city to check on some sugarcane production problems. Renee had been furious that she had to go alone. The next day Parker had apologized but she'd handed back the ring, fury in her green eyes.

Parker still held out the hope that Renee and all the others just weren't right for him and when he found that perfect someone, he'd achieve the necessary balance in his life without prompting.

Last month he thought he'd found a good prospect. Lucille was the rare female who'd reached the position of managing partner of an important law firm, a spot normally held by a member of the old boys' network. True, she worked eighty-hour weeks, but when they met for lunch during the week or dinner on the weekend, she clearly signaled her interest in him as a man.

Three weeks into seeing her, Parker had taken her to dinner at Louis XVI in the French Quarter. She'd been all over him, holding his hand, grazing her leg against his under the table. By the time he'd gotten back to her condo in the Warehouse District, he knew he wasn't leaving that night without them having sex.

He'd packed his condoms. He was ready for action.

As he recalled the scene that had followed their entry into her apartment, Parker groaned, then found himself laughing as he drove.

He had her out of her suit within minutes. He'd lifted her and carried her across the sterile, white-carpeted living room. She had her lips on his in a lock that wouldn't break. He dropped her on the bed and reached for his belt and zipper simultaneously.

She lay back on the bed, wearing only her bra, panties, and nylons—nylons that snaked only to her thighs where they were fastened with beguiling black garters. Parker dropped his pants as he unbuttoned his shirt. He spent far too long between women, trying to find the right one.

"Sugar," she'd said, lifting her foot and stroking his crotch, "there's just one thing we need to do before we proceed."

"Right." Parker reached for his pants pocket and fished out a condom. "Don't worry, we're covered." He winked and ripped open the packet.

She sat up.

Suddenly, she looked a hell of a lot more like a trial lawyer arguing a point with a judge than a passionate woman about to drive him wild in bed.

She pulled out the drawer in her bedside table and tossed a piece of paper towards him.

Parker bent and picked it up. "What's this?"

Fishing in the drawer, she said, "Something you need to read and sign before we proceed. It shouldn't bother you; the word on the street about you is you're the last man in New Orleans who wants to be saddled with a kid." She faced him and held out a pen.

"Read and sign?" He heard the note of danger in his voice, but the lawyer, for all her cleverness, missed the signal.

Leaning forward, she stroked his balls through his underwear and said, "Just a little fine print to make sure we're on the same page."

Her hand was hot and her fingers kneaded him in a greedy, knowing way. Parker squirmed, then crumpled the paper and tossed it over his shoulder.

"What are you doing?"

"Who needs a document at a time like this?" He dipped his head and kissed her leg at the top of her stocking.

She stilled his head with a firm grip. "If you don't read and sign it, you have to leave."

Oh my God, Parker remembered thinking.

She's serious. "Okay, you're the lawyer. Why don't you tell me what it says?" And even as he said the words, his desire waned.

"Sure, but you still have to sign your own name." She leaned forward and cupped him again. Her breasts pushed over the lacy top of her bra. She whispered, "The terms are straightforward. It's a release of liability from any consequences that may result from our engaging in intercourse."

"Such as?" If she'd known him better, there's no way she would have missed the dangerous lowering of his voice.

"Infectious diseases and/or pregnancy."

"You're releasing *me* from liability if *you* get pregnant?"

"Yes, but more importantly, paragraph two, clause two, gives me sole custody should any child result from this coupling."

Parker removed her hand from his crotch and stepped onto the floor. He looked down at her. Her lips were parted, her pupils had grown so dark they'd taken over most of her green eyes. She wanted it, yeah, but what kind of woman acted this way? How had he even considered going to bed with her? "And you thought I'd sign this?"

She wet her lips and lay back on the bed. Her full breasts teased him. "Why not? Mr. Work-a-holic Ponthier couldn't be bothered with a kid."

He reached for his pants. Zipped his fly. His

breath came fast and he was harder than a green stalk of sugar cane. "Babe," he said, "you don't know me well enough for me to screw you."

Then he turned and left her place.

And that fiasco had been the last time he'd been in bed with a woman, successful professional or otherwise.

No wonder he'd reacted so strongly to the woman in Jules's suite. She'd been half naked when he first walked in. He'd caught a glance of a silky garment that scarcely covered her crotch before she grabbed some clothing and then the bathrobe to cover herself.

Yeah, that's all it was, Parker told himself, pulling into the circular drive at Ponthier Place, the family's mansion on St. Charles Avenue. Of all the visits he'd made since he'd moved out of his childhood home, he dreaded this one the most.

Maybe that was why, as he got out of his Porsche and climbed the stairs to the side entrance, he let the image of the dark-haired beauty with her shapely legs drift in, then fill his mind. And as the picture formed, Parker didn't mind at all that he had to return to the hotel in less than an hour to collect the woman his brother had sent tumbling into their lives.

Three

Meg stood under the awning in front of the Hotel Maurepas, shivering from the breeze ruffling her lightweight coat and the maroon material of the overhang that stretched from the door to the sidewalk.

Or was she shivering from something other than the brisk wind? In response to the doorman's whistle, a cab pulled over and Meg stepped toward it. She'd decided to face the Ponthiers on her own, without waiting for Parker.

The power of the Ponthier name both frightened and intrigued her. When she'd called down to the front desk earlier to say she was leaving, she'd had no idea what to say about checking out. The manager had come on the line and assured her he'd have her luggage sent over to the house and she wasn't to worry her head over a thing.

Meg smiled at the doorman, who had just finished instructing the cab driver in a grave voice that he was to deliver her to Ponthier Place. She slipped him a tip from her slim cash supply and settled into the cab.

Out of the breeze, she still shivered slightly, which answered one of her many questions. Well, a little stage fright was good for any performer.

The cab pulled into the traffic on a street whose lanes were separated by a broad grassy area lined with tracks. Good, she was on her way.

And without Parker Ponthier's assistance.

Parker wasn't going to like it when he returned to collect her and found her gone. He'd probably never been disobeyed in his bossy life.

"Good," she muttered. Parker made her feel like she'd gotten dressed in someone else's skin. Right now she needed all the composure she could muster.

Folding her chilled hands in her lap, Meg looked out the window. The cab moved at a sedate pace up the wide, tree-lined street. Leaning forward, she asked the driver, "Why are there train tracks in the middle of the street?"

"Those are the St. Charles streetcar tracks." The driver spoke matter-of-factly, as if the simple description explained everything.

Just then a streetcar lumbered up alongside where the cab had stopped at a red light. With a screeching that would have done an angry parrot proud, it ground to a halt.

The kids would love to take a ride. Meg registered a pang of guilt at that thought. She missed her children terribly. The only times she'd been away from Teddy and Ellen were when they'd gone to sleepover camp last summer and when she'd been in the hospital when Samantha was born. The last time she and Ted had spent a vacation alone had been their honeymoon. And in the last two years before his death, Ted had protested he'd been too busy at work to go away.

Three days felt like a lifetime. Both the cab and the streetcar moved forward and Meg wondered how soon she could extricate herself from the Ponthiers. Mrs. Fenniston was a dear, not to mention a lifesaver, but even a saint wouldn't want to be saddled with someone else's children much more than three days.

She'd console Jules's mother, attend the funeral, then slip out of their lives.

Her attention was captured by an imposing three-story brick building reigning behind an iron grillwork fence. Black shutters emphasized the story-high windows, accentuating the graceful lines of the edifice and drawing the eye upward toward a gleaming cupola and bell tower. "What a magnificent building! What is that?"

"Sacred Heart Academy," the driver rattled off. He half-turned in his seat and pronounced,

"The people that's got money, they like to send their girls there."

"It's an all girls school?"

He nodded.

It sure didn't look like any of the schools in Las Vegas. Meg glanced through the back window of the cab. It looked far too starchy for Ellen's tomboy tastes but she could see Samantha, sweet and precious, modeling a uniform and walking sedately up the broad stone steps.

Then she shook her head. Whatever was she thinking?

The cabbie offered, "I guess you're not from here."

"Oh, no, I'm from Las Vegas," Meg answered, admiring a smooth stone marble gray building that took up most of a block.

"Vegas, eh? You got some gambling there, don't you? I like to play the slots myself, but this city sure has messed up its gambling business."

"Really?" Having grown up in Las Vegas, Meg couldn't fathom any municipality unable to effectively milk such a cash cow. But then, she had no idea how her own husband had mangled his business affairs so badly she now faced bankruptcy, either.

Life had been comfortable, but their postage-stamp three-bedroom house had never been good enough for Ted. Meg had been content, visiting with her neighbors while the children's friends played with them on the quiet street.

But Ted was embarrassed and entertained his business clients at restaurants rather than bringing them to the toy-cluttered house with its tiny dining room.

His financial services company did fairly well but he dreamed of bigger and better things, a dream that grew to an obsession and led him to disastrous borrowing and mis-guided investments that he'd hidden from Meg.

"It's all about politics and greed," the cabbie said, shaking his head. "The rich get richer and the poor just get taken for another ride."

Not wanting to dwell on the poor getting poorer, a thought too close to her own circum-stances, Meg changed the subject by asking how far it was to Ponthier Place. She was get-ting nervous over the cab fare.

"Above Napoleon and below Jefferson."

"And that means?"

He grinned. "Sorry, I forgot—"

"—I'm not from here," Meg finished for him.

"Next block," he said, slowing down.

Looking ahead, Meg saw three imposing houses on the right and wondered which one was Ponthier Place. On the other side of the avenue, a sprawling mansion with broad porches and an inviting circular drive occupied the entire block. "Is that another school?"

The cabbie smiled as if she'd said something clever, then swung in a U-turn to the other side

of the street. Before Meg could register what
he was doing, they'd passed through the brick
posts standing guard at the mansion's drive.

"Here you are," he said.

"This—" Meg swallowed "—this is Ponthier
Place?"

"Was yesterday. Is today. And to hear tell of
that family, it most likely will be tomorrow."
The driver nodded, then threw the car into
park. He closed out the meter and Meg was
fishing in her purse when she heard the cab
door creak open.

Looking up, she saw an older black man
dressed in a double-breasted white jacket and
gray pants holding out a white-gloved hand to
her. She glanced from the cab driver to the
man, then decided to slide out of the car before
she paid the driver. Something about the way
the white-jacketed man waited unnerved her.
He expected, Meg realized, for her to let him
take over.

As she stepped from the cab, accepting the
offered arm of the now gently smiling man,
Meg said, "I still have to pay for the cab."

"You go on inside, Miz Ponthier, and I'll
take care of everything."

"Oh, I'm not—" Meg's eyes widened and
she said, "Call me Meg, please!"

The man nodded. "Very well, Miz Meg. I am
Horton."

And Horton's job was to take care of things.
Meg backed away from the cab up the sweep

of steps that led to the side of the largest house she'd ever been privileged to visit.

Privileged?

Meg shivered again and rubbed her hands together, then tucked them in her pockets. Whoever lived inside this house would take one look at her and know Jules hadn't really meant to marry her. Even the orphanage where Meg had lived her early years hadn't been as large as Ponthier Place.

The double French doors opened and Meg paused halfway up the steps to see who'd come to greet her. After encountering Horton, she half-expected a uniformed maid to drop a curtsy. Instead, she looked straight into the stormy eyes of Parker Ponthier.

The last person Parker had expected on the doorstep of the family home was Jules's post-humous bride. He'd already withstood the condolences of one great aunt, one cousin, Jules's boyhood pal and fellow dilettante Kinky de LaSalle, and Dr. Prejean, all of whom were now gathered in the Great Parlor.

That congregation had him looking forward to the escape offered by the necessity of retrieving the widowed Mrs. Ponthier from the Hotel Maurepas. Now with her arrival he was pretty much trapped. Parker frowned at the thought.

"You're not at all happy to see me, are you?"

Parker ignored her comment and glanced out to where Horton had finished his business with the cabbie and begun his slow walk back

to the steps. Horton never hurried. Facing her,
Parker said, "No doubt that's why you took a
cab." Annoying woman.

Unfortunately, Parker thought, this woman
wasn't just annoying. She was stubborn, gutsy,
intelligent. And attractive. She leaned slightly
forward, and even beneath her coat, her figure
caught his eye. Her dark eyes flashed a challenge at him, as if daring him to continue gazing at her body. Parker mastered his thoughts,
and as he did, he realized he remained in the
doorway, effectively blocking her entry.

By this time, Horton had climbed the steps
and waited, not without a slight frown suggested in his bland expression. Around Horton, the long-time family retainer who
functioned as butler, houseman, and surrogate
father, even Jules had minded his manners.

And so under Horton's watchful gaze, Parker forced himself to move and held the door
wide. "Welcome to Jules's home," he said, the
words almost lodging in his throat.

From Horton, Parker received an approving
nod. From Meg, a wide-eyed stare. She did,
however, precede him into the foyer.

"You might have waited for me," he murmured.

She shot him a look that warned she could
hold her own against him. "I'm not in the habit
of waiting for people who insult me."

Parker raised his brows. She could indeed
hold her own.

"May I take your coat, Miz Meg?"

She smiled and started to shrug out of a lightweight coat that couldn't have done much to shield her from the wind that had kicked up the otherwise calm December afternoon.

"I'll do that," Parker said, catching the coat as she let it slip from her arms. In his mind, he saw himself not stopping with her coat, but moving to free her of her other clothing. He grasped her coat and pushed the wayward image from his mind.

Instead of thanking Parker, Meg bestowed a genuine smile on the houseman as he nodded, loosed the coat from Parker's grasp, and stepped back.

It wasn't at all the same sort of smile she'd given him. No, that had been more of a challenge, a gesture that proclaimed, "You won't catch me at my game and by the way, I don't like you either."

A prickle of pride teased at him and Parker knew himself well enough to know he wanted this woman to smile at him in the same way. Warm and wide and genuine, a smile for a man to drown himself in.

"Truce?" he asked softly.

She glanced at him, then around her new surroundings. "I'll think about it," she said, not at all hard-edged.

He smiled and held her gaze. "Good."

Then she turned away and stepped forward from the side entrance foyer into the Central

Rotunda and any hint of a smile drained from her face.

"This isn't a house—this is a—museum!"

Parker took the three broad steps that led from the entry area to the center of the first level of the house, a rotunda that led in all directions to the primary rooms on the first floor.

He supposed it did resemble a museum, but having played hide and seek and G.I. Joe among the velveteen-covered gilt chairs and nineteenth-century writing desk and antique globe, to name only a few of the pieces cluttering the central rotunda, Parker didn't give much thought to the space.

Or to the impression it might make on someone not from his world.

But Meg's eyes had opened even wider and he knew, as clearly as if she'd spoken the words, that she knew almost nothing about the life led by the man she'd married.

Jules surely would have described Ponthier Place. Parker much preferred the family home in the country, known as Sugar Bridge, to the pretentious showplace Teensy had created at the St. Charles homestead.

But as much as Jules protested against the hold it held over him, as much as he'd tried to run away to the rooms he kept at the Hotel Maurepas, as much as he'd tried to avoid any gathering held in that house, he would have told any woman he loved about Ponthier Place.

For Jules, his life was a love-hate relationship, and nowhere was that more clearly spelled out than in his relationship with his family.

Given the death of their father—by drowning in a boating accident along with his current mistress—and the way Teensy catered to Jules's every whim and clung to him even more, Parker would have been amazed if family hadn't held a tight rein over Jules's actions. Or reactions.

Thankful that as the second child he'd escaped much of the notice of his parents, Parker had watched as his older brother had succumbed to his own confusion and hostility towards his family, a hostility matched only by his seemingly unbreakable need for them.

Horton discreetly bore away Meg's coat, carrying it as carefully as if it had been made from ermine or silk, rather than a flimsy synthetic blend.

She stood staring after Horton, watching her coat disappear as if she'd lost her only friend in the world. The woeful look on her face confused Parker. Perhaps he should have been nicer to her. She was way out of her league and she hadn't even set foot in the Great Parlor yet.

Her lips had parted slightly. She ungripped her hands and ran one lightly over the back of one of the gilt chairs. He liked the picture she made, her tapered fingers unconsciously sooth-

ing the fabric even as she seemed to divine its
nature.

Parker had sensed her hand as she'd lay it
over his arm back at the hotel. She'd offered
comfort and he'd rejected her touch. Watching
her stroke the chair, he pictured her hands
moving over his body, smoothing their way up
his legs, over his thighs, curling around the
part of him that ached from the idea of this
woman touching him.

He was out of his mind. She was not only a
stranger, but a stranger he knew better than to
trust.

But watching her hands, he read a gentleness
that reassured him.

And aroused him. Too much so.

He had to stop himself from thinking of Meg
in this way. To distract himself, Parker mentally reviewed the history of this particular
chair.

His mother had carried on for weeks about
that remarkable find. It matched an original to
the house that sat opposite the Georgian writing desk and Teensy had been quite pleased
with herself when she'd found it in some out-
of-the-way antique shop in Charleston. Dr. Prejean hadn't been called to the house for five
weeks straight after that blessed event. Parker,
now in his mid-thirties, still vividly recalled
that period in his mother's rollercoaster life
and he'd been only seventeen at the time.

"What a lovely chair," Meg said, continuing

to smooth the rounded edge under her hand.

"Tell that to Teensy," Parker said, managing to speak in a fairly normal voice, "and you'll have a friend for life."

"Is that what you call your mother? I mean, to her face?" Meg had dropped her hand from the chair.

Parker wished she'd go back to stroking the velvet, then he frowned. It would be better for him if she didn't resume that sensual motion. In a short tone, he said, "Everyone calls her Teensy."

"Well, I'm not planning to," she said.

"Suit yourself." He pointed to a double-wide archway. "Everyone's gathered in the Great Parlor. Shall we join them? They'll be wanting to express their sympathy."

"Everyone?"

He heard the anxiety in her voice and was surprised to feel a corresponding empathy. "Don't worry, they're family, mostly. You married my brother, Miz Ponthier." He stressed the name. "Don't you have the slightest curiosity to know more about the life he left behind? After all, it's your life now."

He'd moved closer as he spoke and now leaned almost over her. Her chest rose and fell quickly, and even under the armor of the rather demure suit jacket, her lush breasts invited thoughts that Parker had no business thinking. "Whoa—" he muttered.

She'd closed her eyes. He tipped her chin upwards. "Look at me," he said. He waited until her lids lifted and she fixed him with her deep blue eyes. "I don't know what your game is, but Jules was my brother—"

She yanked his hand from her chin. "You didn't know your brother very well, did you?"

"What makes you say that?" Parker gave her credit for her perception on that score. His grief rose as much from guilt as genuine loss. They had never been close; the two of them had nothing in common, apart from a family that embraced its members primarily as business associates. Even in business, they'd disagreed on every decision.

Once again Parker remembered how the day Jules had left for Vegas he'd threatened to do whatever it took to stop Parker's proposal for expansion of the family sugar business. Rather than expanding, Jules was set on getting Parker to agree to the corporate buyout offer they were to have voted on this week. With Jules's death, the family meeting would of course be put on hold.

Over his dead body would he sell, Parker had told Jules in that last argument. Only now it was Jules who lay dead in the morgue.

Meg tapped him on the chest. "I bet you tried to bully him just the way you're trying to bully me."

Parker didn't answer the question. His mind was racing, thinking of Jules's threat. Jules may have had his way eased into Tulane Law

School by family influence, but he had learned the stuff fairly well. And after two previous marriages, Jules definitely knew the unusual terms of the Ponthier Family Corporation dealing with spousal shares. Capturing her hand against his chest, he said, "You didn't marry Jules for love, did you?"

"I-I don't know what you mean."

Parker narrowed his eyes. A much more innocent answer would have been, *Of course I loved him. I love him still.* "Some love match. Where'd he hire you? Between the sheets at the Mustang Ranch?"

Tugging her hand free in a flash, she slapped him hard, fast and furiously, not once but twice.

"Ooh-hoo, Parker, is that you?" A wispy voice preceded the whisper of footsteps across the marble floor.

Holding one hand to his stinging cheek, Parker turned. "Teensy," he said in a drawling voice, "may I present"—he fixed his brother's scheming bride with a look meant to tell her she'd pay for what she'd done—"Jules's bride."

Four

Jules's bride.

Meg blanched. This slip of a woman approaching with a manicured hand outstretched in a languid gesture was technically Meg's mother-in-law. She swallowed. "How do you do, Mrs. Ponthier?"

To Meg's amazement, the petite brunette laughed in a way that sounded not at all musical or amused. "Nobody, but nobody, calls me that!"

Okay. Try again, Meg. She nodded, her mind racing, then decided not to venture any name at all. "Pleased to meet you," she said.

"Much better, dear," Meg's mother-in-law said. "I do so hate to be reminded that I married Jules's—" Her voice broke, and a sob rang from the depths of the woman's throat "—father."

Without realizing she'd done so, Meg had sought Parker's eyes. He stood, unsmiling, silent, watching his mother the way a hiker might eye a rattler asleep in his path. Ahh. Meg glanced down at the marble floor. The solid and elegant foundation might as well have been a bog of quicksand.

Thinking of Dr. Prejean's discussion with her on the phone, she decided she'd best humor this woman and ease out of the encounter. After all, she'd soon be on her way home, free and clear of the entanglements of the Ponthier clan.

What a relief that thought was! Meg managed a smile, stepped forward, and crooking the woman's arm into hers, said, "I am so sorry about your loss."

Teensy teared up and Meg realized no matter how off kilter the woman might appear, she'd loved her son. Her mother's heart warmed to her. "If there's anything I can do to ease your loss," she said, stroking the limp, exquisitely manicured hand, "please let me know."

Teensy sighed and squeezed Meg's hand. "I am just so—" she managed to turn that simple word into about three syllables "—glad that Jules found love in his last hours on this muddled earth of ours. W-h-y"—again, Teensy managed to drag this word out with the breath only a practiced singer or yogi could produce— "it gives me such comfort to know he married the mate of his soul before his untimely demise."

Meg closed her eyes and passed her free

hand over her face. She dared not look at either Teensy or Parker. She had a feeling the highly skeptical younger brother was glaring at her and attempting to read her every thought. And as for Teensy—Meg couldn't live with herself if she destroyed this woman by revealing the truth of her marriage for hire.

Jeez. What had she done!

Teensy didn't give her time to contemplate the answer to that very serious question. Tucking Meg's hand into the crook of her arm, she bussed her cheek and said with a giggle, "You don't look old enough to have married my baby." The last word caught in the woman's throat and suddenly Meg found herself putting an arm around her sobbing mother-in-law. "There, there," Meg crooned, stroking Teensy's short, dark hair. "It's okay to cry. I cry myself, you know."

"But he's never coming back!" Teensy's voice rose to a wail and she clutched Meg's arm tighter.

Meg looked down at the woman holding onto her for dear life, then whipped her head around as she heard a movement behind them. Parker stood staring at the two of them, but he'd clearly been about to bolt.

"Don't go," Meg mouthed, all the while smoothing Teensy's head and shoulders with the same soothing gesture she used when Teddy, Ellen, or Samantha complained of a tummy ache or couldn't sleep.

Parker met her gaze, then his eyes flicked to his mother, then back to Meg. He shrugged, then said, "You've guests waiting, Teensy."

What a stupid thing to say! Meg glared at Parker, annoyed at the dictatorial tone of voice he'd used towards his weeping mother. Well, truthfully, Meg vacillated between being annoyed with him—and fascinated by Parker. His technique worked with Teensy, who dabbed at her eyes, where her eye shadow and mascara had miraculously remained intact despite her bout of tears. She patted Meg on the hand and straightened her posture.

"It is good to meet you, Miss . . ." she smiled vacantly at Meg, then turned to Parker. "Are they in the Great Parlor?"

"Yes." Parker pointed, then after a slight hesitation, added, "Teensy, you'll be wanting to introduce your guests to Jules's widow."

"Oh, of course." Teensy smiled too brightly and Meg felt for this woman who'd just lost her son. Yet though she understood bereavement, something seemed off about the woman. Meg's husband might have died young and left her quite broke but at least he hadn't been nuts! This family, though, was one for the books.

Once again, Jules's mother took Meg's hand. This time she walked them across the rotunda and toward an archway at the far side. From the room beyond, Meg made out a babble of voices, some deep, some high-pitched. But the volume made her think of a PTA meeting much more than a gathering due to the death of a loved one.

Well, perhaps things were different in New Orleans.

Certainly Teensy didn't look like any mother Meg had imagined in all the years of her orphaned childhood. She used to lie awake at the group home after all the other girls had drifted off to sleep. She'd make up stories about her mother and father and the family that really, really wanted her but hadn't been able to keep her. But never in the wildest of those imaginings had she ever concocted a parent like Teensy.

No, her imaginary mother figure hadn't worn an expensive knit suit with buttons that looked like they cost as much as the suit itself, nor possessed a body that must have been engineered in a lab. Neither had her imaginary mother figure sported jet-black hair and a nearly flawless ivory complexion at what must be at least fifty years of age. And she hadn't been called Teensy to her face by her one surviving son, not even in the wildest flights of Meg's imagination.

Neither had Meg married such a woman's son for the sake of earning thirty thousand dollars. That thought sobered Meg and she glanced at Teensy much more sympathetically. Who knew what drove any woman to behave as she did in order to survive?

Just then Teensy paused only a foot or two

from the doorway through which the babble of voices rose. She turned to Meg and said in a low, controlled voice, "Did he die happy?"

The mother's heart in Meg felt with keen intensity the question Teensy asked. It was in Meg's power to ease Teensy's mind. "Oh, yes."

She heard Parker's quick intake of breath and her cheeks flamed as she guessed what he was thinking. Parker assumed Jules had taken her to bed before his death. Well, let him think that. It would take him down a notch or two for him to consider Jules had gotten something Parker would never get to sample.

Meg reminded herself she'd come to the house to help Teensy. She gripped the older woman's hand and said, "I can assure you he was happy."

Teensy had fixed her wide green eyes on Meg. She lifted one finger to smooth the line of her lipstick at the corner of her mouth. Then she said, "Thank you, then. No matter what anyone says about his regrettably impetuous marriage, I forgive you for not doing things the way they should have been done."

Before Meg could react, Teensy moved into the adjoining room, a bright smile splitting her perfectly toned and lifted face. "Darlings," she was saying, "I'm so glad you could come."

Was there some hidden knowledge a mother could detect? Or was Jules's mother only concerned with the niceties expected by society? Meg dearly wanted to understand why Teensy had chosen the words she'd used, but she found herself surrounded by a gaggle of people all talking at once. To assist her in a sanity check, she looked around, seeking—she realized with a funny feeling—Parker's presence.

A strangely comforting presence.

As she digested that thought and shook hands with the first person Teensy presented to her, a soft-spoken woman in her early forties named Amelia Anne, her mind wrestled with that description. Why should she find Parker, a man who'd insulted her and tried to keep her from standing by Teensy's side and whom Jules hadn't trusted one whit, comforting?

Hmmm. She let herself be propelled into the stiff-armed embrace of a portly silver-haired woman who murmured a few polite phrases of sympathy. Meg would rather be pressed against an armoire by Jules's brother, she realized as the stern-faced woman disengaged herself. Surprised at her own wayward thoughts, Meg kept a polite expression pasted on her face as she reminded herself she was playing the role of a grieving widow, a task she'd do well to remember.

But still, despite the condolences on her loss, Meg found herself thinking very little of Jules and far too much of his alive and well and arrogant brother.

Parker opted to remain for the show. He leaned against one of the two marble fireplaces of the Great Parlor, thankful Horton hadn't ordered them lit despite the chill of the day. He, for one, was quite warm enough. How much of that had to do with the woman now standing in the center of the room he didn't quite know.

He had to give it to her. She was handling the greetings and thinly disguised scrutiny of the assemblage without stuttering, faltering, or fleeing out the door. None of his family were the sweet and sympathetic type. Aunt Mathilde, his father's older sister, had no use for anyone born west of the Seventeenth Street Canal, let alone some stranger who hailed from Las Vegas. His aunt was eyeing Meg through the tiny eyeglasses she wore on a silver chain.

Meg gazed straight back. "What a lovely pince-nez."

Mathilde allowed the solid line of her mouth to edge upwards. "It is, isn't it." Then she thumped her cane on the floor and reclaimed her seat beside the fireplace opposite where Parker stood.

Teensy sighed and fidgeted her hands together. "You may as well meet Kinky."

That got her! Parker almost laughed aloud as an expression of astonishment chased across Meg's face. How odd she must find them. Now that she wore that demure suit rather than the Hotel Maurepas bathrobe, Meg demonstrated a squeaky clean, All-American look. She'd no doubt grown up in a tract house with a father who worked a nine-to-five job, and a mother who cooked, cleaned, and read bedtime stories to Meg and her siblings.

So how had she ended up married to Jules?

Parker frowned, then watched as his brother's childhood friend and all-around bad influence Kincaid "Kinky" de LaSalle jerked himself off a sofa and sketched a brief bow to Meg.

"If you were a friend of Jules's," he said, thrusting back the hair that always fell across his forehead, "you may call me Kinky. If not, the name is Kincaid."

"I'm Margaret, but call me Meg, please." In a lower voice, she said, "What do you mean 'If I was a friend?' That's a rather odd thing to say to a man's um"—she stumbled, then finished with—"w-widow."

Kinky kinked a brow, a gesture for which he was famous. "You obviously haven't met your predecessors."

"Predecessors . . ." She trailed off and Parker realized with a shock that Meg had no idea Jules had been married before, not once but twice.

Kinky repeated the brow gymnastics. "My, my, but don't you have a treat in store for you. Well, I do hope Jules found peace in his last days." Kinky's look was close to a leer. Parker thought of moving over, standing beside her to give her a semblance of protection, but checked himself. He smoothed his hand over his cheek where she'd slapped him. Meg could take care of herself.

"If you need any comforting—" Kinky had leaned over and gathered her hands in his "—just give ol' Kinky a call." His innuendo was clear.

Meg extracted her hands. "Please accept my sympathies on your loss. I'm sure you must be suffering."

Kinky shook his head. "Live in the fast lane, die on the curves, I always say."

Meg wrinkled her brow.

Teensy fluttered her hands. "Kinky, do sit down and behave," she said. Then, as if the effort of that command had been too great for her, she said, "I believe I'll have a drink." She drifted to the bar set up at the far end of the room and proceeded to mix a bourbon and water.

Parker shook his head.

Meg now stood alone in the center of the Aubusson rug. Aunt Mathilde had gathered her daughter Amelia Anne to her side and Kinky had joined Teensy at the bar. Isolde, Amelia Anne's sixteen-year-old daughter, hadn't bothered rising from the chair where she sat curled up, her ears covered by her Walkman, her nose buried in a book.

Meg half-turned, glancing towards Parker. In that swift instant, he saw a vulnerability she hadn't so far displayed. No female Daniel in a den of wild animals at this moment. Again, he felt himself softening his stance towards her. Perhaps she had married his brother for love, impetuously, but possibly out of pure motives.

If that were the case, Parker, he said to himself, *where were her tears back there in the hotel room when you broke the news to her?* She'd been shocked, but he'd wager a month's profit that she'd been thinking of her own welfare.

She'd taken a step toward him. Some indication of his thoughts must have shown on his face because she halted and gazed at him with a questioning look. Parker, who prided himself on his poker face, forced a smile into place and decided to play along with her game. Shoving himself from his post at the fireplace, he strolled towards her.

Instead of relief, he saw a hint of nervousness. Good. Let her get a little bit ruffled.

He'd just reached her side when the booming voice of Dr. Prejean split the room.

"Ah, there you are!"

All heads turned toward the doorway. The doctor, one of Parker's least favorite people, stood there, rubbing his hands together. His wisp of a goatee stood almost straight out and his toupee had settled slightly askew on his head. Round rimless glasses winked on his bulging eyes and his red lips formed a pout. His pipe protruded from his coat pocket, so Parker assumed he'd stepped out for a smoke.

"Teensy, why aren't you sitting down, you

naughty patient?" The doctor advanced into the room.

As Teensy hadn't left her station near the bar at the far end of the room, the doctor first encountered Meg and Parker, who'd just reached her side.

The doctor paused, teetering on the balls of his undersized feet. Not only had this man made Parker's life hell as he'd insisted on treating him for illnesses Parker knew quite well he didn't suffer from, but Parker couldn't stand any man with the pretensions Dr. Prejean exhibited. The man had attached himself to Teensy years ago and scarcely saw any other patients, other than the acquaintances Teensy foisted on him. He lived high on the hog off the money the sadly scattered, utterly spoiled, and unstable Teensy funnelled to him.

He held forth both hands, collecting Meg's in his own hammy paws. "You must be Jules's widow." He made a tch-tch sound that set Parker's nerves even further on edge.

"I prefer to think of myself as his bride," Meg answered, in a spirited tone. Parker lifted his brows. This could prove interesting.

Evidently the Vegas vamp was a quick study and didn't care for the good doctor, either.

"Oh, of course," he said, patting her hand. "What a sad loss. Such a young man, in the prime of his life. Taken from us in a tragedy that will live long in the annals of this city's crime-ridden social history."

Meg pulled her hand from the doctor's. "I thought he died trying to score cocaine."

All conversation in the room died. Not a sound could be heard as everyone, but everyone, turned to stare at Meg.

Parker suppressed the smile that wanted desperately to rend his lips. No one, but no one in this room would have acknowledged publicly that Jules had gotten himself into the trouble that resulted in his death. They spoke in platitudes and generalities, murmuring words of sympathy to Teensy and the other family members. For an outsider to call a strike a strike and not dress it up in pretty language shocked them.

They'd have her for breakfast, of course, but Parker had to admit he did find it refreshing. If someone, somewhere along the way in Jules's life, had been willing to speak straight to him, maybe he wouldn't have ended up at the wrong end of a policewoman's gun.

Teensy advanced on Meg, her drink forgotten in her maternal rage. "How dare you say such a thing!" She raced over, stabbing her finger towards Meg. "My baby was a victim. He did nothing to get himself in trouble. Why, I don't know who you think you are, but you're not welcome here at all. Just get your things and get out!" She stamped her foot, then glared at Parker. "You, get her coat and call her a cab. Or have Horton do it." She broke into a sob and Dr. Prejean moved over to her, his arm wrapped tight around her shoulders, crooning words of comfort.

Parker stood his ground.

So did Meg.

Then she turned on him. *Sotto voce*, she said, "Did you make up that story you told me?" Her eyes were wide and large and full of unshed tears.

Parker shook his head. "I told you the truth," he said softly.

She faced the others. "I'm Jules's widow and I'm not going anywhere."

Aunt Mathilde had raised her eyepiece and was studying Meg as if she'd discovered a cockroach on her chandelier. Amelia Anne had retreated to the chair opposite that of her daughter's. Isolde hadn't bothered to glance up. Kinky was looking highly amused and was no doubt about to escape himself, off to score whatever his drug of the moment happened to be.

Teensy lifted her face from where she'd buried it against Dr. Prejean's chest. In a voice that shook, she said, "I asked you to leave!"

Meg looked from her mother-in-law back to Parker. Parker found himself shaking his head in the negative, and wondering at the same time why he did so.

"Of course she's not going anywhere!"

Once more, everyone turned toward the doorway. Framed within the archway sat Grandfather Ponthier, his hands poised on the power controls of his rather souped-up wheel-chair.

"Who is that?" Meg asked the question.

Parker smiled. "Grandfather Ponthier," he said. "He always did have a great sense of tim-ing."

Five

A great sense of timing? Meg had to smother a hysterical giggle. She stared at the wisp of a man advancing on her in a wheelchair. His body looked shrunken, but the masterful way he held his head signaled Meg that here was a man used to being in charge.

"Well, you've got more sense than CeCe or Marianne, I'll give you that," he said as he braked to a stop next to her and Parker, who remained by her side.

Very much used to being in charge. Meg smiled and the old man glanced sharply at her.

"Grandfather," Parker said, "may I introduce—"

"You think you have to tell me what goes on in this house?" He fixed Meg with one eye. The other remained half-hidden behind a drooping eyelid. With the good eye, he winked.

Meg decided instinctively to accept the wink for the friendly gesture it was and ignore the bark. What the heck? If she misjudged him, he'd only snap her head off. After jumping feet first into this misadventure, she might as well shoulder her way through it.

Winking back, she said, "Why, then you know my name is Margaret, but call me Meg, please!"

The old man nodded. Shooting a glance at Parker, he said, "Couldn't help but hear what with Teensy carrying on to wake the dead. So, Meg, what brings you to New Orleans?"

Meg involuntarily exchanged a look with Parker, who was looking just as surprised at his grandfather's question. Why say he knew everything that went on in the house and then ask that question?

Parker lifted one shoulder slightly and Meg figured she was on her own. "Jules brought me," she said. "As I'm sure you know."

He laughed. "Oh-ho, you're no shrinking violet." He slapped his knee with his right hand. Meg noticed his left one lay in his lap, unmoving. That was the same side of his body as the eye that drooped. A stroke for this powerful man must be very hard to bear. Considering that made any strong words much easier for her to accept. Much easier than the coldness of the stone-faced Mathilde, who'd approached them, her grown daughter in tow.

"He may or may not have brought you here," Mathilde said in a frigid voice, "but it doesn't speak well of his regard for you that he failed to notify his family of his nuptials."

Meg heard what Mathilde really meant—
that she held Meg responsible for Jules's decision and for the unnaturally rushed marriage.
Of course she'd blame Meg rather than Jules
now.

As the dead grew colder, their sins forgotten,
forgiveness followed proportionately. Meg had
learned that lesson from Ted's parents after his
death. Somehow the financial crises of his company and personal life they'd pinned on Meg.
She should have done more, been a better wife.
Perhaps if she'd gotten a job and helped out,
the pressure on Ted wouldn't have been nearly
so great. Oh, yes, they might as well have cried
out, "You killed our son."

She shook herself mentally. That was then
and this was now. Meg eyed the group and
noticed even Dr. Prejean had left Teensy's side
to edge closer, as had Kinky. Well, if they were
expecting a scene, they were going to be disappointed.

For once they held silent, waiting no doubt
to see if she'd choose to spar with Mathilde.
And if she lashed out, that would only give
them more reason to lynch her. Parker was
studying her. No doubt he was looking to see
what fib she'd tell next, hoping for something
he could catch her on. Something like "Oh,
we've been lovers for years and just now decided to marry."

Meg said slowly, "Jules thought you would
find his marriage a"—she almost stumbled,

then continued with—"pleasant surprise. He intended to introduce me . . ." then she did trail off. She'd almost said "at the family meeting."

What a faux pas that would have been! Parker would have known in a heartbeat Jules had been intent on using Meg to help him maneuver against his brother in the Ponthier's business dealings.

"Introduce you when?" To her relief the grandfather snapped out the question rather than Parker. But she felt his gaze probing her every expression.

"Today." Meg lifted her hands and let them flutter in a gesture of surrender.

Across the room, Teensy broke into a sobbing wail. "B-but he can't because he's d-dead!"

Meg nodded, lowering her head and dabbing at her eyes. She wasn't actually crying but next to Teensy's sodden display of grief she didn't think she'd be too believable as a grieving widow if she didn't at least try to show some emotion.

She hadn't cried when her husband of twelve years died so she didn't find it at all surprising that she felt no tendency to shed tears at Jules's regrettable ending.

Amelia Anne moved forward and lifted one hand timidly toward Meg's shoulder. "There, there," she said, "we know it must be a painful loss."

"Really, Amelia Anne," Mathilde said, "I

don't see that you need to concern yourself so with this matter."

Amelia Anne dropped her hand and shrank back beside her mother.

Meg raised her head and smiled at Amelia Anne. She wouldn't forget the woman's instinctive kindness. There had been a few people like that in her growing-up years; people whose hearts had led them to extend friendship to an orphan knocked about from foster home to foster home then plopped back in the girls' home. And she'd met more than her share of Aunt Mathildes, those paragons of propriety whose hearts bled lumps of coal.

"I know everyone here has suffered a great loss. Jules was woven into the fabric of your lives." She glanced over at Dr. Prejean, who'd returned to Teensy's side and was standing with an arm draped around her shoulders. His plea was the reason she'd consented to come to the house and continue this charade. "I'll do whatever I can to help in any way."

Mathilde looked down her nose. Meg just knew the woman was itching to say something cutting, perhaps something like "the only help you want to offer is to take away Jules's money." But breeding required her to hold such comments inside. Well, Meg hoped her uncharitable thoughts caused her a nasty stomachache.

She liked to tell her kids that thinking naughty thoughts brewed bad body juices.

They'd wrinkle their noses and make gagging sounds and invariably end up laughing, which chased away the naughty thoughts, of course, and made them feel much better.

Her children.

Meg sighed.

Parker said in a surprisingly gentle voice, "Would you like to get settled in your room now?"

Her room? The words caught her off guard and in a flash she might have been fourteen again and facing yet another new foster family. Strangers who might claim to want her. Strangers who'd never really tried to know her.

Meg found a brief smile for Parker and shook her head. She'd come here in the role of Jules's widow out of a sense of commitment to help ease the situation in any way she could before she left New Orleans.

Sense of commitment? Meg's conscience started giving her a talking to. *You're here because you're guilty over the ten thousand dollars. Give it back and leave now. That's not your room Parker's talking about. It doesn't belong to you. You don't belong here. You don't belong anywhere.*

Yet she did belong to the family she and Ted had created and it was for that family, for her children, she'd leapt into this abyss. And for them, she'd hang onto that ten thousand dollars if she could clear it with her conscience.

"Let's all sit down." From Grandfather Ponthier, the words sounded a lot more like an or-

der than an invitation. He fingered the controls
of his electric wheelchair. Suddenly it skewed
to the right towards Meg.

In a flash, Parker clasped Meg's arm and
pulled her to safety. She slid against him, her
back brushing against his chest, rocklike and
steady under his expensively tailored suit.

Her heart fluttered and she knew Parker's
touch had far more to do with her reaction than
the near-miss.

Safety? Parker's dangerous attraction held
far greater peril than any runaway wheelchair.

"Dang stickshift," Grandfather said. "Excuse
me."

Mathilde raised her eyeglass. "I see you're in
your usual rare form, Augie." She settled onto
a loveseat, patting the space beside her. Amelia
Anne, seemingly ever faithful and obedient,
joined her there.

"Well, at least I'm still alive, which is more
than I can say for my wastrel grandson."

Parker's hold on Meg's arm tightened. She
glanced up at him and saw again the same expression of pain that had etched his face when
he'd first encountered her in the hotel suite. He
truly grieved for his brother. Despite how Jules
had told her the two of them were at odds and
never got along, it seemed Parker had deep
feelings for his older brother.

Meg patted the back of Parker's hand, instinctively comforting him. Unlike earlier in the
hotel room when she'd touched him, he didn't

jerk away, but very slowly released her. With
a brief smile, he said, "Looks like you're safe
now."

Right. Meg's heart skipped and it wasn't
from the shock of the wheelchair just missing
her size-eight feet. If she reacted that way to
that man's touch, she wasn't safe. Far from it.
Then she noticed Mathilde had raised her eyeglass again and fixed it on Meg's face. Choosing bark over bitter, Meg pulled a chair over
next to where Grandfather Ponthier had
parked his wheelchair.

Over by the bar, Teensy had completely collapsed against Dr. Prejean's chest. He now had
both arms around the sobbing woman. Meg
noticed no one else seemed particularly concerned over Teensy.

Mathilde was commenting to Amelia Anne
that she didn't know what that man who called
himself mayor would be up to next. Kinky had
draped himself over the arm of the chair where
Amelia Anne's daughter remained hunched
over her book, oblivious to the rest of the gathering. With his fingertips, Kinky began drumming a beat on the girl's head and even then
she didn't glance up.

Only Parker remained where he'd been, his
inscrutable gaze fixed on Meg.

"Since Jules was going to introduce you to
his family today"—Meg was pretty sure
Grandfather stressed that word—"why don't
you tell us a little bit about yourself?" He

spoke to her, but the way his voice carried, Meg just knew the others would jump in.

Sure enough, Mathilde quit declaiming over the mayor and said, "Good idea, Augie. Why don't you tell us about your family?"

Meg licked her lips, wondering just how to define her family. Springing her three children on them didn't strike her as the best thing to do at the moment. "Um, what would you like to know?"

"The usual things." Mathilde looked at her as if she found Meg extremely dull-witted. "Who your parents are, where you went to high school. The college you attended."

Kinky sat up straighter. "Jules's first wife was a Duffourc and his second a Moisant."

Grandfather thumped on the arm of his wheelchair. "And a lot of good their pedigrees did them. Neither one of them lasted two years. I guess CeCe couldn't fight her own nature, but why that Marianne didn't stick by him six months after—"

"Really, Augie, must you air all the family linen?" Mathilde spoke even more sharply, her patrician eyes narrowing.

It had been like that in the foster homes. Meg was used to conversations that broke off, to whispered endings of sentences. Those hurts had faded over the years as she nurtured her own family, but watching the Ponthiers brought back the ghosts of those feelings. Well, the Ponthiers couldn't inflict any wounds she hadn't already grown scar tissue over.

But she'd be willing to bet none of them had ever met anyone like her.

In her sweetest voice, she said, "I finished high school with a GED."

Mathilde glanced from Grandfather to Parker, then towards Kinky. The effete young man shrugged one shoulder. Mathilde clearly had never heard of a GED and Meg was sure she was too proud to ask what it meant.

Not so Amelia Anne. In a soft voice she asked, "Is that some sort of honors program?"

For Meg it had been.

She nodded. It had been a major accomplishment. She'd dropped out of school at sixteen—not that she'd attended regularly. When she was ten, the wonderful long-term foster parents who'd taught her to love and to laugh at life's problems were killed in a car crash. After that, it seemed the families who took her in were always more interested in her as a babysitter than as a daughter of their own. She'd always been good with kids. Everyone said so.

The teenage girl lowered her earphones for the first time since Meg had entered the room. "A GED is a test you take to get a diploma when you've dropped out of school."

Meg nodded. It didn't surprise her that the girl followed the conversation under the armor of her music and book. "That's right. It's a General Equivalency Diploma."

"And you said it was an honors program."

Mathilde's accusation rang clear in her voice. *Lie about this, lie about anything.*

Grandfather slapped the arm of his chair. "Better than not finishing what she started."

Meg smiled at him.

The teenager said, "That's what I wish I could do. Take one test and have the whole thing over with."

"Isolde, really," Amelia Anne said, a hurt look on her face, "you're enrolled in the best school in the city. You'll enter the college of your choice and enjoy a wonderful debutante season. How can you make such a thoughtless statement?"

Without another word, the girl pulled the earphones over her ears and buried her face in her book. Kinky, who'd quit drumming on her head while she spoke, resumed his tapping rhythm.

Amelia Anne sighed.

"What you should ask your daughter," Mathilde said, "is where she learned about a GED. Whoever heard of such a thing!"

Without removing the earphones, the girl said, "Astor's older sister did it after she got pregnant."

"Isolde, mind your manners, please," her mother said in a weak voice, glancing more at her own mother than at her daughter.

"I suppose that nixed college," Kinky said, at last stopping the nervous dancing of his fingers.

Meg wondered whether he referred to Isolde's friend or to herself for "only" holding a GED. She stared at his hands, moving so restlessly. An image took shape in the reaches of her memory but she couldn't quite place it. What was it about that nervous gesture that seemed familiar?

"Did you go to college?" Grandfather asked the question.

"UNLV."

"I don't believe I know that school," Mathilde said.

"University of Nevada at Las Vegas." It was Parker who answered, his slow, deep voice a welcome contrast to the strident tones of most of the others.

She flashed a glance at him, grateful he hadn't disappeared and left her to face the wolf pack on her own. She had the distinct feeling he'd rather be anywhere else than in the middle of what he'd called the Great Parlor.

"Good basketball team." Dr. Prejean stuck in, steering Teensy into the family circle.

There was something unhealthy in the overly solicitous manner the doctor adopted toward Teensy. Meg had a feeling he made every detail of the Ponthier's lives his business and meddled far more than any doctor she'd ever known.

At least they seemed to take the doctor's pronouncement as approval of sorts. And no one asked whether she'd graduated. Meg watched

them watch her and asked herself whether she
would be able to help Jules's mother in any
way. She seemed to live pretty much in her
own little world and the others seemed content
to let Dr. Prejean handle her.

"Well, that's high school and college,"
Grandfather said. "So tell us about your parents."

Meg hesitated.

Kinky said, "First tell us how you and Jules
met."

Grandfather glared at the young man.
"Never could wait your turn. Neither you nor
my grandson ever learned a whit of respect."

Kinky produced his one-shouldered shrug.
"Our parents never stressed that lesson."

Mathilde said, "I find it much more likely
that you closed your ears to that particular lesson."

"Ooh, don't go grouchy on me," Kinky said.
"I do know where the skeletons are buried."

The look of disgust on Parker's face was
clear. Meg wondered what Kinky meant, but
she didn't really want to know. She really
wanted to go home, to hold her children in her
arms and breathe in their innocence.

"Where did you meet my grandson?"

Should she let them down gently? Meg
glanced around the elegant room, at the priceless antique furnishings. Through windows
that stretched from the floor almost to the high
ceiling she glimpsed a broad porch and beyond

that the expanse of lawns and gardens that she knew occupied the entire block. Yet for all the wealth of their surroundings, these people were miserable.

She took a deep breath and started to answer bluntly. But then Teensy lifted her head and the look of anticipation on her face jolted Meg. The mother wanted a fairy tale ending for her son.

"I met him"—she cast about for words she could use that weren't too far from the truth—"at a social event."

Parker's brow quirked upwards. She wondered how far off his forehead that brow would have traveled if she'd stated the truth as baldly as she'd been tempted. *He came into the bar where I was slinging drinks.*

"A dance?" Teensy had sat forward. Prejean had to drop his arm from her shoulders when she moved abruptly.

"A musical evening." There, that ought to satisfy her. The band had been playing when Jules had settled into the corner table, ordering round after round of bourbon and water. The group had overwhelmed the lobby bar of the casino, playing too loudly as usual. But they were good as most of the small acts in Vegas were, the talent drawn there in the hopes of striking it rich.

"Did you dance?" Teensy asked wistfully.

"We talked." And they had, for so long Moose the bar manager had yelled at her twice.

He only quit yelling when Jules tossed a hundred-dollar bill at him. *Then we kept on talking and then he asked me to marry him for three days for thirty thousand dollars and I did and he got himself killed and here I am. Am I nuts?*

"I think you're making her sad," Amelia Anne said.

Meg gave her a small smile. "I'm okay," she said.

Teensy burst into tears. "Well, I'm not!"

Talking over her sobs, Mathilde said, "Do tell us about your parents."

Meg gestured towards Teensy, but the doctor had taken her in hand again.

She knew she didn't want to tell this group of piranhas that she was an orphan. They could probably trace their family line back further than the antiques clustered about the room.

She parted her lips, wondering whether she shouldn't just make up yet another story. But she hated lying and she'd spun such a web already.

Parker moved from the position he'd been holding beside one of the fireplaces. Stepping over by her side, he said, "Meg probably doesn't want to talk about her parents because she wants us to welcome her on her own worth."

Meg stared up at him. What did he mean? How could he know anything about her? The shock had to show on her face.

"What do you mean by that, Parker?" Mathilde glanced from him to Meg.

Meg tried to compose her expression. Unless Parker employed investigators who worked at the speed of light, he couldn't know one fact about her personal history.

"I mean," Parker said, smiling down at Meg in quite a nice way she hadn't seen him do before, "I'm well acquainted with Meg's parents."

Six

Parker could have choked his words back but it was too late. He hadn't been able to restrain himself. Watching his family weighing and measuring her and being so open about finding her unsuited to the world of the Ponthiers rankled him.

Doubly so, because he realized he'd been doing exactly the same thing. From the first moment he'd seen this woman in Jules's suite he'd assumed the worst of her. He'd judged and labeled her exactly as Mathilde and Teensy were doing. Only his grandfather showed any signs of independent thinking, which shouldn't surprise Parker. Grandfather Ponthier followed no other man's course.

With the rest of them, though, no matter who Meg's family was, it wouldn't have been good enough.

Nothing ever was for the Ponthiers.

His mouth tightened and the smile he'd produced to reassure Meg vanished.

"You know my parents?" A curious mixture of excitement and disbelief flashed in her eyes. It was as if she wanted to believe him but found it impossible. Well, it was pretty preposterous. She had to realize he'd lied to protect her, and he wondered if the gesture would cause her to think better of him.

"Which business are they in?" His grandfather directed the question to him. Naturally he would assume Parker knew them through one of the Ponthier business connections. His grandfather made it a habit to tell Parker at least once a week that his entire life consisted of work and he ought to learn to enjoy himself.

"Sugar," he answered, noticing how sweet Jules's widow looked smiling up at him.

"Well, at least that's respectable," Mathilde said. "You'll have to invite them to the wake." She narrowed her eyes. "Did *your* side of the family receive an invitation to the wedding?"

Meg shook her head.

Mathilde looked slightly mollified.

"Actually," Meg said, "they don't even know Jules and I m-married."

"You were going to tell them today, too?" Grandfather jabbed at the controls of his chair. "You two sure got things all out of order."

"I know. And I'm really sorry, sorrier than you can ever know." She sounded so contrite Parker almost forgot his suspicions. Could someone so innocent be a schemer who'd entrapped Jules and lured him back into cocaine?

Parker hated to think of the situation in such dire terms but the woman had been with Jules when Jules had been using. His brother hated to get high alone, which accounted for his long-standing friendship with Kinky.

"Call your parents," Grandfather said.

"Call them?" Meg blinked. "Uh—"

"Is there some reason you don't want to involve them in your life?" Mathilde had long ago mastered the art of loading a question with a range of implications, all of them negative.

"Oh, no, but they're . . . out of the country right now."

"Traveling abroad?" Mathilde seemed pleased at that news. Parker figured she didn't want the family embarrassed at a big event that Jules's wake and funeral would turn out to be.

Meg nodded. She did that a lot. But then, withstanding an assault from the collective Ponthiers tended to produce that reaction. Most strangers wouldn't have held up nearly so well. Parker hadn't forgotten the first time he'd brought a date home in high school. Teensy had criticized her makeup; his father, still alive at that time, had flirted with the child; and Grandfather's barks had reduced her to tears. She'd called her parents to come rescue her. Parker hadn't even gotten to kiss her.

Dragging his attention back to the present, Parker wondered who Meg's parents were and what her life had been like. Why had she dropped out of high school? Did she like ice

cream? He smiled. There was so much he
wanted to discover about Meg.

"I do have some other relatives I need to
call," Meg said.

"Good," Grandfather said, "wouldn't want
to think you're all alone in the world."

Parker watched the play of emotions passing
across Meg's face. She was a funny blend of
nerves and steel. One moment she'd stand up
to all of them, the next he had the feeling she
wanted to flee back to whatever safety her real
life offered her.

"There's someone else you need to tell,"
Amelia Anne said.

Mathilde glanced at her daughter. "Why
that's a silly thing to say. There are lists and
lists of people to notify. I don't know why
we're sitting here when we should be organizing things." She lifted her eyeglasses that
lived on the chain around her neck. "Kinky, be
a dear and ring the bell for Horton."

Amelia Anne had lowered her face. Addressing her hands folded in her lap she said, "I was
thinking of Gus."

Mathilde let her spectacles fall to her chest.

Grandfather swatted at his controls as if a
dozen mosquitos had settled there.

Kinky made no move to ring the bell for
Horton.

Teensy lifted her head from Prejean's shoulder.

Even Isolde glanced up, her bright and too-knowing eyes checking the reactions of each of the adults.

Parker was interested in only one reaction. He swiveled his head to study Meg. Her puzzled expression made it clear—she didn't know about Gus. Even for Jules this behavior was beyond all bounds. He'd married this woman without telling her he had a son. And not just your run-of-the-mill happy little boy.

"Um," Meg began.

Parker cut her off before she could ask the fatal question "Who's Gus?" Again, he didn't know why he protected her, except he couldn't stand to watch his family pouncing on her.

"You know him as Auguste Jules IV," Parker said. "But everyone else calls him Gus."

"Oh. Oh, of course." She smiled at him and he thought again how sweet she looked.

"You did know your husband had a son by a prior marriage, did you not?" Mathilde never missed a trick.

"Of course she did," Parker said.

"You have a problem letting her answer questions for herself?" Grandfather was studying Meg. Parker was pretty sure the old guy already liked Meg better than both of his brother's former wives put together, but his grandfather lived by his own set of rules. He either accepted people outright or he blocked them out.

Funny, but Parker wanted his grandfather,

whom he admired despite his caustic tongue, to put her on his A-list.

"So he doesn't know about his father's death?" Meg spoke slowly, as if assessing the ramifications of that truth.

They all stared at her.

"*We* only just found out," Mathilde said.

"What about his mother? Won't she be the one to tell him?"

Kinky laughed. "Darling, I don't know what Jules told you about Marianne Duffourc, but the woman's incapable of dealing with life on a good day let alone a bad one."

Parker had to agree. To Meg he said, "She's a bit of a child herself." Like his own mother, he thought. Jules had succeeded in marrying a woman exactly like Teensy in at least one of his marriages.

CeCe, of course, was a different matter altogether. She'd not only divorced Jules after only two months, she announced to whomever would listen that two months with Jules had caused her to renounce not only her husband but men in general. To the immense relief of the Ponthier clan, CeCe had removed herself to San Francisco and at last report was working as a massage therapist. But though she'd sworn off Jules and his gender, she continued to cash her alimony checks.

Meg was looking more and more concerned. "The loss of a parent for a child his age . . ." As she trailed off she glanced straight at Parker and he read the question in her eyes. Between those thick lashes and those unusual blue eyes that blended from azure to midnight near the irises, he saw her seeking the answer to the question of the child's age.

"Ten is tough." Parker wondered how she did what she did to him. Perhaps she'd put the whammy on Jules, too, and he'd married her out of sheer old-fashioned desire, because he simply couldn't help himself against her appeal. Parker couldn't blame his brother. Not one bit.

"Oh, ten is very tough," she murmured.

He thought he saw a glisten of moisture in her eyes, the first sign of pure grief she'd yet to show.

Isolde said in a voice that carried across the room despite the fact she still had her nose buried in her book, "I don't think ten is harder or easier than any other age. I think it's got to be hard no matter when." She lifted her head, a look of surprise on her face, then she retreated into her pose over the book, earphones firmly in place.

Amelia Anne smiled at her daughter.

Parker couldn't help but think his much put-upon cousin was probably grateful that her daughter acknowledged the sentiment. Amelia Anne was accepted as the type of doormat no one would miss if she simply drifted off into the night. Parker had often found himself wishing she'd find herself, perhaps through entering therapy or joining a feminist group. But she remained firmly within the shadow of her mother, her only social outlet the genteel, white-gloved gatherings of the ladies of the Orleans Club. And as that bastion of old New Orleans respectability lay a mere block from Ponthier Place, and Amelia Anne's husband's family owned the house opposite them on Soniat, the orbit of Amelia Anne's life was not large.

"You know, Isolde," Meg said, answering the teenager despite her withdrawal, "I think that's a valid point. Ten is tough. And so is thirty-two," she added softly.

Parker thought he saw a smile flit across the girl's face, but he couldn't have sworn to it.

"Well, I've heard some of my friends say they spend their days going to funerals and they say it like they're talking about getting up a foursome for golf," Grandfather said. His jaw worked. "Don't understand that myself. A death lessens us all, old or young." He cleared his throat. "Enough philosophizing." He pointed to Meg. "You and Parker will have to break the news to Gus."

She merely nodded.

Parker wasn't sure why, but the idea panicked him. What did he know about telling a ten-year-old his dad had died? And it wasn't as if Gus were your average well-adjusted kid. Marianne did nothing but ignore him, then fly into town with an armload of presents, then when Gus erupted with rage, she claimed not to be able to do a thing with him.

She and Jules had packed him off to school in Mississippi before the child had turned seven. Parker had seen Gus on holiday visits to Ponthier Place, but not for more than an hour or so at a time. Parker's own home lay safely across town near Bayou St. John. Since Grandfather's stroke, Parker spent a lot more time at Ponthier Place, discussing business in the library, but during the past two years, Gus had remained most of the year at the school.

Knowing how ill-suited he was to the task of handling the child, Parker waited for Meg to object, to say it wasn't her responsibility. He'd wager Marianne wouldn't even fly back from Switzerland for the funeral; CeCe might show up, but no way would she bother with a stepchild, especially a boy. Hell, neither one of them had ever wasted any affection on Gus in the past.

But instead of objections, he heard her say, "Perhaps we'd better get going. I'm sure I'll be of more help with Gus than with everything else that needs to be done here."

"Sensible," Mathilde said, practically a compliment coming from her.

Meg rose. Parker tried to think of some way to stall. "Perhaps we should call his therapist."

Prejean nodded. "Excellent idea. Given the child's volatile nature, professional help is most definitely wise. I have a friend I can call,

someone I like better than that man Gus has
been seeing."

Parker glared at the doctor. If Prejean rec-
ommended a therapist, Parker would handle
Gus on his own. "Never mind," he said, reaching his decision. "Loving concern will serve the
child better than an army of doctors."

Meg smiled at him. "I just need to make a
phone call, then I'll be ready to go."

"I'll show you the library," Parker said, smiling back, thinking how typical it was he'd been
chosen to bear the family burden and how nice
it was that for once he didn't have to do it
alone.

Meg followed Parker out of the room, grateful to escape. She had no idea whether the mission she'd accepted would prove harder to
handle than that room of critical, self-absorbed
people, but she'd opt for working with a child
over an adult any day. With a child there was
so much more hope.

She shivered slightly. That Mathilde! And
the way she treated her daughter.

Parker must have noticed her physical reaction. Pausing before a pair of dark, ornately
carved doors, he said in a dry voice, "Nice welcome home."

Home. Meg glanced up at him in surprise.
Uh-uh, this palace wasn't home. Home was a
jumble of toys and books and half-finished pro-
jects. Home was a house full of laughter despite the tears that came with the bumps and

losses of life. Even though she'd been reduced to living in Mrs. Fenniston's extra rooms after Ted's death, Meg still made sure her home was fashioned by love.

"A death in the family," she said, choosing her words carefully, "sometimes brings out elements of ourselves that may not show us in the best light."

Parker pushed open the double doors. "Are you always so forgiving?"

Meg shrugged. She wasn't sure how to answer him. She certainly didn't feel it her place to criticize his family, no matter how insufferably rude they were. Her own guilty knowledge of her terms with Jules made it pretty tough for her to blame them for scrutinizing her.

"The phone's on the desk." He pointed across the room to a massive piece of furniture that dominated the far end. It gleamed from polishing. Several stacks of file folders, neatly arranged, covered one side of the surface.

Meg approached. "Do you work out of your home?"

"I grew up here," Parker said, "but I have my own home elsewhere in the city. I consult with Grandfather here, and I have an office in the CBD."

"CBD?"

"Central Business District. Sorry, I forgot you wouldn't know."

"Just a stranger in town," she said, itching

to reach for the phone but at the same time curious to know more about this man.

"I think of New Orleans as a city of subsets." He folded his arms across his chest and settled against the edge of the desk. "There's the parish of Orleans, and then there are all the neighborhoods or subsets. For instance, you're Uptown. My original family settled in the Vieux Carré almost two hundred years ago. And between here and there is the Garden District."

Meg nodded, following his words but of course not really understanding what he described. "So much history. I can tell you like your city a lot."

"I do." He smiled at her. "I'm glad that's obvious." Moving away, he said, "You'd better make your call. We need to get going to see Gus."

She picked up the phone, then hesitated. No way was she talking to her children in front of Parker Ponthier. What he didn't know about her personal life she preferred to keep secret. That thought reminded her she'd have to ask him why he'd said he knew her parents. Her heart had leapt at his statement, reminding her that as an orphan she still held the secret wish that she'd be reunited with her birth family.

"I'll meet you at the side door where we came in," he said, turning and striding across the room.

She dialed Mrs. Fenniston's number, racking

up yet one more long distance call on the Ponthier bill. She had a feeling that before she backed gracefully out of this entanglement she'd be calling home many more times.

Mrs. Fenniston's voice came over the line.

Meg gripped the phone in relief. "Oh, Mrs. Fenniston, I'm so glad you're there."

"Is everything going well?" Nothing ruffled Mrs. Fenniston's calm. "I do hope so."

"I guess so," Meg said, wishing she could spill out the entire story. Over the past several months she'd grown close to the dignified widow, but she hadn't been able to confide the details of her "job" in New Orleans. "But not exactly as planned."

"I believe that's one of the reasons the colonel loved to study quantum physics," Mrs. Fenniston said. "Well, you mustn't worry about the children. We are having a fabulous time. They introduced me to the water park yesterday."

Meg smiled. She admired and loved this woman who'd taken her and her children in. Both of them had been widowed at almost the same time, Mrs. Fenniston after fifty-five years of marriage to a brilliant British scientist who'd been conducting research in Nevada's nuclear testing industry.

"I bet they loved the water park."

"Yes they did. And I found it quite refreshing. Someone's dancing a jig to talk to you."

"I just want to warn you I may be delayed."

"Well, you do what you need to do there and don't worry about us. We're having a peach of a time. But you do sound a bit unlike yourself."

"Oh, I'm fine," Meg said, wishing she could pour out her troubles to Mrs. Fenniston. But she'd gotten herself into this mess and she'd see herself out of it.

"Here's Ellen, then."

"M-o-m! We went to the water park and Teddy was such a b-a-b-y. Why, even Samantha went down the big slide but not Teddy."

"And did you go down the big slide?"

"Of course." Her ten-year-old daughter sounded indignant. "Only a baby wouldn't go down that."

Meg heard a commotion and wasn't at all surprised to hear her son's voice next. "My sister is too stupid to understand that I'm far too mature to need to scare myself in order to enjoy my day."

Meg sighed. Teddy had grown up far too fast in the past year. She knew he felt he had to take on the role of his father and she tried her best to allow him to grieve in his own way, while also encouraging him to be the little boy he still was.

"And you did enjoy yourself?"

"Yep. And Mrs. Fenniston let me have three hot dogs."

"Good." That was more like a ten-year-old boy should act.

"Here's Samantha."

"Mommy, I had a tummy ache last night but Mrs. Fenniston fixed it."

"Oh, that's good, sweetie. Are you better now?"

"Yep."

"I miss you," Meg said, clutching the phone so tightly she thought it would pop from her grasp.

"Agamem-mem threw up," Samantha said.

Agamemnon was Mrs. Fenniston's twenty-pound tomcat, who ruled her house.

"And I love you," Meg added, wishing she could gather her children close and never let them go.

"It was a hairball, Mrs. Fenniston said."

Meg had to laugh despite the tears in her eyes. Her children were carrying on quite well without her. "Let me speak to Mrs. Fenniston," she said.

"Bye, I love you," Samantha said.

"Well, dear, are you feeling better now?"

"I can't thank you enough."

"It's not a bother at all. I feel younger than I have in years."

"I'll try to be home within two days. I'm really sorry to stay longer but things are much more complicated than I expected." Now that was an understatement!

"You just let us know and we'll pick you up at the airport."

"Thank you."

"I promised the children they could construct a lemonade stand, so I'll say good-bye."

"Good-bye, Mrs. Fenniston." Mrs. Angel, Meg might have said. She closed her eyes, murmuring a brief prayer of appreciation for the woman's steady friendship.

Just before she lowered the phone, Meg thought she heard a click on the line.

Alarmed, she stared at the phone, then around the room. Had someone listened in on her conversation? Shaking her head, she rose and crossed the room.

In the foyer by the door, she came across Grandfather Ponthier. He was sitting there in his wheelchair staring out the broad windows that ran floor to ceiling across the front of the house. His brows were drawn close. When he caught sight of her, he stared hard.

He wasn't such a bad old man, just bossy. She was relieved there was no sign of a telephone anywhere near his wheelchair. Had it been her imagination or had she heard that click on the line? Probably just her guilty conscience. Meg summoned a smile. "I'm ready whenever Parker is."

"Hmmph." He lifted his right hand toward his face. As he did, she caught sight of a portable phone tucked against the side of the wheelchair.

Grandfather said, "As soon as you get back from Mississippi, I'd like you to come talk to me about those children of yours. In private."

Seven

In private? Did that mean he'd keep his discovery to himself? Possibly, Meg thought, as rather than the show of temper she expected to see on the Ponthier patriarch's face, Meg sensed a grudging respect. "No wonder you agreed to break the news to Gus," he said.

She flashed him a smile but she couldn't help retorting, "Didn't anyone ever tell you eavesdropping is very bad manners?"

He chuckled. "Sure and people who were more concerned with success than manners taught me it was a damn good way to learn about the competition. Referring to the business arena, naturally."

"Naturally." Meg was dying of curiosity. How much had he overheard? How much would he keep to himself? "Umm—"

Just then Parker came bounding down the staircase that rose from the far end of the foyer.

Great. Meg had gained enough impressions of Jules from his family to conclude that Parker would never believe his brother had married a widow and mother of three from an unknown family out of love and desire. A man who shipped his ten-year-old to boarding school wasn't exactly a prime candidate for taking on three more youngsters.

Meg admitted she didn't want Parker to revert to the suspicious, arrogant jerk he'd been at the hotel, questioning her motives and treating her like a call girl. Since they'd come to this house, he'd shown he could be nice in a way that surprised Meg. And impressed her.

He drew on a pair of black leather gloves as he approached. She noticed he had a dark blue overcoat and her own wrap tossed over one arm.

Meg shot a look at grandfather, who was staring hard at Parker, the same intensity with which he'd greeted her a few minutes earlier etched on his face.

Please don't say anything about my kids, she said to herself, holding her breath.

With a smile, Parker said, "Ready?"

Meg glanced again at grandfather Ponthier. He drummed his fingers on the arm of his wheelchair. Looking straight at Meg he said, "Remember to come see me when you get back. No matter how late it is."

"Sure," Parker answered for them.

Meg licked her lips and nodded, wondering why he'd chosen to hold his fire. No doubt some business mentor had told him to accumulate knowledge as well as wealth. Well, she'd take the gift for the moment.

Parker held her coat. She slipped into it, appreciative of the simple courtesy, then followed Parker out the side door where she'd entered earlier, feeling in a very strange way as if crossing that threshold with Parker were the most natural thing in the world.

"We'll take the Infiniti," Parker said. "You'll probably find it more comfortable."

Meg had managed to hang onto her ten-year-old Corolla. Ted had driven a leased Mercedes, a luxury the dealer had wasted no time in relieving her of after the funeral. Outside of an advertisement, Meg wasn't sure she'd ever seen an Infiniti. The families in her old neighborhood favored Toyotas and an occasional Chevy wagon.

Following him along the wide drive toward a rustic-looking carriage house, Meg asked, "More comfortable than what?"

"I usually drive my Porsche."

"Ah," Meg said, thinking that explained the black leather driving gloves. "Isn't that a two-seater?"

He nodded, then pushed a button on his key ring and one of the ancient-looking carriage house doors eased silently upward.

She must have looked impressed because he said, "Retrofitted. I designed it myself."

"Nice."

A gleaming black car sat inside the garage.

Peering around, Meg saw three other cars, one of them a low-slung sports car. "Your car does look like it's fun to drive but Gus wouldn't fit."

"Gus?" He held the car door open for her and she slid in. The soft leather of the seat embraced her and she let out a small sigh of appreciation. Then as Parker walked around the car she said sternly to herself, "Don't get spoiled. You're going home to your Corolla very soon."

Parker tossed his coat into the back seat and took his place behind the wheel. He filled the space in a commanding way and Meg suddenly felt as if the spacious interior of the car had shrunk. She scooted just a bit sideways, her face turned towards him. She wanted to study Jules's brother but the way he had of crowding in on her made her want to protect herself. It also left her breathless in a way she found surprisingly pleasant.

Pulling from the garage, Parker said, "Gus may not want to come back with us."

"Not come to his father's funeral?" Meg heard the shock in her voice.

They left the drive and turned onto a side street with few curbs and no sidewalks, the surface pitted with broken paving, an odd contrast to the quality of the homes lining the block. Parker managed to miss most of the potholes. He turned onto the broad avenue Meg had traveled in the cab before he spoke again.

Staring ahead, Parker said, "I don't know

what my brother told you. Sometimes I'm not sure my brother told you anything about himself, except it seems he said 'I do,' based on that paper you flashed in front of my face."

Meg made a sound of protest.

"Please, let me finish. You asked why Gus might not want to come to his father's funeral and I'm answering your question. Jules lived for himself. He and Gus's mother, Marianne, are—were—two of the most self-centered human beings who ever walked this planet." Parker shrugged and flashed a glance at Meg. "In short, lousy parents."

"But family is family." Meg heard the stubborn note in her tone and knew she argued purely out of her own lack of family during her childhood. She knew quite well many children were better off away from the parents who'd brought them into the world.

"Family," Parker said slowly, "can drive you nuts."

Meg thought of the group in the Great Parlor. "You do have a point."

"What about yours?" He looked at her, curiosity in his eyes. Then he turned his attention back to the road, where they were merging onto a freeway.

"You mean my parents with whom you're acquainted? Why ever did you say that?" She tried to keep the question light.

"Truthfully, it just popped out." He glanced over at her. "It was the least I could to to protect you. I take exception to my relatives when they marinate and grill guests."

"Thank you for the helping hand. It can get pretty hot on a grill." She smiled and was pleased when he smiled back.

"Especially when Mathilde and my grandfather are cooking. But don't change the subject. Tell me about your family."

"Why?"

He looked surprised. "When someone defends the institution as strongly as you do, I can't help but think you must have discovered some secret the rest of us could benefit from. You know, how to achieve the perfection of one mother, one father, two-point-five children, one dog, one cat, oh and don't forget the parakeet."

"A little bitterness there?" Meg murmured the words but she could tell he heard her by the face he made.

"Are you married?" He wasn't wearing a ring, but Ted never had.

"Me?" He shook his head. "No. I was engaged once, but as it turned out—to the wrong woman."

"Ah." She wanted to know more, but it wouldn't be polite to pry.

"Stick around the Ponthiers for awhile and you'll be glad you're—" He stopped, chagrin overtaking his features. "I am so sorry. I can't believe what I was about to say."

"Glad that I'm a widow." Meg nodded. "After someone close to us dies, we say things that are true but we don't want to let ourselves acknowledge any truth if it's ugly or detrimental to the person who died. But it's okay to say what you feel. It's better really than pretending.''

"How'd you get to be so wise about death? It can't be from losing Jules. You only found out today." He narrowed his eyes. "And . . . you didn't even ask to say good-bye or to see the body.''

Meg stared at her hands. She hadn't even thought of going to see Jules's body. Not once had it entered her mind. She'd been far more concerned with trying to reach her children over the phone. But how out of character that lack of attention was for a brand-new bride. She could feel him staring at her, the earlier suspicion flooding back to fill the space between them.

She knew she had to say something. Why not tell him the truth? The question whispered in her mind. She opened her mouth, then stopped. He'd despise her. He'd probably head straight to the airport and dump her there. So why not tell him? She should go home, back to Las Vegas, and let the Ponthiers solve their own problems.

"Or is all that wisdom pure theory?" Parker was gripping the wheel with both hands. "Ever seen a dead man? Ever seen a face that used to laugh and cry and shout with joy that's now a mask? A dead man, Meg, is no longer there. The spirit is gone and it's as if that person never existed because the shell isn't anything at all like the person in his life." He swallowed hard and Meg felt tears steal up behind her eyelids.

"I know what you're describing," she whispered. "I was married before and that's how Ted looked."

"You've outlived two husbands?"

She nodded.

He moved one hand from the wheel and touched her briefly on her folded hands. "Forgive me for judging you. Once you've seen death, it's nothing you want to see ever again. It must have been too much for you to think of seeing Jules like that."

Meg nodded, feeling worse than ever. She dabbed at her eyes, thinking that if Parker ever found out the truth he wouldn't just despise her, he'd probably run over her with his Porsche.

Back and forth until she was really, really flattened. What a skunk she was! "I'm sorry you had to see him like that," she finally managed to say.

"Me, too. And it was such a waste." He jabbed at the wheel with his right hand. "Just like my father."

Meg had wondered about this missing member of the family. "What happened to your father?"

"I think," Parker said in a dry voice, "that story falls into what Mathilde would definitely call the dirty linen."

Of course that made her even more curious. She wanted to press him but it wasn't polite. Instead she looked out the window. They'd been moving swiftly through the traffic and were now on a bridge that seemed to go on forever. "Where are we?"

"Lake Pontchartrain. Headed east."

"Gus's school is a long way out of the city."

"Actually, it's in Mississippi."

"Mississippi!" Her voice rose.

"Perhaps I should have told you just how long of a trip this would be but I was grateful for your help." He flashed that grin that made him look like a young man without a care in the world, rather than the burdened executive he seemed so much of the time.

"And afraid I'd back out?"

"Well, I didn't know that you'd want to be locked up in a car with me for two hours each way."

Meg thought of the way he'd backed her against the armoire and suppressed a shiver. But she couldn't say it sprang from distaste. Far from it. "Well, I can't turn away from a ten-year-old in need," she said, sticking carefully to the legitimate reason for this time spent with Parker.

"Your parents teach you that?"

"You're good," she said, laughing. "Are you a lawyer?"

He made a face and shook his head. "I left that to Jules."

"And did what instead?"

"Engineering at MIT. Then an MBA from Tulane."

"I see." No GED and state college for Parker Ponthier. "Which do you like better?"

"Both." With a pleased look, he said, "I have the perfect job, running companies that make both products and money."

Companies. Plural. Meg was impressed. Ted had bungled his one business. Then she thought of Ted's work schedule and how she'd never seen him. "Do you work a lot?"

He shrugged. "To hear my grandfather tell it, I do. But work makes me happy."

"How many hours a week?"

"Tell me about your parents and I'll answer your question."

She smiled. "You win this round." The smile fading from her face, she admitted, "I'm an orphan. The kind who never knew who her parents were."

"Left on the doorstep of a foundling home?" He sounded aghast.

"Pretty much. Just substitute foundling home with Department of Social Services."

"How could someone do that?"

"I spent a lot of nights making up reasons," Meg said. "And then I got over it."

He glanced over at her. "No wonder you put such importance on family."

Oh, he was not only smart, but sensitive. Meg sighed and wondered how she'd landed up in this dream car with a man who could see right to the heart of the matter. A man to whom she'd already sold a bill of goods and told more fibs than she'd uttered in her previous thirty-two years.

"So tell me how many hours a week you work."

"Oh, it depends."

"Sounds like waffling to me. Are you afraid your grandfather is right?"

He scowled. "A little too smart for your own good, aren't you?" But he said it in a teasing voice, in a way that showed he appreciated her insight.

"It must be more than forty," Meg mused.

He nodded.

"Fifty?"

"Maybe."

"Twelve times five is sixty."

"Good at math, are you?"

Meg nodded. She spread her fingers wide. "I always carry my own calculator."

He grinned. "Okay, Mathematician Meg, I probably work six days a week, ten to twelve hours a day."

"Hmmm." Meg thought of Ted, always absent from her life and the lives of their children. She thought of the bulging briefcase he'd bring home at night and how he'd sometimes fall asleep over reports. She remembered the evenings she'd tuck the children in, sharing their nightly pillow talk, then wander into the den to curl up with a book.

"I like my work," Parker said, sounding slightly defensive.

"That's good, but isn't there more to life than working all the time?"

"I don't know, you tell me." His mouth had taken on a stubborn line.

Meg realized she'd hit on a sore spot. Well, it was a sore spot with her, too. Just as well she'd discovered this horrific flaw in Parker. She'd been sitting there feeling pretty cozy and forgiving towards him, a trend in her emotions that would do her no good at all.

"Oh, you know, there are things you'll miss out on. And one day you'll look up and realize you've made a ton of money and you don't have anyone to leave it to."

He glared at her. "Rub it in, why don't you?"

She produced a sweet smile. "Just trying to help." Yeah, help herself not like this man too much.

"You sound like Grandfather."

"He does make a valid point once in awhile."

"True, but he does it in such a crusty way."

That was for sure. Meg didn't like to think of what the old guy might have to say to her when they returned to the house. She pointed out the window. "Would you look at all these trees! For someone who's lived in the desert forever, this is the most amazing sight."

"So you've lived in Las Vegas all your life?"

"One of the tiny percentage of natives. Or at least the state assumed I'd been born there, since I was found there."

"Is it hard, not knowing anything about your family? Your heritage?"

"Sometimes. And there are times I do silly things as a result of wishing it weren't true." She hesitated, but then decided to tell him. "Like today when you said you knew my parents. I got all excited thinking by some fluke you did know someone who'd been searching for me and just hadn't found me."

He looked at her with such compassion she had to glance away. "I can't stand it when someone feels sorry for me."

"You're pretty tough, aren't you?" It sounded more like an exploration of the possibility, rather than a condemnation.

"I do what I have to do to get by," Meg said, thinking just how true that was. Why, if she hadn't been willing to take the chance on Jules's offer, she'd be home fighting off the barrage of bill collectors. "And it sounds as if working serves that purpose for you."

"I'm sure you're right," Parker said, still looking a bit stubborn. "And I guess if I ever found the right situation I might not work as much."

"Situation?"

He flashed her that sexy smile again. "Oh, you know," he said lightly, "the woman of my dreams."

Eight

The woman of my dreams. Parker mulled over his words as he drove on toward St. Suplicius School. Meg, having warned him that driving always made her drowsy, had indeed given in to sleep, lulled by the rhythm of the road.

He found himself watching her. Oh, of course he paid attention to the road, but just when he thought, *She's sleeping, there's no need to look again,* he'd let his vision take her in. Each time he glanced over, her expression had changed ever so subtly. When she first closed her eyes she hadn't relaxed much.

He couldn't blame her for being tense, not after losing her husband and meeting the family. All in the same day, and here she was en route to break the news to a stepson he could swear she hadn't known existed.

Her breathing shifted, slowing its pace, and the line of her mouth softened. He saw her in profile, as she'd half turned away from him. Her hair lay against the line of her cheek, a gleaming dark contrast to her pale skin. For someone who lived in the desert, she didn't spend much time in the sun.

He wondered why he'd chosen to answer her question about working so much the way he had. At his age he'd had plenty of time to meet such a woman if she really existed. He'd finally concluded that the perfect match for him was as elusive as it had been for every other member of the Ponthier family.

They were cursed by bad choices and Parker would rather remain alone than mimic any of the mistakes to which he'd borne witness. Parker's earliest memories of his parents were screaming matches. Teensy had claimed to do her best to ignore his father's womanizing, but it had taken its toll on her.

As an adult, Parker was well aware of his father's infidelities. They were famous in the city. Teensy's, he only suspected. But he couldn't imagine the good doctor, who'd been a fixture in the Ponthier household for years, was paid only in U. S. dollars.

When Parker's father died in a boating accident, everyone expressed the appropriate sentiments, but Parker felt almost nothing except shame and a guilty sense of relief. The woman who died along with him had been married to one of the Ponthiers' closest business associates. Parker had to smooth over the scandal and mend the business relationship.

Parker to the rescue, just like today.

Meg stirred in her sleep and turned. She was curled facing him now, her lips parted softly, her breath coming slowly and evenly. Her dark eyelashes accentuated the creamy skin, almost baby soft. He felt desire mingled with a curious sense of protectiveness stir within him and forced his attention back to the road.

She didn't look old enough to have been married once, let alone twice. He wondered, with a quick spurt of jealous curiosity, whether either of her husbands had been the man of her dreams.

Not Jules. No way. Parker shook his head. He mourned his brother but he knew his faults too damn well. So who was the other guy? Not that it mattered one whit, of course.

His grandfather liked to tell him he had to think of finding a wife the way he would undertake any other business enterprise. But the old man didn't know just how many women Parker had dated before abandoning the quest. He'd been a lot more selective after the disaster of his engagement to Renee, but he'd yet to meet a woman he could picture himself married and faithful to for the rest of his life.

Parker had sworn long ago that once he married, he'd never become like his father. That was not a vow he took lightly.

He slowed the car and took the exit for Bay St. Louis. Meg was sleeping so peacefully he hated to wake her, but they were within a few miles of the school.

Turning his head, he found her watching him, blinking her eyes sleepily. "Are we almost there?" She hadn't moved from her semi-curled position.

"Yes." Funny how she opened her eyes exactly when he was about to wake her. "It's just down this side road." How well he remembered the route, too.

"Do you come over here often?" She yawned and stretched her arms over her head.

"Not anymore."

"Did you go to school here?" She sounded surprised.

"For a year."

"How old were you?"

Parker grimaced, remembering the year he'd turned ten. Jules, two years his senior, had gotten bounced from his school in New Orleans yet again and their father had reacted by sending him to St. Suplicius. And of course he sent Parker along to keep his older brother out of trouble. "Ten."

"How awful!" She straightened her suit jacket. "That's how old Gus is now. That should help you relate to him. Why did you only stay for a year?"

"Teensy said she'd take out an ad in the *Times-Picayune* listing every woman my father had had an affair with if he didn't let her baby come home again."

"So she wanted you with the family."

Parker shrugged. "She wanted Jules back. It was a package deal."

She murmured something, but he couldn't make it out. Probably more sympathy, which he didn't want. He should keep his problems to himself. After all, that's what they'd taught him at St. Suplicius. Stand up straight and act like a man.

"I take it your father didn't mind having affairs, but he still preserved some level of discretion?"

"That's the way of the polite world, isn't it? Do whatever you want as long as you dress for dinner." Parker realized in a flash of insight one of the subconscious reasons he'd broken his engagement to Renee. Married to her, he would have ended up like his father. The thought came out of nowhere, but he knew the way he knew a good business deal that his instincts were right.

"But didn't he care that your mother knew?" Meg sounded troubled.

"The best advice I can give you, Meg, is don't try to understand my family." He swung the car onto the tree-lined drive leading to the school's main building.

He spoke without thinking that she'd joined the family. He waited for her to protest his exclusion of her, but even though she wrinkled her brow in thought, she said nothing.

Funny how she didn't do some of the most natural things one would expect of a newlywed. Like not saying good-bye to her dead husband or crying over his death or assuming she'd be included in the family. Back at the hotel, she'd seemed almost surprised to be invited over to the house. For someone who made such a fuss over family, not plunging herself wholeheartedly into belonging to the Ponthiers was rather odd behavior. He tucked the thought away to pursue later as he parked the car in a visitor's slot.

Turning off the ignition, he reached for the door handle, eager to get the scene he dreaded over with.

She reached out and caught his hand. "Please, before we go in. When was the last time Gus saw his father?"

He let go of the handle, thinking back. "I'm not sure I know." Jules hadn't been present at Thanksgiving dinner. Lucky him. Parker had stayed at the table for the barest minimum of time required by social rules and regulations. He had no interest in the five couples Teensy had invited to share the meal with the family. The women looked a lot like Teensy, polished but not too happy. The men talked money and business interspersed with golf and sailing. Parker had known them all for years. He'd heard it all, every conquest, every close business call. At similar events in the past, he used to while away the time by trying to pick out which woman his father was screwing.

"Parker?"

That dark thought must have chased its way across his face. "Sorry," he said. "It's been at least since August. I remember that Gus came home for his birthday then."

"Hmm."

"Is that good or bad?" For whatever reason, he accepted she'd know what was best for Gus.

She shook her head and opened the car door. He made it around the car in time to hold the door for her.

"Thanks," she said, surprised. "That's nice."

He smiled. "You bring out the best in me."

She flashed him a look that held as much fright as pleasure, but said nothing in response.

They walked toward the double doors of the central administration building, Parker kicking himself mentally for scaring her off with his comment.

"It looks like a fort," Meg said.

"Actually, it was a monastery. Monks still live here, along with the priests who run the school."

"Monks and priests. What an odd influence for ten-year-olds."

"Not for a child from New Orleans. We're probably the most Catholic city in the country."

"Are you Catholic?" Meg asked.

Parker stared at her, wondering if she knew what an odd question that was to ask of a Ponthier of New Orleans. He paused before opening the door. But of course she had no way of knowing that. He looked down at her wide-eyed gaze. "I gather Jules didn't mention religion either," he said dryly.

"Oh!" She looked guilty, as if she'd made some sort of slip.

Parker reminded himself to take a good look at that marriage license and send an investigator off to Nevada. He also reminded himself he had no business being drawn in by Ms. Meg's surface charm—not until he had all the facts in hand.

Meg fixed her gaze on Parker's hand where it now rested on the heavy brass door knob. She didn't dare lift her head until she composed herself. She was doing a good job of showing just how little she and Jules had known one another. 'Course, that didn't mean they couldn't have married impetuously, love at first sight and all that that implies, in a city where wedding chapels sprouted on every block. Why, she thought she'd known Ted, whom she'd dated for two years, only to discover she'd married a man she'd invented in her mind, a man far different from his true self.

Slowly she squared her shoulders. Right now they had to think of Gus. Meeting Parker's eyes she said quietly, "I'm ready if you are."

He swung the door open. Something about the imposing nature of the doors sent prickles marching along Meg's neck. The sweep of marble floor in a large entry chamber did nothing to dispel the feeling she'd stepped back in time,

back into the dreaded world of institutional-
ized children.

A young man in a blue wool uniform rose
from behind a desk. He couldn't have been
more than a year or two older than Teddy, but
his air of disciplined seriousness aged him.
"May I help you, sir?"

Sir. Meg restrained her reaction at the blatant
sexism.

Parker said, "We'd like to see the headmaster."

The young man pointed to a bench along the
wall. "Please have a seat. Your name, sir?"

"Parker Ponthier. And Mrs. Ponthier." He
looked as if the words had taken him off guard.
"Mrs. Jules Ponthier."

The boy nodded. "Yes, sir."

Meg thought he shot a not-so-polite glance
her way. What kind of reputation did Jules and
his child have?

They'd barely settled on the bench when a
silver-haired man with an elegant bearing appeared from one of the halls branching off the
entry area. He wore an impeccably tailored
charcoal suit.

"Parker Ponthier," he said as he approached,
hand extended. "What a pleasant surprise."

Parker rose as did Meg. He shook the offered
hand and said, "May I present Mrs. Jules Ponthier? Meg, Brother Calax."

A slight lift of the brow was the only slip of
surprise the man showed. "Delighted," he

said, taking Meg's hand and clasping it gently. Looking deep into her eyes, he said, "May you have many blessed years in your sacred union."

Something about the man struck Meg as phony. She retrieved her hand and said, "Thank you, but it seems the universe had other plans for us."

The man turned to Parker. "Let's step into my office."

He led the way through the same door from where he'd come. More gleaming marble floors. Pictures of sad-faced, dark-eyed men in brown robes lined the walls. Along the way, lights burned in wall sconces. Meg heard not one sound she associated with children.

The headmaster ushered them into a room done in dark woods and crimson velvet, the walls lined with bookshelves from floor to ceiling. He indicated a grouping of chairs in front of a fireplace.

Once seated, Parker said, "Jules is dead."

Meg saw Parker's jaw working. She had to quell the urge to reach out and take his hand. Parker needed to be comforted and she knew enough about the Ponthiers by now to understand that there was no one there to perform that function for him. No one would hold his hand while he grieved for his brother.

"I see." The silver-haired man rose and opened a panel set among the bookshelves. When he turned back around, he held a silver tray with a decanter and glasses on it. He set it on the table in front of them and poured some of the liquor into three crystal glasses. "It is God's will," he said, then lifted the tray and offered it to Meg and Parker.

She accepted one of the tiny glasses, as did Parker. She didn't really want a drink but this man made her feel as if she was supposed to do whatever he told her. That thought put her back up and she set the glass back on the tray.

Again, the man lifted a brow. Meg knew she was reacting to authority the way she used to when one of the families would trade her in for another foster child and she'd end up back in the girls' home.

Parker was watching her, cradling his glass. Meg realized she'd better soften her behavior. She had no business revisiting old wounds when she was here to help someone else.

"I suppose you're here to break the news to Auguste the Fourth." The man sipped from his glass.

"Yes." Parker and Meg answered in unison.

The man nodded. "I'll call him in. I'm due at a very important engagement with the governor but I'll wait until you've seen Auguste."

"Oh, you don't need to wait," Meg said. "We'll be okay."

"My dear Mrs. Ponthier," the man said, "in times like these, spiritual guidance can make all the difference in the world."

"Thank you, Brother Calax," Parker said.

Meg knew he'd jumped in to keep her from
disagreeing with the man. But there was no
way she was going to tell a ten-year-old his
father was dead while this bag of wind prosed
on about God's will. It wasn't anybody's will
that Jules was lying in the morgue in New Orleans. It was tragically stupid behavior that had
gotten him there. His own tragically stupid
patterns of living had caught up with him.

The man lifted a phone receiver from a small
table beside his chair and said a few words. To
Parker, he said, "He'll be here momentarily.
Tell me, how did Jules die?"

Parker clasped his hands. "Gunshot."

"Mugged?"

Meg wondered whether Parker would clean
up the version of the story for this man. What
would the family say? Would they admit Jules
had died trying to buy cocaine and been shot
struggling over an officer's gun? Or would
they circulate some story, for instance, that he
was killed in a holdup? And what were they
to tell his son?

Meg was in way over her head. She'd have
to follow Parker's lead. She believed the truth
was best, but given her current complicated situation, there was no way she could judge anyone for any fabrication.

Parker looked straight at the man. "My
brother," he said slowly, "suffered from a drug
addiction that no one ever liked to talk about.
If we had, he might be alive today."

"Ah, I see." The man nodded sagely and polished off his glass.

Meg smiled at Parker, offering him her support. She was impressed with him for speaking the truth.

The door opened. A young boy stood in the doorway. He wore the same uniform as the youngster in the reception area. Heavy blue wool, shiny brass buttons. "You wanted to see me, sir?"

The man beckoned him in.

When he stepped into the room, Meg could see the child was painfully thin. And his right eye was black, blue, and purple.

"Have you been fighting again, Mr. Ponthier?" The man spoke sharply, in a voice he hadn't displayed before.

"Yes, sir." The child stared straight at the headmaster, not even glancing over at Parker and Meg.

"And what was your punishment?"

"Two days in the brig, sir."

He shook his head and sighed. "When will these youngsters ever learn?"

Meg gripped the arms of the chair where she sat. "What's the other guy look like?"

The boy looked from the headmaster over to her, as if awaiting permission to speak.

"You can tell me," Meg said.

The boy broke into a grin. "He's got two shiners, ma'am."

Meg smiled back. It was always good to win a fight.

"Mr. Ponthier, your visitors have something to say to you."

Parker rose and crossed over to Gus. He shook hands with the child. After one darting glance of recognition toward his uncle, Gus kept his gaze fixed squarely ahead, not displaying any emotion.

"Have a seat," the headmaster ordered, apparently planning to orchestrate the entire discussion.

"No!" Meg jumped up. "We're not staying. Thank you, but we need to rush right back to New Orleans."

"Auguste the Fourth isn't going anywhere," the headmaster said, using that sharp tone he'd used to speak to Gus.

"Oh, yes, he is," Meg said. "He's coming home with us."

Parker was looking at her as if she'd gone nuts. But then he started to smile. He handed his untouched glass back to the silver-haired man. "Meg's right."

The man rose from his seat. "No child leaves this school until the end of term."

"Don't worry, his bill will be paid in full," Parker said. "Gus, get your things."

The child looked from the headmaster back to Parker and then up at Meg. She caught her breath. He looked so young and vulnerable, despite the black eye and the military posture.

She waited for him to react, knowing that if she were in his shoes, she'd be thinking it was too good to be true but hoping all the same it was.

When he finally spoke, he looked from Parker to Meg, then flipped a middle finger towards the headmaster. "If you're really taking me home, Uncle Parker, there's nothing I need here."

Nine

There's nothing I need here.

That statement alone was enough to break her heart. Gus was silent as the three of them swept from the headmaster's office. They cleared the front hall and passed by the student on duty, who looked at them with longing in his eyes as they opened the front doors.

In silent agreement they kept a brisk pace. Even though the headmaster had remained behind in his office, seemingly defeated, resigned to the company of his decanter, they all moved as if they sensed he would stop them if they gave him half a chance.

Brackets of concentration lined either side of Parker's usually generous mouth. He stared straight ahead, and he walked purposefully. To Meg's discerning glance he moved with the stance of a man finally paying back a long overdue debt.

In unison, they cleared the building and stepped onto the front drive. Meg chose and discarded words of comfort for the boy. She knew only too well what it was like to be abandoned in a place run by rules and regulations without regard to the fears and joys of children.

Before she could decide what to say, Gus stopped and turned to face the building. With his pitifully thin arms hunkered to his hips, he called out, "Starve me, beat me, make me dance with girls, but I am never going back to that hellhole." With a grin, he pivoted 180 degrees, then said, "Hey, dude, I see you brought granny's hearse." He flipped a bird towards the school and cartwheeled across the grass toward the Infiniti.

Meg looked at Parker.

Parker looked at Meg. "Any ideas for Act Two?"

"WalMart and McDonald's. Or maybe the other way around."

Gus had ripped open the front of his jacket. One of the shiny brass buttons spun into the air and winked as it caught the late afternoon sun.

Parker grinned. "Food. Good thinking. But does it have to be McDonald's?"

"For a ten-year-old?" She considered. "Either that or pizza."

"Then we tell him about Jules?"

"After he's fed and clothed." Meg considered, wishing she had the wisdom Parker granted her credit for. "I think so. But we need to do it before we drive back."

"Why?"

Meg shuddered slightly. "I hate to say it, but it's in case he does want to stay at his school."

"Now I'm confused. You just incited a jail-break back there in the headmaster's office. You gave me the clear indication it was a fate worse than—" a shadow passed over his face and he continued "—death, for him to stay here."

She stubbed at the concrete of the drive with her toe. "It's hard to explain but sometimes the safety of the dreaded known is preferable to the dread of the unknown."

Parker repeated her words under his breath. "Convoluted reasoning, but I guess I see your point. Though you don't think he'd really want to stay?"

"Oh, no, but he may feel better if offered the choice. I firmly believe children need to be of-fered choices in some things. Not in all matters, but since this school is where he's been and he's going to a home without a mother or a father, it seems like one possibility he might cling to."

They'd started walking again, but Parker halted abruptly. In a curious voice, he said, "It's true his natural mother won't be there, but what about his stepmother?"

"I thought you said she was in San Fran-cisco."

He touched her shoulder. "I guess it must be hard to think of yourself as the stepmother of a child you didn't know existed."

"Oh! You mean me?" Meg watched Gus, who was busy hacking at his jacket with a pocketknife he'd presumably had stashed away. "I-um-you're right. I don't think of myself as Gus's stepmother. Jules and I weren't married long enough for me to think in those terms."

"How many hours were you married?"

"Days. We were married several days."

"It's funny, Mrs. Ponthier," Parker said, that tone of disbelief back in his voice, "but most young lovers can count the days and hours since they've said 'I love you' or since the time the minister said 'You may kiss the bride.' But not you. I'm beginning to think you don't have a very romantic nature."

"That's me. Ms. Pragmatic." Meg tried to laugh it off, but she knew exactly what he meant. She used to commemorate the anniversary of her first kiss with Ted, the first time they said I love you, the first time they made love. That all slipped away as the kids came, and Ted worked all the time, and their conversations degenerated to who was teething and who made the honor roll, but she remembered the sweet tenderness those early romantic feelings had created in her emotions.

She even kept trying but it was tough with a man who didn't notice and didn't reciprocate. She remembered wishing those feelings hadn't gotten lost in the shuffle of life, remembered thinking that if she'd chosen more wisely that slow death wouldn't have occurred.

And after Ted's death, Meg had promised herself if given the choice she'd go without a mate rather than settle for anyone who wouldn't go the distance in a relationship.

She sighed. That sentiment was well and good and so far she had stuck by it. But her subsequent financial mess had caused her to muddy the waters with her marriage for hire.

"Maybe you just weren't in love with my brother."

Meg frowned and said somewhat crossly, "Don't be silly. Why wouldn't I have been in love with your brother?" She started walking then, eager to reach the safety of the car and the shield of Gus's company.

"Having known Jules all of my life, I could draw up quite a list of reasons why not." He unlocked the car with his remote.

Gus raced up, jerked open the front passenger door, and flung himself inside. "But let's review that list later," Parker said, pulling open the door Gus had just closed. "In the back, Gus."

Meg started to protest, but she didn't want to send mixed signals. Gus climbed out. He winked at Meg, and said, "Guess my uncle finally scored." Then he jumped into the back seat.

Meg and Parker entered the car. Parker turned around and said, "Gus, this is Meg. She and your father were married last week."

"And you're moving in on Uncle Parker already?" Gus stared at Meg, a storm clearly gathering in his eyes. "Guess you didn't last even as long as the other two."

A knot worked in Parker's jaw. He glanced at Meg, the plea for help clear.

She slipped out of the car and reentered in the back seat, beckoning to Parker to do the same. They'd have to break the news to Gus now. Waiting wouldn't be right.

He followed her move. Gus looked from one to the other and said, "Okay, what's the deal?"

Meg said, "I did marry your father. And I'm here with your uncle because your great-grandfather asked me to come with him. He did that because we have some hard news"—she swallowed and hoped she was doing this right—"to break to you."

"Yeah, what? Granny cried herself to death?" He sounded tough, but Meg noticed how white he'd gone.

"Teensy's fine," Parker said gently, "but your father is gone."

"No shit." Gus laughed, a hard-edged sound that broke Meg's heart. "He's always off somewhere. Anywhere but where I am, that's for sure."

"Gus, I know this is hard to hear 'cause it's

so hard to say, but your father—my brother—
is dead."

Gus stared at Parker, his eyes wide, his
mouth silent. He checked Meg's expression,
too. She nodded.

"No fucking way!" Gus howled the words
and kicked at both of them.

Parker reached for him and took the flailing
child in his arms. He let him kick but from
within the safety of his embrace. Meg tried to
show her support by keeping her gaze steady
on Parker's anguished eyes. Gus didn't need
the confusion of a stranger trying to comfort
him physically at this point, so she sat still.

"He said he'd come back for me. He said he
wouldn't leave me in that hellhole forever."
Gus was sobbing. "He lied and I hate him. I'm
glad he's dead!"

Smoothing Gus's crew-cut hair, Parker murmured, "I know. I know. It hurts bad."

Gus beat his fists on Parker's chest. "You
don't know shit. Nothing hurts. I don't feel
nothing." Then he folded his arms across his
chest and thrust his jaw out at a definitively
obstinate angle.

Despite his shuttered body language he did
remain within the circle of Parker's arms. Parker, his mouth a grimly thin line, continued to
smooth his hand over the child's head.

A tear welled in Gus's eye and he sniffed
thunderously. "Are you sure he's dead?"

Meg and Parker both nodded. Meg said,

"We wouldn't tell you such a sad thing unless it was true."

"Oh, yeah? Well, it would be just like my dad to make up a story like this so he could start a new life without bothering about me. He probably did it just so he wouldn't have to take me fishing. He kept telling me he would but now"—Gus's eyes overflowed and he finished angrily—"now he never will!"

Meg knew what it was like to be cast off. Many times she'd wished for reassurance that she was wanted. Tentatively she reached out her left hand to Gus. She knew what she was doing was dangerous. She was crossing a bridge in her mind by even thinking of using her pretense of a marriage to reassure the child. But comforting him came first with her. And instinct—and her own early sense of abandonment—drew her on.

She lay her hand on Gus's bony knee. The plain gold band Jules had purchased at the wedding chapel circled her ring finger. "Your father married me in Las Vegas," she said slowly, not quite meeting Parker's searching gaze. "He brought me back to New Orleans. So he wasn't trying to run away or start a new life without you."

"Yeah?" He looked at her, then up at Parker.

Parker nodded, adding credence to Meg's story.

"And you won't put me back in that hell-hole?"

"School," Meg said gently. "No, we won't put you back in that school."

He worked his jaw again. In a funny way, the gesture reminded Meg of Parker. She'd seen him do the same thing when clamping down on his emotions. Maybe it was something they taught boys in that hellhole, as Gus so aptly referred to his school.

Gus loosened the grip he had on his crossed arms. In a voice barely audible he said, "How did my dad die?"

Meg looked to Parker. There he was doing it again—that toughening of the jaw. She gave him a smile both sad and encouraging, letting him know this question was his to handle.

"It's hard for me to say this, Gus, but your dad had some problems. He was my brother and I loved him very much. But his problems led to a scuffle over a gun. He was shot and killed."

Gus's eyes grew wide. He touched his bruised eye. "Was he in a fight?"

Parker nodded.

Meg realized she was holding her breath. How much should they tell him? He'd hear the whispers and the stories as he grew older. Telling her children Ted had died from an aneurysm had been hard enough and that was straightforward compared to Jules's death as the result of a drug deal gone bad.

"I guess that's why he used to tell me I shouldn't fight," Gus said in a small voice.

Meg sensed that Gus was about to make the leap of logic that if he hadn't fought—if he'd been a better kid—maybe his dad would still be alive. It was a terrible thing, this burden children took on trying to adjust the outcome of adult behavior. But Meg had seen it in her own children. And more than that, she'd lived it.

To Gus she said, "We each have a time on earth and when it's time to pass from this life, it's going to happen no matter what. Nothing you did or didn't do could ever change that."

Gus glowered at her. "But if I'd have been better he might have come back for me and then I could have saved him." He stuck up his fists, brandishing his grazed knuckles. "I would've fought off those bad guys!"

Meg smiled despite herself. "You're a tough kid, but there's no need to fight."

"He loved you, Gus," Parker said.

"Ha!" Gus's arms clamped back across his chest. "What's love when you're an orphan and you've never been fishing."

"Everything," Meg said, the word slipping out before she thought.

"And you're not an orphan," Parker said. "You've got a mother and now you have two stepmothers."

Gus looked at Meg with curiosity. "Are you going to stick around?" He sounded tough, but Meg didn't buy the bravado. Here was a kid who'd been dumped and passed on to others far too often.

She thought of her children back home in Las Vegas, of her life and how she needed to go home soon. Very, very soon. Her hesitation must have shown because Gus scowled. "You're just like the rest. Take the money and run."

"Meg's different."

She glanced in surprise at Parker.

"Yeah, well, we'll see," Gus rubbed his eyes, then his stomach.

"How about a burger?" Meg asked.

His face lit up. "With a chocolate shake and extra-large fries?"

She nodded.

He wiped at his eyes.

Parker shifted so that he no longer held Gus within his arms. Gus settled on the seat between them, looking younger than ten in his white t-shirt and heavy wool trousers. Meg could count his ribs through the thin fabric of his shirt. "What did they feed you at that school?"

He made a face of disgust. "Vegetables. And chicken. Chicken. Chicken. Chicken!" He stuck a finger down his throat.

Meg and Parker smiled and moved together out of the back seat and into the front. Parker turned the key in the ignition, then smiled at her and mouthed, "Thank you."

She smiled in return, grateful for his acknowledgement, thankful for his support, and all too aware of his presence.

"McDonald's here we come," Parker said. "And then, Gus, we're taking you home."

Ten

We're taking you home. Parker tasted the words again as he watched Gus chow down on not one but two double cheeseburgers. Meg had done justice to one of the chef salads in a plastic to-go box. Parker, who hadn't set foot in a McDonald's for more years than he could remember, tried to appreciate his chicken sandwich but found it fairly unpalatable. Maybe that had more to do with Gus's finger-down-the-throat routine at the mention of chicken than the cook at McDonald's, though.

He smiled at the thought and tossed a napkin to Gus as his nephew slurped the last molecules of ice cream and chocolate from his cup. Gus caught the napkin, waved it towards his face, then sat back with both hands on his skinny waist.

"Now that's some *food*," he said. "Weren't you hungry, Uncle Parker?"

Parker shook his head and caught Meg hiding a grin. She probably found him too uptown for her tastes, but for his part, he was ready to forgive her almost anything for coming with him on this mission and sticking by him as they broke the news of Jules's death to Gus.

It amazed him that Gus had reacted as well as he had. Jules had been pretty much an absentee father, but he'd spent more time with Gus than Marianne had. Gus's mother had consigned the baby to round-the-clock nurses and gone back to work on her waistline and her golf handicap.

Parker watched as Meg and Gus began negotiations surrounding a game to be played with a wadded-up paper cover of a straw. She was at ease with the child in a way he envied. There were some women who should've been sterilized at puberty and Marianne was one of them. Meg, on the other hand, took to children so naturally Parker found himself thinking the crazy thought that maybe his brother had married her because she would make a good mom for Gus.

Gus flicked the wad of paper toward Meg. She bounced it back with a flick and cried out as it crossed an imaginary goal line.

"No fair," Gus said. "You cheated." Then as Meg protested, he whipped the paper past her and off the table. That must have been a score because he yelled, "Gotcha!"

Parker dropped his notion. His brother had never thought of anyone other than himself and Gus was no exception. He sure hadn't been thinking of his son when he'd gone out on Jackson Avenue to score a fix.

Gus was giggling and his blue eyes, so much like Jules's, were alive in a way Parker didn't remember seeing since Gus had been a toddler.

Not that you've paid much attention to him. Even when Gus had lived at Ponthier Place a few years ago, Parker had pretty much ignored him during his visits to the house.

Meg snatched the paper missile heading toward her face and waved her clasped fist triumphantly. "I win," she said. "About ready for a trip to WalMart?"

"WalMart?" The way Gus said the word you would've thought it ranked below chicken in his world view.

Meg nodded.

"Do you think it's open on Sunday?" Parker asked, having no idea. They could easily wait until tomorrow. Teensy would take Gus shopping or have Horton do it.

"Sure they are," Meg said. "Sunday is the day America shops."

Gus had stuck his nose in the air. "Only low-class people shop at WalMart."

"Is that right?" Meg tossed the crumpled paper projectile from one hand to the other, eyeing the child.

Parker heard the dangerous note in her voice. If he were a betting man, he'd lay money that Gus was about to get a lesson on snobbery. Well intentioned and well deserved.

"Everyone knows that." Gus sucked at the remains of his shake through his straw, setting off a barrage of sucking noises.

"And everyone knows that's a low-class noise so let's get going." Meg stood up.

"Hey, I'll have you know I'm a Ponthier." Gus stuck his hands on his waist. "And Ponthiers don't shop at WalMart." He sat back against his chair. "You tell her, Uncle Parker."

Parker couldn't actually remember the last time he'd stepped foot in one of the discount stores. Instead of fabricating his response in order to support Meg, he said, "Did you know the guy who founded WalMart was one of the richest men in the world when he died?"

Gus's mouth twisted. "So big deal. He went and died then he couldn't spend the money anymore. Just like my dad." He rubbed his hand across his mouth, pressing his knuckles against lips that quivered.

Parker could have kicked himself for his choice of words. Sending a mute apology and yet another plea for help across the table to Meg, he reached out a hand and touched his nephew's shoulder. "I'm sorry, Gus."

Gus kicked the base of the table and shrugged away from Parker's touch. "It's okay. Shit happens." Then he glared defiantly, obviously anticipating a reaction to his words.

"Gus—" Parker started.

"When you were at that school swearing got you in trouble, didn't it?" Meg interrupted.

Gus nodded.

"And when you got in trouble people paid attention to you, didn't they?"

He nodded again, a small smile lifting the corners of his still trembling mouth.

"Well, that's not how we're going to react," Meg said briskly. "Parker and I respond to polite, intelligent word choices. Language appropriate to a Ponthier of Ponthier Place."

Parker stifled a grin. He admired the way she wasn't above using the child's snobbery to win her point. Gus did have a mouth that could use some cleaning up. To Gus, he said, "Meg's right."

Gus looked from one to the other then down at his hands. "No friggin' way I believe that," he said.

Meg gathered the remains of the sandwich wrappings and discarded catsup packets onto a tray. "I noticed a WalMart off the freeway not too far from here. I saw it just as I was waking up."

"I said"—Gus raised his voice—"I'm not going to any damn WalMart."

The couple at the next table turned to stare at them.

Parker began to wish he'd never entered the universe of McDonald's, WalMarts, and impossibly spoiled nephews.

"Ready?" Meg asked.

Parker rose, wondering what they would do if Gus refused to vacate his seat. He'd started drumming his heels against the base of his chair with an alarming intensity.

"They have pretty cool pocket knives at WalMart," Meg said, addressing Parker without looking at Gus.

He had to hand it to her. She'd noticed Gus's knife earlier.

Parker dumped his tray.

Moving about as fast as an alligator sunning itself on a summer afternoon, Gus dragged first one foot then the other from beneath the table and pushed his skinny body from the plastic chair. "I'll go," he said, mutiny in his eyes, "but don't expect me to like anything they have there."

Meg smiled. Parker pushed open the door and held it open for the woman and the child. It was a pleasantly odd notion, but he felt a little bit like he'd gained an impromptu family.

Almost three hours later, Meg held open the side door as Parker led a sleepy Gus into the house. Gus wore the baggy shorts and knee-topping sweatshirt he'd selected at WalMart. He'd also picked out hiking boots, gray socks, and a pocketknife.

Meg had tossed in underwear, pajamas, and a toothbrush, items Gus understandably refused to be concerned with as he played with his new knife. All in all, the shopping spree set Parker back about $150, a bargain considering not once during the drive back to New Orleans did Gus reiterate his protests against shopping at the discount store.

Cars lined the drive and lights burned in every room of the house. The last thing Meg wanted to do was meet more friends or relatives of the Ponthiers.

"Let's get him to bed," she whispered to Parker.

Horton appeared from a side hall. "Good evening, Miz Meg, Mr. Parker, Mr. Gus."

"Who do we have?" Parker asked.

Horton raised one hand and began ticking off his list against his fingers. Meg was amused to see he still wore white gloves that somehow managed to remain spotless. "The Graviers, the Millicents, the Bennings, the Duffources. Ah, and Miss Laisance called, too. She asked particularly for you."

And who was Miss Laisance? Meg shot a glance to catch Parker's reaction but he merely said, "I'll be back down in a bit. We've got to get Gus to bed and he could use a bath."

"Hey, I don't go to bed this early." Gus jerked wide awake and shook free of Parker's arm. He crouched in a fighting stance and said, "Just try to make me."

"Any word in response to that telegram, Horton?"

"No, sir." Horton held out a hand toward Gus. "Shall we get your bath out of the way?"

"Oh, you don't have to do that," Meg said.

Parker looked surprised. "Horton raised us, you know."

"Oh." Meg was confused. Was Horton a butler? A maid? A nanny? He seemed far too dignified to be assigned to overseeing the bath of a ten-year-old.

"If you'd rather do it yourself?" Horton asked politely.

Meg thought of facing the crowd he'd described. No doubt all the well wishers were dying of curiosity over Jules's surprise widow. "Yes. Yes, I think I would."

Gus stared at her open-mouthed. "You can't see me naked. I don't even know you."

Meg rolled her eyes. "Puh-lease, Gus. I've no interest in seeing you naked. Only clean."

"Thanks, Horton. I'll show Meg to Gus's room." Parker pointed to the large stair rising from the end of the entrance hall. "March," he said. "We'll be right behind you."

"I like being dirty," Gus said, but he took off, leaping up the elegant staircase two steps at a time.

"Have Meg's things been sent over?" Parker asked Horton.

He nodded. "They're in the Burgundy Suite."

Parker looked tired, Meg thought, watching him confer for a few minutes more with Horton. She quit listening and glanced around, noticing several new floral arrangements had arrived since they'd departed for Mississippi earlier that afternoon.

"About time you two got back here!" Grandfather wheeled across the entry way and braked to a halt in front of them. "They could use some more food in there," he said to Horton, who nodded and withdrew.

"What did you do, stop and gamble?"

"Hello, Grandfather," Parker said.

"Hi, Mr. Ponthier," Meg joined in.

He glared at her. "You may as well call me Grandfather. Everyone else does."

"I guess you want to know how Gus took the news," Parker said.

"You always did know how to get to the point." Grandfather nodded and Meg saw through his gruffness. He was concerned about Gus.

"I'll tell you, but let me show Meg to her room first," Parker said. "She's had a long day and before she takes on any more new faces, I'm sure she'd like to freshen up."

Meg glanced at him, touched by his thoughtfulness. Or did he say that because she looked raggedy and he didn't want the family embarrassed? Whichever it was, she was happy to take him up on the offer. Delay served her purposes.

"Okay, okay, but come right back down here. And you, young lady, don't forget you owe me a conversation."

"I won't," Meg said meekly and followed

Parker across the hall and up the stairs. Unlike Gus, she walked slowly, drained by the experiences of the day and feeling oddly shy alone with Parker as they climbed the stairs to her room.

Yet she felt inexplicably comfortable with him. She had stood beside this man's brother in a wedding chapel and sat within inches of him on the flight from Las Vegas to New Orleans. Not once had she been at ease with Jules. And it wasn't enough to attribute the difference to the circumstances of the marriage for hire.

After his earlier arrogance, Parker had shown her a softer, more approachable aspect of himself, a most appealing self. She wanted to walk by his side and learn more about this man.

"The Burgundy Suite is at the back of the house," Parker said in such a matter-of-fact voice Meg felt foolish over the direction her thoughts had taken.

He pointed to the right down a long hallway that ran in both directions from the top of the stairs. Even on the second floor the ceiling arched far overhead. Lights glowed in sconces along the walls. "It'll be quieter there," he added.

"That's very thoughtful. Where is Gus's room?"

Parker pointed towards the door they'd just walked past.

"Wouldn't it be better for me to be closer?"

"To Gus?" He sounded surprised, but then he paused, weighing her question. "You wouldn't mind?"

"Not at all." Not that she'd be there much longer, but she wanted to help the child in any way she could. She could picture him getting quite forgotten in this house, especially with all the bustle that would result from his father's funeral, an event that would leave him emotionally more needy than usual.

Parker pushed open the door across the hall from Gus's room. "Teensy got a little carried away with yellow when she redecorated this guest room," he said. "Do you mind it? It's not as large as the Burgundy."

A vision of yellow the color of morning sunlight met Meg's eyes. She took in a four-poster bed covered in frilly yellow fabric, an armoire, a chaise covered in yellow velvet, and a skirted dressing table. Here and there splashes of white and cornflower blue relieved the yellow. The effect was startling, but definitely cheery. "It's perfect," Meg said.

"Yes, it is, isn't it?" But Parker wasn't looking at the furnishings. He gazed straight at her with an expression akin to hunger in his eyes.

Meg gazed back, unable to break the connection. His blue eyes had darkened, turning almost inky. "It's my favorite color," she whispered, meaning the blue of his eyes.

"Mine, too," he said. He raised his left hand

and with a touch as light as a butterfly grazed her cheek. "You were terrific with Gus."

Meg's cheek sizzled from the simple contact. "It was nothing—" she caught herself from finishing the sentence. She'd been about to say nothing I wouldn't do for my own children. But Parker, despite his dutiful errand to break the news to Gus of his father's death at his grandfather's behest, didn't strike her as a man who'd take to a woman with three children of her own. Driven purely by her instincts, she chose to rely on them and keep the knowledge of her family to herself.

Parker stepped back. In a brisk voice, he said, "Well, you may call it nothing, but the family owes you a tremendous thanks. So the room will do? There's a bathroom attached." He pointed to one of two doors. "I'll go get your bags and be right back."

"Sure." Meg wondered what had shifted his mood so abruptly. Had he frightened himself? She certainly had. What was she doing thinking about what type of woman Parker Ponthier might be interested in!

The door across the hall burst open and Gus sauntered out dressed in his WalMart garb. "At least I've got cable in my room here," he said. He pointed to the yellow finery. "Is this your room?"

"Yes. And does your room have a bath attached, too?"

He grimaced. "Sure we can't forget about the bath?"

"Sorry," Meg said. "A bath can be a lovely experience. Think of it as pleasure rather than punishment."

Gus wrinkled his nose. "Sometimes you talk like a teacher," he said. "Is that what you were before you married my dad?"

"No, but I plan to be a teacher." Which is one of the reasons she had married Jules, ironically enough. She'd hoped to pay off Ted's mountain of debts and have enough to return to college for her degree.

Gus blew air through his mouth and nose in a rude fashion. "Ho, you don't have to work now. You'll just spend your time drinking martinis and screwing your personal trainer."

"And not paying attention to Gus?"

He nodded, then picked at the hem of his sweatshirt. "That's what my mom does. I mean my real mom. And CeCe, too, except she likes women."

Meg hoped her reaction didn't show. Thankfully, Parker was headed up the hall, her Saks boxes piled high.

He put them in her room. She said to Gus in a low voice, "I don't drink martinis and I've absolutely no use for a personal trainer."

"Yeah?" He shrugged. "You'll just find another way to spend your time."

"Let's go start that bath water and let Meg have a well-deserved rest," Parker said to Gus.

"You're sure, Parker?" Meg was surprised at how good it felt to hear Parker's name on her lips, and she was also pleased by the way he was jumping in to help with Gus. "I am the one who turned down Horton's services."

He nodded.

"Hey, I can take my own bath," Gus said. "I'm not a baby." Looking from Parker to Meg, a crafty grin lit his face. "If I go take a bath right this minute, will you hide me from"—he bugged his eyes out and made a fake sobbing sound—"Teensy!"

Parker raised his eyes upward, obviously seeking patience. Meg smiled and watched as Parker pointed his nephew across the hall. Gus, carrying on at top volume with his fake boo-hooing, marched, with Parker falling in behind.

Twenty minutes later, revived by a shower and a quick change of wardrobe, Meg paused at the open door to Gus's room. Parker stood beside one of the twin beds. The bathroom door remained shut and from behind its protective muffling, the booming of a radio pounded.

As if he sensed her presence, Parker turned from the window. A smile lifting his lips, he said, "Parenting must be a full-time job."

From the doorway, Meg nodded and said, "Oh, it is!" Then to cover her far too expressive statement, she moved forward into the room and said in a much more subdued voice, "So I'm told."

He dropped to the edge of the bed. With a rueful smile, he said, "I can't even begin to pretend to know the first thing about helping out with a child. I plead complete ignorance."

"Oh, it's not so hard to learn," Meg said, approaching the bed.

"Sugar production, real estate, finance"— Parker grinned, almost mocking himself—"I can master those easily enough, but somehow I've never understood children."

"Do you want to?" Meg told herself his answer did not matter, yet she knew she lied. Holding her breath, she said, "Do you want to have children of your own?"

Parker regarded her, a serious, thoughtful expression in his eyes. "You know, I do. But I honestly can't say I'm qualified."

Meg smiled. "You learn as you go."

"Perhaps." Then he flashed one of those dangerously seductive smiles, especially seductive because he didn't seem to realize the effect he had on her. "But all that aside, I wish I could do more for Gus."

"What would you wish for?" Meg had moved so that she stood beside the end of the bed. Parker sat midway up its length.

He was silent for awhile. The thumping of bass reverberated through the bathroom door. Meg waited for his answer, curious as to what he would say.

Suddenly, he rose and said, "Where are my

manners?" He gestured to the bed and said, "Please, have a seat."

Meg smothered a smile, but was delighted nonetheless. "Thank you," she said, seating herself primly on the foot of the bed.

Parker dropped down and the bed bounced softly. Meg felt the movements echoing within her body and wished to the high heavens that his good manners and breeding hadn't asserted themselves. She'd felt much safer standing.

Slowly, he said, "I'd wish for wisdom, to start with. You showed me the value of that."

"I did?"

He nodded. "At the school, then by the way you convinced him to go to WalMart."

Meg waved a hand, wishing Parker weren't sitting quite so close to her, wishing he didn't look nearly so delectable. "Merely a bit of applied psychology."

"Hmmm." Parker stared towards the windows, then said, "I'd wish for knowledge."

"You were a ten-year-old boy yourself," Meg pointed out gently.

"So I should look within for answers?"

She nodded. "But wishing is good, too." Feeling more relaxed with him, she turned sideways on the bed so she faced him. Tucking one foot under her, she said, "I believe very much in the power of wishes. Some people think of them as affirmations, but I like to call them wishes. We—" She stopped, realizing what she'd been about to say.

"We?" Parker leaned closer, his eyes fastened on hers.

"I"—Meg corrected herself—"I have a tradition involving wishes."

"And what's that tradition?" Parker asked the question in a low murmur. By this time, he'd moved much too close for comfort. Meg hadn't once seen him scoot or edge over, but the fact was when she looked up at him, her own eyes wide and her heart pumping in response to his nearness, Parker was only inches from her. What she ought to do was wish him away.

"I call it pillow talk," she said softly, then raised her chin. If he made fun of her now, it wouldn't matter how fast her heart raced in response to him.

"And it has to do with wishes?"

She nodded and reminded herself to speak in the singular. She was so used to thinking of herself and her children as a unit that the "we" slipped naturally off her tongue. "Wishes for dreams." Meg pointed to the pillow tucked under the bedspread. Feeling more than a little bit shy, but wanting to share her tradition with him, she said, "If you hand me that pillow, I'll show you the best way to make a wish."

Without taking his eyes from hers, Parker reached around, yanked the pillow out from beneath the covers, and handed it to her.

Meg tucked the pillow against her chest. There, at least it would protect her from Parker getting too close. "So, you hold onto the pillow"—Meg began—"and so does . . ."

Parker touched the pillow just above where her hand clasped it. "Let me guess," he said in a low voice, "if you're sharing pillow talk with someone, that person holds onto the pillow with you?"

Meg tightened her grasp on the pillow. As she did, her hand brushed Parker's. "You're pretty smart, aren't you?"

He shook his head. "No, you're a good teacher." Touching her lightly on the back of her hand, he said, "You led me straight to the answer."

Meg glanced down to his hand beside hers and in a wild moment of desire, wished the pillow weren't separating their bodies. Then she reined in her imagination. In a controlled voice, she said, "With pillow talk, you could wish to find more ways to spend time with Gus."

Watching Meg fondle the pillow, Parker stroked the bottom side of Meg's pinky finger. "And can I wish for more than one wish?"

"One or two," she said, her gaze fastened on his hand. He moved his explorations of her soft skin to the top of her hand, then skimmed her forearm with his palm.

Before she could consider objecting to his caress, he tucked her hair away from her cheek, and leaned close to kiss her. His seductive lips hovering above her mouth, he whispered, "And could I wish that I can spend more time with you?"

She parted her lips, considering her answer. She could feel the heat of him—the expectancy.

The bathroom door burst open. The radio blasted into the room, as did Gus, wearing only a towel.

Meg jumped back.

"Dudes!" Gus grabbed at his towel. "What's a guy have to do to get some privacy around here?" He backed into the bathroom and Meg dropped the pillow on the bed and fled the room.

Parker picked up the pillow and hugged it.

From the bathroom, Gus said, "See what happens when you make me take a bath."

Parker chuckled and left Gus to his privacy. But Meg was indeed a very good teacher; Parker couldn't wait to make some wishes for his dreams.

After the feelings Parker had aroused in her, Meg felt it was less risky to face Grandfather Ponthier than to remain in Gus's room with Parker. Descending the elegant staircase, Meg tried to compose her expression, but it was tough. The man had gotten to her! Glancing downward, she found a pretty silver-haired woman watching her approach. Remembering she was supposed to be a grieving widow, Meg schooled her features.

"You must be Jules's widow," the woman said in a well-modulated voice. "I'm Julianne Soniat. Please accept both my felicitations and my condolences."

"Thank you," Meg said, relieved that the woman wasn't a clone of the harsh-tongued Aunt Mathilde. Even her shower hadn't prepared her to face that member of the Ponthier clan.

"My grandson Michael went to school with Jules at Country Day. He's out of town but I'm sure he won't miss the wake."

Meg nodded. When was the wake? She hoped this nice woman wouldn't ask her. And what did one do at a wake, anyway? She'd never been to one as it wasn't a custom observed by the Protestant families she knew in Las Vegas. For Ted, there had been visitation hours at the funeral home, then a graveside service. Perhaps a wake was a New Orleans custom or a practice followed only by Catholics. She'd have to ask Parker.

"I'm just leaving," the woman said gently. "I'll tell Michael we spoke."

Meg realized the woman thought she was lost in her sorrow. She repeated her thanks, thinking that if she kept her conversation to those two words she might escape the next few days without committing too many blunders.

The wheelchair appeared from the direction

of the library. "Julianne," Grandfather called, "thank you for coming."

The woman had been pulling on her gloves. She stopped and turned to face Grandfather, a lively glow sweeping over her face. "Wild horses wouldn't have kept me from your side, Augie."

Grandfather wheeled to her side. Taking one hand in his good one, he kissed her knuckles.

"But you'd run away without saying goodnight."

She tugged on her gloves. "Guilty there."

Meg recognized personal history when she saw it on stage. Had they been lovers once? Or was it unrequited?

"Goodnight, Augie, and you too, dear," she said, and walked gracefully toward the door.

Grandfather shook his head. "What a waste," he muttered.

"An old flame?"

"Nosy sort, aren't you?"

"As Mrs. Soniat said, 'Guilty there.' "

He shot her a sharp look and wheeled his chair around. "Into the library. Now."

Eleven

Parker stood in the shadows, watching Meg follow his grandfather into the library. What were the two of them conferring about? He found himself wanting to know everything about Meg and even considered either joining them or eavesdropping on their discussion.

Eavesdropping would serve his grandfather a proper turn. The old guy was quite proud of his ability to scope out the moves of his business and familial opponents through exactly that tactic.

Parker took one step forward, only to find himself stopped in his tracks and stymied in his intent by the arrival of Becca Laisance, the last person he wanted to see at that moment.

"Parker, I've been looking everywhere for you," she sighed, opening her arms to him, her upper body managing to graze his chest. "You poor, poor dear. Where have you been hiding?"

Why had he ever invited her to accompany

him to that upcoming winter ball? One look at
her self-satisfied face after he'd asked her and
he'd known immediately he'd made a mistake
of monumental proportions.

The breasts that had helped lead him into
that error pressed against him. "I am so, so,
sorry about Jules," she cooed, embracing him.

He patted one hand and extricated himself.
"Thank you, Becca," he said. "It's sad but
we're coping."

"I do hope I can help," she said, far too
archly for his taste. He asked himself for the
second time why he'd asked her to dinner.
Then he remembered he'd needed an escort for
a charity dance he hadn't been able to avoid.
Thank Teensy for getting him into that one, he
said to himself and tried again to produce a
smile for the simpering, yet very beautiful
Becca Laisance.

He suddenly remembered he'd asked her to
the charity ball right after the lawyer had
whipped out that ridiculous release of liability.
He'd done it on the rebound. Well, at least that
made him feel as if he hadn't quite lost his grip
on reality. Smiling broadly, he flicked a lock of
blond hair back from her face, and said, "You
help just by being your gorgeous self."

She performed an amazingly agile shimmy
and gave him an angelic smile that promised
she could behave very much like the devil herself. Amazed that he found himself unmoved

by her performance, Parker said, "Have you
seen Gus?"

"Gus?" She twirled her hair with one long
ruby-tipped finger.

"My nephew," he said briefly, hoping Gus
hadn't fallen into Teensy's clutches. There was
no telling what crime the kid would commit in
order to free himself from that fate.

"Jules's little boy?" She looked at him, all
wide-eyed. "He's here?"

He nodded, glancing around and moving
them into the center of the hall, then closer toward the Great Parlor. He longed to do whatever it took to edge them towards the library,
but he sensed Meg wouldn't be too receptive
if she discovered him with Becca in tow.

"I thought he was away at school." She
pouted and stopped twirling her hair long
enough to sneak a glance at the diamond-
studded watch on her right wrist. "Want to escape for awhile?"

He shook his head. "He was at St. Suplicius
but we brought him home tonight."

"We?" She went back to twirling her hair.

"We. Yours truly, with help from Jules's
widow."

Becca laughed. "I can't believe anyone Jules
married is capable of giving help to anyone!"

Parker stared at her. A dark cloud rose in his
mind. "By the way," he said slowly, "remember that charity event I asked you to attend

with me? I won't be going, on account of
Jules's funeral."

"Oh, no." She really pouted this time. "And
I was so looking forward to it."

"It just wouldn't be right, though, would it?"
He knew his mouth had formed a grim line.

She completely missed the nonverbal cue.
Tapping him on the chest, she whispered, "I'll
make it up to you. Our own private charity
event."

Out of habit, he flashed her a smile. "I'll take
a rain check," he said, stepping back and turning away.

Straight into the path of Meg, who'd been
standing behind him for who only knew how
long.

Her eyes were bright, and Parker knew instinctively the image was caused by unshed
tears. Continuing in her approach, she held out
a hand and said in a throaty voice he didn't
recognize, "Parker, introduce me to your
friend?"

Ooh, she was mad. Parker hadn't been born
yesterday. Either grandfather had done it to
her, or she'd been listening in on Becca's at-
tempts to woo him. Amazed at his own self-
confession, he hoped fervently that it was the
latter that had her riled up.

"Becca Laisance, Margaret Ponthier." For
whatever reason, he used her formal name.

Meg smiled and held out a hand. "How do
you do, Miss Laisance?" It was the first time

Parker hadn't heard her say, "Call me Meg, please."

Becca nodded, not deigning to lift her own hand. "So sorry to hear about Jules. I guess you'll be going back home soon, since he's not with us anymore?"

Meg fluttered her lashes and sighed.

Parker almost laughed out loud.

Meg said, "Why, I haven't decided. I think that's up to the family. You understand that, don't you? I've just been having the most heart-warming chat with Grandfather Ponthier." She smiled up at Parker. "He's so happy we brought Gus home with us."

Becca practically glowered. Parker knew Meg was putting on a show, but instead of being annoyed he was enjoying the performance. It served Becca right. He hadn't even been on date one with the woman and she'd been acting as if she were God's gift to Parker A. Ponthier.

And the only gift Parker wanted, he realized with a searing flash of insight, was the chance to get to know Margaret "Call me Meg, please" Ponthier a whole lot better.

Meg stared at the retreating backside of the blonde, too embarrassed to let Parker see her face. If Grandfather hadn't gotten her so worked up, surely she wouldn't have carried on like that. But that woman wasn't a good-hearted sort. Meg had heard what she'd said about Jules.

"I guess I owe you yet another thanks," Parker said.

"You do?"

He tipped his head in the direction of the blonde. "Meg's search and rescue."

She smiled but said, "I'm sure you can fend for yourself with the opposite sex."

"Some days I'm not so sure," he said, his blue eyes fixed on her face. "Did you and grandfather come to terms?"

Meg shifted her gaze to her feet and studied the conservative black pumps she'd worn for the first time that day. She'd never owned shoes so plain or boring in her life, but Jules had dressed her for the role he'd hired her to play. Staring at the shoes reminded her to toe the line and escape with her emotions intact. "We talked about the funeral," she said.

Sadness settled into his eyes.

Meg reached out and squeezed his hand. "You've had a hard day, too, you know."

He not only accepted her touch this time, but returned the gentle pressure on her hand.

"Well, well, back at last I see."

Meg started to yank her hand free at the sound of Dr. Prejean's voice but Parker clasped it tight.

"Hello, Prejean," he said, his voice none-too-warm.

The doctor made a point of staring at their

joined hands. "Teensy was feeling just a bit stronger so I left her in the salon with the visitors and came out for a pipe." He pulled a pipe from his jacket pocket and began filling it.

Meg wondered how long Parker was going to hold her hand. It felt good, and natural, as if her hand belonged in his. Was he holding her hand because he wanted to? Or was he using her to make a point that Prejean couldn't push him around?

"I've been thinking about doctors for Gus," Prejean said.

"He doesn't seem sick to me," Meg said.

"He's not," Parker said.

"With Teensy's blood in him and with all he's been through," Prejean said, "it's best to put him in therapy. Think of it as a preventive measure."

The pressure on Meg's hand intensified. Parker said in a dangerous voice, "Teensy's blood runs in my veins, too."

Prejean gestured with his still unlit pipe. "You're an anomaly, Parker. Always said so."

"Why, thank you, doctor," Parker said. He glanced down to where his hand covered Meg's, then slowly let go. "Sorry," he murmured, not sounding sorry at all.

Meg clasped her hands together, thinking how cold they felt as soon as Parker released her.

"Join me on the porch?" Prejean said, looking straight at her.

"Thank you, but I don't smoke."

"I'll puff in the opposite direction." He was eyeing her like she was a prime guinea pig. Meg couldn't help but feel he wanted to psychoanalyze her or perhaps to win her over to his point of view regarding Gus.

"She's expected in the Great Parlor," Parker said. "If you'll excuse us."

Without waiting for the doctor's response, Parker turned and Meg followed. Parker's hostility to the doctor was clear and readily understandable to her. Besides, given the choice, five minutes by Parker's side was worth more to her than an hour's free treatment with any doctor.

As they reached the double doors of the parlor, Meg hesitated.

Parker must have sensed her stage fright. "There aren't so many people left now. It'll be okay."

"It's a little like being in a fish bowl," Meg said. "And I'm the new fish and everyone's swimming around to take a look."

"Can't blame them for that," Parker said. "Jules always did have good taste."

Meg blushed. She started to mumble a thank you but Teensy pounced on them in the doorway.

"How was my little grandbaby?" Teensy's eyes were open way too wide, her mouth too brightly smiling. She wore a tailored black silk dress with a hem that almost swept the floor.

"Gus is fine," Parker said.

Meg nodded, wondering where Gus had gone. He wasn't with Parker, he hadn't been in the library with Grandfather and Teensy's comment confirmed he'd escaped her notice. She'd go check on him as soon as she could gracefully excuse herself. All the same people from the afternoon were in the room, plus several other couples. Bolstering herself, she listened to Teensy ramble on about her grandbaby. To hear her talk, you'd think Gus was still in diapers.

She shook hands and smiled with the visitors, grateful that Parker remained by her side. She found it hard to keep the names and faces straight. They all said the same sorts of things. *Sorry for your loss. What a tragedy. To be taken from you when you were just married. You were married only recently, weren't you?*

Feeling like the biggest impostor ever, Meg held her own, but just barely. Another blonde, almost as beautiful as Miss Laisance but slightly less aggressive, had managed to sidetrack Parker.

As soon as Meg had met the last of the visitors, she murmured an excuse and slipped from the room. At least with Gus she felt she possessed an honest purpose. Trying to help the youngster deal with his loss gave her a reason for her presence in the house. Teensy didn't need her and Dr. Prejean must have known that when he'd called Meg at the hotel that morning. The doctor clearly liked to meddle in the family's affairs and his call to her had no doubt been prompted by that trait, one she could tell Parker despised.

Had it only been that morning? It seemed like weeks since she and Jules had left Las Vegas. She was caught in a time warp where the most amazing things happened.

Amazing things, indeed, she repeated to herself, thinking of the way Parker had been looking at her earlier and of the intimate reflections they'd shared in Gus's room. Only yesterday she'd agreed to help Jules save his family business from his greedy brother Parker. And today, she admitted, if she didn't watch her p's and q's she'd find herself falling under Parker's spell.

Gus wasn't in the other downstairs rooms. She peeked out on the porch and saw the bobbing glow of the doctor's pipe but no sign of Gus.

Grandfather Ponthier had been direct and to the point with her in their discussion in the library. He'd wanted to know when Jules had intended to send for her children. Meg, in turn, had been stumbling and evasive, finally coming up with a weak "at the right moment."

Perhaps she should have confessed then and there, but she still thought she could exit from the Ponthiers' lives gracefully and spare the family the knowledge of why Jules had married her. Of course, she still had no facts on the buyout Jules had described, but clearly he had wanted badly enough to take the extreme measures he had employed. *Not that it's any of your business*, she scolded herself, heading up the staircase. Sign your shares over and let the Ponthiers decide their own fate.

Grandfather had ordered her—yes, that was the best word to describe his brusque behavior—to send for her children, but she'd put him off. She did so by using at least a partial truth, telling him she didn't want them to have to live through another funeral so soon after their own father's death.

That had won him over. For all his bossiness, he had a good heart. That had shown when he'd thanked her for helping with Gus, letting her know that as much as he admired Parker he attributed Gus's return to the family to Meg's intercession.

Meg knocked on the door of Gus's room. No one answered. She turned the knob and cracked it slightly. "Gus?"

"Go away and leave me alone."

She heard muffled tears then the slamming of a door. "It's Meg. May I come in?"

"I told you to go away!" The voice was even fainter. He'd probably shut himself into the bathroom.

Well, he hadn't said she couldn't come in. She pushed open the door. A bedside lamp burned but other than that the room was dark.

"If you come one more step closer I'll—I'll—"

Meg paused, waiting for him to finish his sentence.

A door flung wide and Gus stepped out, not from a bathroom, but from the closet. His face was splotchy, his eyes puffy. "I told you to go away."

"I know," Meg said, "but I wanted to make sure you were okay before I did."

"Why?" He rubbed at his eyes.

"When I'm sad, I want someone to check on me." Meg moved slowly forward.

"Well, I'm not sad." He stuck his chin out at a defiant angle.

"Then maybe you can comfort me."

"Why?" He sounded less angry and slightly curious now.

"Because it makes me sad when I feel someone in pain." She sat on the side of one of the twin beds.

He edged closer. "You mean me?"

She nodded.

He flung himself onto the bed. His feet bounced against the comforter. He still had on the heavy hiking boots. "I don't need anybody."

"Well, just in case you decide you do, you come find me, okay?"

Gus had folded his hands on top of his chest. Meg thought he looked eerily like a body laid out in a casket and wondered if he realized the posture he presented. She sighed and let her shoulders sag and her head drop into her hands, feeling sad for him, for Jules, and for her own children who had also lost their father.

He sat up and, sticking out a hand, patted her on the shoulder. "It's okay to be sad."

Twelve

It's okay to be sad.

Two nights later, Parker wandered down to the library around midnight. They'd buried his brother that afternoon, saying good-bye with pomp and ceremony before he joined his father in the family mausoleum at Metairie Cemetery.

Old New Orleans had rallied around the Ponthiers before and they did so again; as scandalously as both Jules and his father had lived, just as decorously was the equally outrageous son laid to rest.

Even though CeCe had flown in from San Francisco for the event, Gus had ignored his former stepmother and clung to Meg throughout the wake and service. Marianne had sent a wreath as large as the casket, but had not bothered to fly back from Switzerland, a point not lost on Gus, whom in the early moments of the wake Parker had found stabbing at his mother's floral offering with his prized WalMart pocketknife.

Parker hadn't interfered. Meg had returned soon after from the ladies room, taken one look, and held out her hand.

Gus had handed over the knife, though with great reluctance.

That he did it at all amazed Parker.

Meg had said in a soft voice, "It's not the flowers you're angry at," and slipped off with Gus in search of a Coke.

Crossing the room towards the refuge of his desk, Parker wondered who it was he was angry at.

Jules for wasting his life and getting himself killed?

Their father for doing the same thing?

Teensy for looking at him as if she couldn't figure out how the wrong son had died?

Himself for thinking such a horrible thought?

Parker dropped into his leather desk chair and swiveled to the right. In his line of vision stood a suit of armor Jules had picked up on one of his junkets to France. As the library served as an office away from the office for all the Ponthier men, the room represented their range of tastes.

Uncomfortable with the empty eyes of the visored armor, Parker shifted to the other direction, only to find himself staring at the portrait of four generations of the Ponthiers Teensy had commissioned when Gus was born.

She'd never liked the result and Parker had salvaged the painting.

Grandfather had been vibrant, Parker's own father showing the wages of his sins. Jules held Gus in his arms, the child's fat cheeks bracketing a smile. Parker stood to the far side of his grandfather, away from Jules.

Which was fitting. They'd never gotten along, never come together as brothers. Parker exhaled a long breath. As messed up as his brother's life had been, he'd done one thing right. He and Marianne had created Gus.

Studying the chubby baby in the portrait, Parker wondered whether he would ever know what it meant to be a father.

He cut short his dismal thoughts and switched on the computer; perhaps he'd check the overnights on the London and Tokyo exchanges. That should occupy his mind.

Anything was better than the weight pressing on his spirits, threatening to smother him like a soggy rug snuffing out a flame.

The computer whirred and clicked as it performed its startup routine, checking its internal elements. The virus scan software flashed its progress across the screen, reassuring all was safe to proceed.

Parker stared without seeing at the monitor. Instead of the program manager with its array of tools and services, he saw Jules's body as he'd viewed it at the morgue.

A computer virus created havoc by entering

a system and multiplying itself until eventually all the disk space had been claimed. Jules's addiction to drugs had done the same thing. After gaining a hold, its demands had replicated themselves, increasing exponentially as the habit grew.

And ultimately it had brought Jules to a crashing halt.

Parker sank his chin onto his hands, his elbows propped on the surface of the desk, trying to erase the images of his lifeless brother that filled his mind. For all his faults and foibles, Jules had possessed a nervous energy that kept him charging about and produced a charm that attracted people to him like bead-seekers to a Mardi Gras float.

That Jules was no more.

Parker thrust his chair back from his desk and jerked his body upwards, out of the seat and towards the fireplace. Rubbing his chilled hands together, he concentrated on lighting the fire that some considerate and knowing person had laid earlier. Parker suspected Horton, who'd orchestrated the work necessary for the Ponthier household to deal with the solicitous stream of visitors who'd made their way through their doorway over the past several days.

Horton would have guessed Parker, who suffered from sleeplessness, wouldn't close his eyes nor rest his head on his pillow this night.

A strip of kindling caught and held. Steadily

the flame inched its way, then suddenly the
piece curled and flared and fell in a scatter of
fire onto the log beneath.

Parker stared at the sparks, letting their light
and fire consume his visions of his brother. In
a crackle and spurt of heat, the log caught and
began to burn.

Think of something else, he told himself.
Think of something good. Think about something that gives life, rather than takes it away.

Parker closed his eyes. The warmth from the
fire began to chase the chill from his body.
Raising his arms, he rested them outstretched
on the mantel, his forehead on the cool marble.

The image of Meg standing by his side for
the endless hours of that day and evening flick-
ered to life. There had been so many people
through the house Parker had wanted to bolt
the doors by eight o'clock. Many of the visitors
had come out of curiosity as well as custom,
Parker had suspected, curious to see this outsider whom Jules had brought back to New Orleans the day he'd died.

Meg nodded and thanked the mourners for
coming. She hadn't talked much, not even to
Parker. But she'd been there beside him, steady
and calm and bright-eyed.

Teensy had picked out the black suit Meg
wore. Parker knew this because his mother had
complained to him that she'd never met a
woman so uninterested in shopping. She'd also
marveled that Meg hadn't wanted to wear the

Ponthier pearls, an earring and necklace set that contained more diamonds than pearls.

She'd finally yielded to the earrings and against her pale complexion and dark hair, the jewelry looked better than Parker had ever seen it. Not even Marianne, whose goal in life was that of fashion plate, had shown them to such advantage.

Parker raised his arms over his head and stretched. Then he smiled. Between the fire and thinking of Meg, he was beginning to feel much better. It didn't take away the loss, but he could begin to feel as if life would go on.

And it could be even better.

The black suit had a prim high collar but the jacket hadn't concealed the swell of Meg's breasts or her narrow waist. And the proper knee-length skirt might have attempted to avert attention from her legs, but the snug fit showed the curve of her derriere to advantage.

Parker wondered what she did for sport. With a body like that, she had to be into something vigorous. He hoped she played tennis. With a smile, he realized he'd have to ask her.

Ask her what, Parker? His smiled faded. What was he thinking? Meg was Jules's widow. Widow, you fool. Like she's going to be interested in you.

But the funny thing was, he felt she was. Which was his pride, of course. Parker Ponthier, the man who only had to crook a finger and any woman in the city would come run-

ning. He grinned ruefully. Of course she was
nice to him; he was her brother-in-law. And
she valued family, that was clear by her standing by his side as the mourners had called at
the house. And by the way she looked after
Gus.

Yeah, Parker, she's interested in you.

He turned his back to the flames. The front
of his body had more than enough heat. Heat
that only built as he let his mind drift to the
pleasant what-if of a woman like Meg standing
by his side not just for one day, but day after
day.

Headed back to the staircase from the kitchen,
a mug of warm milk in her hand, Meg paused.

Light filtered from the doorway of the library.

Parker.

It had to be. Couldn't be anyone else. Teensy
had been put to bed with a sedative. And
Grandfather had chugged several bourbons
and disappeared to his room at an early hour.
Not too long after the funeral, Meg and Parker
had been left along with Mathilde, Amelia
Anne, and her husband to greet the friends
who'd stopped by to express their condolences.

Parker, who'd stoically helped carry his
brother's coffin, had refused any numbing liquor. Now, Meg sensed, Parker would be sitting
up late, his only companions the ghosts of his
memories.

She inched forward, the dim yellow light beckoning her.

In the morning, she was going home. She had enough cash for a one-way ticket to Las Vegas. If they needed her to sign any legal documents or sit in on the family business meeting, she'd come back. But her children needed her. And she needed them. The life she'd made for herself was in Las Vegas.

Her only regret was leaving Gus behind.

She stopped just outside the library door, then with the mug clutched close to her chest, peered in.

The sight of Parker, his chin propped on his hands, his eyes closed, pain etching his forehead, prompted her to admit that leaving Gus behind was not her only regret.

Parker pushed back his chair and crossed the room to the fireplace. He knelt by the fire. Meg saw the flicker of a match, inhaled a faint drift of the sulphurous sting. A fire crept to life, licking at the kindling.

He must be planning an all-night vigil.

Sitting up with thoughts she sensed weren't pleasant. Even though he'd been the picture of civility throughout the day, he'd held himself apart. He kept his true feelings locked within him, presenting to the world what he needed to in order to do the right thing.

That stolidity had helped her manage the ordeal. Since she'd gotten herself into this predicament, she felt it her duty to see it through as gracefully as possible. She'd stayed close by him, murmuring polite responses to the callers' words of sympathy. Rather than her usual talkative self, she'd followed his example and been grateful for his presence.

She'd never met a man like Parker.

And, she thought with a reluctance greater than she'd ever known, she wasn't likely to again. He exhibited a curious mixture of old world courtesies and an assumption of rightfully and naturally being in charge of any situation. Except for Gus; he didn't seem too sure of how to interact with his nephew.

But more than any other attribute, his dedication to his family impressed Meg. In some ways, he indicated he thought most of his relatives were slightly batty; yet he stood by them. He'd never gotten along with his brother; yet he grieved his loss.

Parker cared for those he loved.

Not everyone followed through like that. Marianne's telegram from Zurich had said, "Please tell Gus I'll be in New Orleans when I can." She might as well have said when it's convenient. What about now when her son needed a structure, a foundation, a family? Meg had stood beside Parker when he crumpled the message and tossed it into the fire before Gus could see it.

Inching farther into the doorway, she wondered whether she should interrupt him or slip away, leaving him to his memories.

Parker stood at the fireplace with his back to her, his face turned down toward the budding fire. A family portrait dominated the wall above his head.

Meg had figured out during her session with Grandfather the other day that the painting represented several generations of Ponthiers. The artist had either been psychic or had known the family well. Grandfather dominated, Jules hovered with an infant Gus held at an awkward angle in his arms, a man whom Meg assumed to be Parker and Jules's own father stood between Jules and Grandfather. And slightly separated, yet somehow bridging the physical distance, Parker loomed.

Still wondering whether she should go in or mind her own business and creep up the stairs to bed, Meg watched as Parker stretched his arms over his head. The fire was licking at the logs, creating a rosy halo behind his body.

Meg had never known a brother or a sister, nor a mother nor a father, but she could imagine the loss he had experienced. He must be very, very sad.

She took a step forward.

Parker turned and rather than the sorrow she expected, his mouth curved in a smile. And then even as she gazed at him, the smile faded. He shook his head slowly and thrust his hands into the pockets of his suit trousers.

Since she'd last seen him, he'd discarded his somber tie, unbuttoned the top of his dress shirt, and rolled back the cuffs that had been fastened with plain gold links.

A dark look that reminded her of their first encounter in the hotel room crossed his face. His mouth twisted and he kicked at the rug next to the fireplace.

No one should have to grieve alone. "Parker?" she said, easing forward into the room, calling his name softly to keep from startling him.

Perhaps he'd already seen her hovering in the doorway, because he didn't seem surprised. "Couldn't sleep?" he asked.

She shook her head, one foot off the ground, suddenly unsure she should have intruded. Even if he didn't mind, she wasn't sure it was the wise thing to do for herself.

He looked too good standing there, all dark clouds chased away, a welcoming smile on his face. He held out a hand. "Join me by the fire?"

Nodding, she crept forward, her mug of cooling milk clasped to her chest.

He shifted slightly, making space for her in front of the center of the blaze. The logs hissed and popped and she breathed in the unaccustomed smell of genuine wood smoke. The fireplace in the Las Vegas home she and Ted had owned had been powered by gas, the fragrance fake.

"I saw the light," Meg said, glancing shyly up at Parker, admiring the play of light and shadow on his face.

"I'm glad," he said.

"I wasn't sure if you'd want company."

"Not just any company, but yours, yes." He gazed at her when he said the words. "Thank you for sticking by me today."

"You're welcome." Jeez, she was supposed to be comforting him and she couldn't think of anything better to say than that? She sipped at the milk, but found she no longer wanted it. Still, holding it gave her something to do with her hands other than stuff them in the pockets of the plush velour robe Teensy had given her to wear. Having run into Parker, Meg was thankful she'd thrown it on over her UNLV t-shirt when she'd gone in search of the milk.

The light had gone out of Parker's eyes. He was still looking at her, but almost as if it weren't herself he was seeing.

Meg gazed back. Parker didn't need words of sympathy; he'd heard enough of those today. He didn't need to be told the pain would go away; he'd discover that for himself as the weeks and months passed. He didn't need to be told to cheer up and think about the good times of his brother's life; those were stored in his heart.

She set the mug on the mantel. Carefully, she turned back to face him and opened her arms.

He walked into them, laying his cheek against her hair.

"Oh, Meg," he whispered, "you are so good."

Thirteen

Good or not, Meg clung to Parker, her arms wrapped around his waist. She'd meant to offer comfort, yet she realized she wanted more than that from him.

What she wanted she couldn't have put into words. But it felt so good to be held by Parker, to feel his strong arms around her. Ted had been gone more than a year. During that time, she'd marched onward, keeping the family together, struggling with the financial mess Ted had left behind.

Not once in that time had anyone put their arms around her, smoothed her hair and whispered, as Parker was now doing, "It's okay to be sad."

She nodded, her face brushing against his chest where the top two buttons had been unfastened. She breathed in the distant hint of a subtle cologne applied hours earlier when the day had yet to be gotten through. The aroma mingled with wood smoke and a musky maleness that spoke to a feminine awareness she had thought buried along with Ted.

Savoring the sensation of his touch and scent, she relaxed against his chest. It was only for a moment, a very long, sweet moment.

Parker continued to smooth Meg's hair. He reasoned that the least he could do was comfort her. He'd lost his brother, but she had lost her husband. If he sought his own solace, and if her touch felt a whole lot better than he had a right to experience from an embrace offered out of innocence, then he'd deal with the guilt later.

Right now he wasn't letting go.

"You really are good," he murmured, breathing against her hair. "You were such a trouper today." Running one hand in a gentle circle on her upper back, he said, "You don't have to be strong right now. I promise you're safe with me."

She snuggled against his chest in a way to which his body couldn't help but respond. But then she dropped her hands from around his waist. Still within the circle of his arms, she looked up. Softly, she said, "I'm supposed to be comforting you."

"Oh, but you are," Parker said. He traced the outline of her lips with a fingertip. Then, taking her face in his hands, he kissed her.

It was a kiss that lasted an eternity.

Yet only the briefest of moments.

Her lips were tender, and the way she parted

them slightly as his mouth brushed hers set off
a searing hunger within him. Parker wanted to
crush her to him, but he sensed her hesitation
and he pulled back, the kiss over before it had
really begun.

He wanted more.

She gazed at him, eyes wide and dark and
inviting. Or did he only imagine the invitation
because he so desperately wanted to lose himself in her? With the little finger of her right
hand she touched her lower lip.

"I suppose I should say I'm sorry for that,"
he managed to say, "but I'm not."

"Then don't."

He forced himself to edge out of arm's
length. "Do you never say what you don't intend?"

"Well, I do try to say what I mean . . ." She
hesitated and her glance clouded.

"—and mean what you say?" Parker finished for her.

She smiled at that. Backlit by the crackling
fire, snuggled in the forest-green velour robe,
her bare feet peeking from beneath the hem,
she reminded him of a child up early, eager for
Christmas morning.

Only she was no child. The feel of her lips,
the curves of her body, the wisdom of her actions all reminded him of that.

And it's not Christmas, Parker.

It wasn't Christmas, but he wanted a pres-

ent—the gift of forgetting, of blotting the loss
of his brother from his mind.

Meg could give him that gift.

A temporary respite, but one he craved.

They'd shared the loss and now they could
share their solace.

Right, Parker. As if your motives could be
called pure and unselfish. Still watching her
gazing back at him, he tried to remember how
suspicious he'd been of her at their first meeting. Tonight it was damned hard to remember.

A log sizzled and a shower of sparks burst
forth.

Meg jumped slightly.

"Sit down?" he asked abruptly, hoping she'd
stay with him. He indicated the loveseat beside
the fire.

She glanced from the fire over her shoulder
towards the doorway. "If it's not too late?"

"Not for me." Taking her lightly by the arm,
he led her to the loveseat. "I promise to let you
go at the first sight of a yawn."

Meg smiled; she collected her mug and settled on the loveseat, knees together, legs
crossed primly at the ankles.

"I'm going to pour a cognac. Would you like
some? Or would you like me to warm your
milk?"

"Cognac would be nice," Meg said.

He took her mug from her and moved to the
bar tucked in a ship captain's locker on the far
side of his now-neglected desk. His computer

still whirred and as he glanced at the image
flashing on the screensaver, Parker was more
grateful than he could say for Meg's presence.
She was saving him from himself.

When he returned to the loveseat with two
snifters of cognac, Meg accepted one, then said,
"You know, I thought you didn't drink."

Parker heard the curiosity in her voice. What
he also heard was that she observed and noticed his behavior. "I don't much," he said,
standing beside the sofa but not yet joining her.
He wanted to admire the picture she made and
had a feeling getting too close to her would be
a mistake.

"Because of Jules?"

He almost couldn't hear her question she
spoke so softly.

"Partly."

She half turned towards him. The relaxing of
her proper posture gratified him. "And the
other part?"

He shrugged. "Alcohol can get to be habit
forming for any Ponthier."

Meg laced her fingers around the bowl of her
crystal glass, picturing Teensy over the past
two days and the way Jules had guzzled bourbon and water the night at the Pinnacle when
he'd hired her to marry him.

That thought caused her gut to tighten. Her
job was done. She had ten thousand Ponthier
dollars waiting for her in a Las Vegas bank. She

had no business getting to know Parker Ponthier one whit better.

There was no future in such knowledge. Nonetheless, she stroked the sides of the glass with her fingers and inhaled the pungent liqueur.

"I've never seen a Baccarat snifter displayed to such advantage," Parker said, his low-pitched voice breaking in on her thoughts.

"And I've never sipped brandy from Baccarat before," she said, tucking her bare feet beneath her and fussing over the adjustments as she kept her head bowed in embarrassment at her forthright words. *Wow, Meg. Make him think you're straight out of Poverty Park.*

She loved fine things. Her life with Ted had been a huge step above what she'd known as a child but no way had she been able to afford crystal that cost a hundred dollars a stem. But she'd coveted it, pricing it at the fancy mall in Vegas where the wealthy tourists shopped. Well, heck, why be embarrassed now. She took a tiny sip and smiled at him. "You know, it tastes better out of Baccarat."

Parker smiled and joined her on the loveseat, leaving a careful six or seven inches separating their bodies.

That distance both relieved and annoyed Meg. She had absolutely no business letting him touch her again. Yet she couldn't stop herself from lightly tracing her lower lip with her pinky finger. Gosh, but he'd tantalized her

with that kiss. His lips were warm and tasted
of the promise of passion.

Don't go there, Meg.

She lifted her gaze from the warm amber of
the brandy. She hadn't heard him move, but
the six or seven inches of space had disappeared, swallowed up as he'd leaned closer.
His arm now lay behind her back atop the
loveseat's mahogany scrollwork.

She gulped a mouthful of brandy.

And promptly choked.

He leaned even closer, patting her sharply
on the back.

Her face flushed, still gasping, Meg slowly
brought her coughing spell under control.

He kept his arm over her shoulders. "Better?"

His voice was so tender Meg wanted to melt
against him. But she was made of sterner stuff
than that. Sitting forward, just out of range of
his warm hand, whose strong fingers had
cupped her face when he'd kissed her, she said,
"I guess I'm not used to the finer things."

He scowled, which surprised her. "Well, you
would have gotten used to them if Jules hadn't
gotten himself killed."

What could she say to that? *No, I wouldn't,
because I planned to leave the minute he
forked over the thirty thousand dollars he offered me and pay off the creditors who won't
quit hounding me?*

For a wild moment, she did consider telling

him the truth and ending her charade.

Then he brushed her cheek with his thumb. "Forgive me," he said, "and this time I mean it."

She melted then.

Just one night.

His hand left her cheek but lingered over her shoulders. He circled his thumb lazily on the back of her neck.

Meg tried not to hold her breath.

He took a sip of his drink. "I want to thank you again for the way you've handled Gus."

Meg wondered if her surprise showed. A ten-year-old nephew was the last topic she expected from a man with his arm around her stroking the back of her neck in a way that made her crave his touch on other, even more sensitive spots.

She sighed and settled against his hand. She might as well face the fact that she was the mother-figure type. Why should she expect Parker to see her as some alluring and sexy woman who was already dissolving into a puddle of desire under his touch?

Because I want him to.

Just this one fantasy, this one night.

She was going home tomorrow. She'd be sensible then. Parker's strength, the way he stood like a rock while the turmoil of his family swirled around him—these qualities appealed to her.

And face it, Meg, he's sexy as all get out and you've denied yourself for so long.

Just one more kiss.

She wouldn't ask for more than that. She took a sip of cognac, savoring its sweet warmth. Then she realized Parker must be waiting for her to respond to what he'd said about Gus. Summoning her attention, she said, "Gus is a child. A child needs his family. It was pretty straightforward."

Yes, as straightforward as her longing for Parker to hold her, kiss her, pull her close and make the world go away. She would never have this moment again.

A feather light touch beneath the collar of her robe flamed her senses even higher.

He walked his fingers up the vertebrae of her neck. "I have a confession to make," he murmured.

Her eyes widened. Did Parker want the same thing she wanted? Trying not to sound too hopeful, she said, "You do?"

"Mmm, hmmm. If it hadn't been for you, I would have left Gus at that school."

"You what?!" Meg sat upright. Brandy sloshed up the bowl of her glass then trickled down the crystal sides. Her estimation of Parker mirrored the slow downward crawl of the liquid. "Why ever would you have done that?"

"I'm ashamed of it now, especially after seeing how good you are with him." He shifted and his hand no longer touched her neck.

Strangely lost without the contact, Meg said, "Don't you like children?" Waiting for his answer, she scolded herself for caring what it would be.

Irrelevant, Meg McKenzie Cooper Ponthier. Completely irrelevant.

"I don't dislike them," Parker said slowly. "I just never know what to say or do. And with my family background"—he paused for a taste of his drink—"the only thing sure with me and a child is that any input from me would no doubt uphold the family tradition of screwing up the next generation."

Meg played with her glass, wondering if Parker really believed what he'd just said. She watched the play of the firelight on the amber liquid and told herself Parker's reaction to Gus was of little importance. She was going home tomorrow and all of the Ponthiers would be left to fend for themselves, as they'd been doing for generations. But in the back of her mind, she couldn't walk away and leave Parker thinking he was hopeless when it came to kids.

Why, Meg? Because you think he's going to follow you back to Las Vegas and woo you?

"Did I stump you?" Parker asked.

"What?" Meg looked up. He'd put his arm back around her shoulders. She blurted out, "Do you think you're screwed up?"

He laughed. "Not exactly." He grinned in a disconcertingly charming way. "Not unless you count my bad points."

"Which are?"

Hearing the sincere interest in her voice, Parker shifted on the couch and considered telling her his number one fault at the moment was admiring the way her hair curled over her shoulders and led his eye downward to where her robe was slowly loosening from the grip of its sash, which led his mind to thoughts of her hair spilling over his body, her robe abandoned on the rug beside the fire.

"That many?"

He shook his head in an attempt to clear the image of her naked before the fire. "Left alone to run a company, I do fairly well, but I do have trouble with women and children." He kept his tone light.

"You're afraid you'll screw up the kids and—" She stopped, blushing.

He put his arm back around her shoulders and pulled her to him. "And I have a way of falling for women I shouldn't."

He kissed her again. This time there was nothing tentative or fleeting about the meeting of their mouths.

He drew her lips in to taste them. He parted them to mark her. He plunged his tongue in to claim her.

And she answered him, taste for greedy taste.

Her breasts pushed against his chest and even through her heavy robe he felt the rounded weight of her flesh and the eager invitation in the way her hand curled around the back of his neck.

With a hungry groan, he reached without seeing for the glass she held. Without letting go of her mouth, he swayed their bodies to the edge of the loveseat, abandoned the crystal to the low table and moved them as one till she lay beneath him on the loveseat.

If he didn't taste more of her, he'd explode. He parted the lapels of her robe. To his surprise, she wore a ratty t-shirt under the elegant robe. But it suited her so much better than the silk camisole she'd been modeling when he'd burst in on her at the Hotel Maurepas.

Parker ignored the voice in the back of his head that told him he shouldn't be reaching for the sash. But she wasn't pushing him away.

Instead, now both hands were lifted to the back of his head. She drew him downward into another kiss that consumed the rest of what little caution remained to rule his actions.

Meg tangled her fingers in Parker's hair. She should have taken her hot milk straight back upstairs and avoided this man because now she wanted more than a few kisses on the couch. Which meant, of course, she ought to sit up, cup her hands primly back around the bowl of her brandy snifter, and quit kissing him back.

Surely he'd come to his senses soon, she thought even as he pulled back slightly and tugged at the knot in her sash. His breath was

coming quickly. The firelight softened the lines
of his face. As he worked on the knot, she
moved one hand from the back of his head and
traced the line of his nose.

He smiled at her, and said, "I broke it when
I was a child."

"It's beautiful," Meg said. "I hope it didn't
hurt too much."

Parker's smile faded and he let go of her
sash. "Jules hurt worse."

Meg dropped her hands, reminded of how
outrageous her behavior was. Parker gazed
down at her, obviously unwilling to let her go,
but struggling with himself.

If she'd loved Jules of course she wouldn't
be on the couch with Parker. Meg opened her
mouth to speak, then slowly thought better of
it. If she told him the truth, he'd be off the loveseat faster than a flea jumping onto a dog.

"We shouldn't be here," Parker said, still not
moving.

"No." Meg touched her lips with the tip of
her tongue, wondering how she'd gotten herself into such an awkward situation. Here was
a man she genuinely wanted. And couldn't
have.

"Do that again and I'll forget myself," Parker
said in a low voice that sounded a lot like a
growl to Meg.

So she did.

He pounced on her. Her body pinned beneath his, he said into her ear, "So help me

God, I can't stop myself. I need you tonight."

She nodded her head, the long day's growth of beard chafing her ever so slightly as she moved against the side of his face.

He kissed her lips, her eyes, her throat, and she felt the urgent desire of his body as he pressed against her on the couch. Would it be so wrong to give herself to a man who wanted her? Who needed her, if only for one night?

Suddenly he lifted his body from hers and Meg almost cried out in loss as he strode across the room. But he paused only to shut the doors to the library and turn the key in the lock.

Standing above the loveseat, he looked down at her, hunger in his eyes.

Watching him, Meg shrugged out of her robe. Her UNLV t-shirt skimmed her thighs.

Parker reached over and trailed a hand up her calf, alongside her knee and a slow inch at a time up her inner thigh.

Meg caught her breath.

Parker knelt beside the loveseat. "I should wait, you know, but I'm not going to unless you tell me to."

"Wait?"

"Until a proper time has passed. Until after the company affairs and Jules's estate are settled. Until after you've had a chance to grieve and come to your senses and save yourself from a mistake."

"No mistake," Meg said.

Parker didn't smile.

Meg stifled a sigh, realizing Parker was right, for more reasons than he knew. "When will those things be settled? After the company vote?"

He'd lifted his hand back to her thigh. He stilled it and said, "Company vote?"

Meg could have bitten her tongue in half. "Oh, you know, the one that was supposed to be this week."

His eyes narrowed and he lifted his hand from her leg. "You know about that?"

She nodded.

"What did Jules tell you?"

How much should she say? He told me you were a hard-headed obstinate son of a bitch bastard who refused to accept the best buy out offer in the history of corporate acquisitions and he'd do whatever it took to consummate that offer. "Something about a merger?"

Parker leaned back on his heels, still on the floor beside her but no longer touching her body, no longer looking at all like the same man who'd been kissing her senseless. He murmured, almost to himself, "All business, aren't you, Meg? Everything else is just pretend."

She shook her head but he was beyond paying attention to any protest.

Two lines had formed on his forehead between his eyes. "It seems odd to me that my brother told you about a proposed merger when he failed to mention, among other details, that he was the father of a ten-year-old or that he'd been married twice before."

"Really?" Jeez, but she'd blown it. Meg sat up and reached for the arms of her robe.

"You know what I think?" Parker rose and looked down at Meg from his full height.

"What?" She knew her voice sounded very, very tiny.

"I think my first suspicions about you were damned well founded. I think you and my brother were in cahoots and I intend to figure out just exactly what game the two of you were playing." He strode to the fireplace, his jaw working.

Facing the fire, he said, "Whatever it is, I'll catch you at it and put an end to it. And that will be that. But you know what I won't forgive you for?"

Meg held her breath, cursing herself, knowing what he would say, feeling the pain of it in her own heart.

Parker swung back to face her, his eyes blazing with a mixture of fury and desire. "You made me like you."

He bent and gripped her by the shoulders. "I ought to take you now just to punish you, to punish myself, to get you out of my system."

She stared, wondering wildly if he'd really do that, even as she sensed he would never touch her out of anger. She couldn't say anything to proclaim her innocence. She had none. Sick with regret, she whispered, "Parker, I'm so sorry."

He crushed her against him, bruising her mouth with his. She cried out as he devoured her with his tongue. Panting, wanting, hating herself for her deception, Meg struggled against him. This was not a kiss; this was a punishment.

He let go. She fell back against the loveseat. Staring down at her, he said, "Sorry won't do. Save your excuses for the lawyers."

Fourteen

Very early the next morning, Meg huddled in her room, waiting until it was time to leave for the airport. Over and over she replayed last night's encounter with Parker. Each time, her thoughts followed one of two forks.

Her fantasies wondered what would have happened had she not mentioned the buyout vote. And her fears crystallized around what he could and would do to her if he discovered the truth of her marriage.

She'd have to give back the ten thousand dollars but that was probably the right thing to do anyway. But could he have her sent to jail?

She chewed on the tip of her thumb. No matter what, he'd never forgive her. She'd never know the touch of his lips, the urgent demands of his hard male body pressing against hers.

Meg sighed and got up from the bed and paced to the window and back. She'd told Grandfather Ponthier she had to go home and check on her children the day after the funeral.

What she hadn't told him was that she had no plans to return. Feeling a need to clear her conscience as much as possible, she decided to slip downstairs and let him know this. As the patriarch, he could break the news to the rest of the clan that Jules's widow had declined to join the family. Legal matters they could handle by FedEx.

A loud knock on the door interrupted her thoughts. She smoothed her hands on the lap of the dark blue dress she'd worn on the flight from Vegas to New Orleans with Jules. Everything he and Teensy had purchased for her she'd left hanging in the closet.

The knock sounded again, much louder. "Yes?" A day ago she would have called come in. Today she held back. "Who is it?" Silly question; she knew who it was. Even his knock sounded angry and authoritative.

"Parker."

"Can you come back later?" Like maybe after I'm gone. She despised herself for chickening out, but she was afraid to face him.

Silence answered her.

She held her breath. Maybe he had gone away. Disappointment welled even as she strained for the sound of receding footsteps.

"It's about Gus."

She left the bed and moved to the door. She cracked it open.

He hadn't shaved and his eyes looked the way hers felt at the end of a long shift in the smoky lobby bar of the Pinnacle Casino. The same two buttons of last night's shirt were still unfastened.

Without looking directly at her, Parker asked, "Have you seen Gus this morning?"

She shook her head, unwilling to trust her tongue.

He jammed his hands in his pockets. "Any idea where he might be?"

"He's not in his room and no one else has seen him?'

Parker shook his head.

Meg wasn't inclined to become alarmed. Ponthier Place had so many rooms, so many places a child could lose himself in make-believe. Why, her three kids would have built a fortress in the library and turned the Great Parlor into a schoolroom or theater. "When did you check?"

"An hour ago." He glanced across the hall then back. "I was going to take him fishing. If he wanted to go."

This from the man who assumed he'd screw up the next generation. "That was sweet," Meg said.

His shoulders stiffened. "I wouldn't have bothered you but if he's not with you I think he may have run away. Or worse."

She opened the door so they stood fully facing one another. "Why do you think that?"

Parker beckoned with his finger. "Take a look and tell me what you think."

Meg followed him across the broad hall. Parker pushed open the door and stood back for Meg to precede him.

She knew at a glance Parker was right. That was no child under those blankets. A pile of pillows had been stuffed under the covers of the bed.

Parker yanked back the covers and that's exactly what lay beneath them.

She eased into the room. The hiking boots from WalMart no longer sat beside the bed.

Meg knocked softly on the closet where Gus had tucked himself away his first night out of school. No answer. She looked in. The package that had held his prized pocketknife sat empty on the floor.

Sorrow gripped Meg, a sadness tinged with fear for Gus's safety. For all his bravado, he was only ten. Teddy and Ellen's age. She scooped up the empty box and held it out to Parker.

"Don't touch anything," he said.

"Parker, you don't think someone's taken him!"

His mouth a grim line, Parker said, "With Jules dead, Gus is one hell of a rich kid."

Meg opened her mouth to state what she thought was an obvious point. Until she turned any inheritance back to the family, which she knew in her heart she would do, Gus wasn't the sole heir to Jules's wealth. Not unless she was really confused over the law.

And not unless Parker knew something she didn't know.

Wiser after last night's fiasco, she kept those thoughts to herself. "Perhaps he's gone outside to play. That would explain the shoes, clothing, and knife being gone."

He nodded. "Sensible, but I've already walked the grounds."

Meg felt her calm beginning to wilt at the edges as her concern mounted. She closed her eyes and tried to remember what Teddy and Ellen had done the day after Ted's funeral, trying to use that behavior as a clue towards what Gus might be doing.

Teddy had gone to the garage and spent three hours cleaning his father's golf clubs. Meg had checked on him every so often and seen him crying a few times. It broke her heart, but she left him alone with his grief. When he finished, he came inside and buried his head in her lap. His dad had promised to teach him to play golf as soon as he was twelve, a promise that could never be fulfilled.

Meg had stroked his hair and vowed to herself that if he wanted them, she'd get him golf lessons, no matter the cost.

Meg pressed her fingers against her eyes, the memory of her son's grief too raw to bear. Slowly she opened her eyes, to find Parker looking at her, his expression a mix of curiosity, concern, and impatience.

"Let me think," she said.

Ellen had handled her grief very differently from Teddy. She'd blamed her dad for leaving them, even though Meg had tried her best to explain that an aneurysm wasn't something one got because of bad diet or poor health habits.

Anger and fury had fueled her daughter's reactions, emotions that had eased themselves from Ellen's system over the past year until at last she'd become more accepting of her loss. But as the bills had mounted and Meg and the kids had been forced to sell the only house Ellen had called home, her anger had kindled anew.

Meg suspected Gus had more in common with Ellen than with Teddy.

"Was there any place special Jules used to take Gus?" Meg asked.

Parker shook his head. "Nothing that comes right to mind. I wasn't around them much when they were together."

"Did they go fishing?"

"Gus always wanted to, but that was just one more thing Jules didn't do with him."

Feeling braver despite Parker's aloofness, she said softly, "That's why you were going to take him fishing today, isn't it?"

"Be that as it may, this isn't getting us anywhere."

Ooh, he wasn't defrosting at all. Meg said, "It might be. Gus may have taken off to someplace special, someplace he associated with his father."

"You may be right, but I'm going to call in the police just in case."

The police! Meg licked her lips. Parker probably wanted to turn her over for impersonating a Ponthier. She glanced around the room, seeking more clues. A corner of a book stuck out from beneath the bed. She retrieved it and read out loud, "*Huckleberry Finn.*"

Parker had headed out of Gus's room but when he heard the title he turned back. "He might have gone to the river."

"The Mississippi?"

"That's the only one around here."

He sounded vaguely sarcastic but Meg decided to ignore that. "How would he get there?"

"Easily on the streetcar." A dark look crossed Parker's face. "Are you coming or staying?"

He was walking down the hall as he asked the question, not even waiting for her answer. Meg wheeled after him, thankful her dress shoes had such sensible heels.

Grandfather Ponthier was parked in the hallway near the door. "What's up with you two?"

Parker said, "We think Gus may have gone to the river."

"The river's a big stretch. You have any idea where?"

Parker stopped. He studied his hands then

glanced back at his grandfather. "I was going to check the levee off Carrollton and St. Charles."

"Where Horton used to take you fishing?"

Parker nodded.

Meg couldn't help but wonder at that. She'd expected to hear "Where your father used to take you?"

"And you figure that makes sense?"

Meg started as she realized Grandfather had barked the question at her. She nodded.

"I'm going after the car," Parker said. "I'll pull up in the drive in two minutes."

Meg nodded.

Grandfather said, "Weren't you due at the airport in about an hour?"

In her concern over Gus, she'd actually forgotten. She gasped. "I can't go now! But I'll lose my ticket."

"Tell you what," Grandfather said, "you run along and look for Gus and I'll call your little ones and let them know you've been delayed."

The horn honked.

Meg hesitated. She should call Mrs. Fenniston, but there wasn't time. She thought of Teddy or Ellen or Samantha running off alone to a dangerous river full of what had to be nasty and powerful currents.

"Just leave it to me," Grandfather said. "I'll call 'em up and set things right."

The horn honked again and Meg ran to the door. "But you don't have the phone number."

He smiled. "Just tell me their babysitter's name. There's more than one way to leap a frog."

Meg called out Mrs. Fenniston's name and number, then raced out the door. She hoped the crusty old patriarch didn't scare Mrs. Fenniston silly.

But then, one of the things she respected about Mrs. Fenniston was that nothing, but nothing, ever seemed to ruffle her.

Parker gunned the engine of his Porsche, roaring down the drive before Meg was barely settled in the seat beside him. He hated having her there beside him, yet he was damn grateful for her presence.

What if they were wrong and Gus hadn't ambled off to the river? What if he had been lured from the house in some bizarre child snatching? The house had a security alarm, but Parker knew it hadn't been set last night.

An oversight that was completely his fault. He'd been so upset with Meg, so supremely furious with the scheming woman for suckering him into believing she was some innocent, and even more upset with himself for forgetting his own code of honor and making a play for his dead brother's widow, that he'd been the one who hadn't set the alarm.

He'd been out on the porch for hours after Meg had fled the library, wrestling with his feelings about her, wondering how in the hell he could go from wanting her with every fiber of his being to believing in his gut that she'd married his brother under very suspicious circumstances.

He wished she'd said nothing. He wished she'd kissed him and opened her arms and her body to him and said not a word about Jules and about business machinations she should have had absolutely no knowledge of. That thought reminded him that he needed to get a copy of her prenuptial agreement from her.

His lawyers would be wanting to take a look at it.

Jules always used the same one. Having been married twice before, Jules insisted his prospective spouse sign a prenuptial agreement he'd drafted himself. The tradition itself was a longstanding one; any Ponthier male asked his wife-to-be to sign a contract ensuring that the shares of Ponthier family stock bestowed upon marriage reverted to the company upon death or divorce.

Parker wanted Meg's copy of that agreement. He didn't want to do any business with her. The sooner she was out of his life the better off he would be.

Glancing over at her, sitting so silent in the low seat beside him, he wondered whether he knew what was best for either of them. He wondered whether Jules had married her just to double his voting shares in order to sell out the company to the international consortium that had been courting the Ponthier holdings of sugar, commercial real estate, and hotels.

If he had, then Jules would have won the battle if he hadn't gotten himself killed. Married, he could outvote Parker. Dead and with the standard prenuptial agreement in place, the shares reverted to the company, to be settled on Gus, but not until he was of legal age.

Both Grandfather Ponthier and Parker's father had settled their shares equally on Parker and Jules. Grandfather had done so reluctantly, but after his stroke, he hadn't wanted to end up helpless and still in voting position. He'd told Parker, speaking even more gruffly than usual, that he wished he could give him all his shares, but it wouldn't be right not to divide them evenly.

Parker had understood, even though he regretted the sense of tradition that overruled common sense. It was Parker who managed the business, oversaw the sugar production facilities, the real estate holdings, the hotel managers.

Jules partied, and married, and divorced.

Parker toiled.

He sighed and shut his mind to that pointless direction. All that mattered now was finding Gus.

He'd turned left onto St. Charles Avenue, heading farther uptown parallel to the streetcar tracks. Gus could have paid the fare and trundled riverbound without anyone looking twice at him.

He just hoped the boy had gone towards the river, a place he considered less threatening than heading downtown, towards Canal and the French Quarter.

Fishing was far preferable to the vices to be found in that direction.

"Didn't Huckleberry Finn and Jim build a raft?"

Parker gripped the wheel. He'd been so lost in his reverie he'd almost managed to crowd Meg from his mind.

Almost.

He turned and watched her gazing at him as if he knew the answer to questions he didn't even know existed.

"That sounds vaguely familiar."

"Maybe that's what he's doing."

"Why would he do that?" Parker knew he sounded irritable, but he couldn't think of anything more pointless than building a raft on which to navigate the Mississippi. The river would tear it to bits. He gripped the wheel and braked to an abrupt halt at the light at State Street.

"To forget? To dream?" Meg turned her body towards him, the way she'd sat during their ride to Mississippi to collect Gus only a few days earlier. "Didn't you ever do that when you were a child?"

He shook his head. He'd spent his childhood dragging Jules out of trouble and getting blamed by Teensy for his efforts. Eventually he'd abandoned Jules to his own follies and buried himself in sports and studies.

They'd passed Loyola and Tulane universities at last. The traffic crawled and Parker fought the desire to jump the car onto the neutral ground and drive along the streetcar tracks to bypass the cars, all of which seemed to be driven by tourists admiring the Audubon Park oaks.

To his surprise, Meg reached over and touched his hand. "He may not be there, Parker."

He noted the white flesh of his fingers as he tightened his hold. "Maybe, maybe not. But we have to try. And I respect your instincts enough to check this out before we call the police."

She nodded. "I hope I'm right and that he hasn't done anything foolish."

"Like launching himself into a river that's been known to suck the strongest swimmer into its depths and not let them go?" He heard the desperation in his voice and wondered when Gus had claimed such a part of his heart. He'd largely ignored the child but after watching him with Meg, he'd begun to feel an attachment for him that he couldn't quite understand.

"We'll find him," was all she said.

He bumped over the tracks across from River Road and yanked the car out of gear. He pulled on the parking brake and said, "Let's go."

She jumped from the low seat, amazingly graceful in the slim-cut skirt of the dress she wore. Without complaint, she crunched across the gravel and onto the banks of the grassy levee.

She kept pace with him as he climbed the rise. Horton had taken Jules and him fishing many times during their childhood. The two of them had tossed the fish about and laughed, but Horton had carefully retrieved them. It wasn't until much later that Parker realized Horton took the fish home and fed them to his family.

He'd always thought of Horton as part of his own family and had learned to his surprise during his teens that Horton had a wife and five children, the oldest two of whom were already in college when Parker was still in high school.

A man and a woman on horseback crossed in front of them. The sun shone, a beautiful, mild December day. Ahead on the crest of the levee two dogs chased one another. To their right, another dog leapt for a frisbee.

Several hours of searching later, Parker and Meg reached the top of the levee and stood looking down. Parker collected his bearings, tried to calm his fears, and gazed to the right. Then, down below, far too close to the waterline for his comfort, Gus appeared.

He sought Meg's hand, almost unaware that he did so.

She clasped his hand in hers, her fingers warm and reassuring.

"He's okay," Parker said. "That's Gus."

She nodded. "Looks like he's building his raft, too."

"Little bugger," Parker said. "Wait till I catch him."

Meg tugged at his hand and he turned and looked into her eyes.

She was smiling at him and he found it impossible to remain angry with her, to think of her as a possible enemy. "Thank you for coming with me," he said.

"Any time."

He smiled, and fought a desire to kiss her, fought off the feeling that if he stayed around her she'd make him forget every detail he needed to investigate.

Just then, Gus shouted, and Parker watched in horror as the child tumbled into the water.

Parker raced down the bank, Meg fast behind him.

"Hold on," he cried, pausing to kick his shoes off.

Just then a mongrel bounded up, barking furiously, and dove into the water. He plunged straight for Gus and the child cried out, coughed up water, and clung to the dog's fur.

As Parker jumped into the water, the dog paddled towards shore, towing Gus.

The three of them ended up on the bank, gasping like fish. Parker grasped Gus in his arms, their clothes dripping wet. The dog stood over the boy, his tongue hanging out.

Meg fussed over them. Grateful for her help, Parker smiled at her. She smiled back, wringing the water from Gus's wet sweatshirt.

"Where were you going to go?" she was asking Gus.

The boy only shook his head and clung to the smelly, shaggy dog. The only thing he had to say for himself was, "Can I keep him?"

Fifteen

"Can you keep him?" Parker spit both the words and the water out of his mouth and stared at his nephew. The child looked so disarming, one skinny arm thrown around the neck of the Heinz 57 Variety dog, that he had to smile. One of the mutt's ears pointed skyward, the other drooped towards its whiskered face. But a dog!

Parker had never had a dog. Teensy wouldn't take the chance of having her antiques shredded or her floors scarred. And if she had allowed her sons to have a dog, it would have been a purebred, too tiny to be of much interest to boys.

He tried to let Gus down easily. "You know, he probably belongs to someone."

"Oh, he doesn't," Gus said, hugging the dog to him. "We've been playing for hours. No one's been by to claim him and he doesn't even have a collar. It's a good thing he found me or the dog catcher might have ground him up for sausage."

Parker exchanged glances with Meg, who was studying the soggy dog with a bemused expression. He wished he knew what to do, wished he possessed the wisdom to answer Gus as he should. He also wished he had the words to tell Gus what the time he and Meg had spent searching for him had taken off his life.

"Well, he did save Gus from the river," Parker said, feeling a need to defend his inexplicable desire to befriend the mongrel.

Meg nodded. "And I'm sure he'll clean up nicely."

"Though probably not to Teensy's standards," Parker said.

Meg pulled him aside. "Don't encourage him if it's only going to break his heart. He's had enough disappointments."

"I know. You're right." He gazed at Gus, who was busy throwing a stick that the dog chased and returned with something akin to a smile on his goofy face. "If no one claims him, I'll take him to a groomer. And I suppose, if Teensy throws a real fit, he can come to my house."

"I think you're sweet on him," Meg said.

"No way. But the mutt did jump in at just the right moment."

Meg looked a little too smug for his comfort. "Right," she said, drawling out the word. Then she turned her back on him and knelt down beside Gus. "You feeling better?"

He nodded and sniffed loudly. "I wanted to go where my dad said he'd take me. I've been here before, but never with my dad. But somehow I thought . . ."

Meg pulled him close to her. "You thought maybe some miracle would bring your dad back here to be with you, huh?"

He nodded, his head bobbing against her side. "But I knew better all along. I know my father is dead. And that means no one is ever going to take me fishing." He sniffed again and Meg caught back a strangling sound that threatened to escape her throat. He reminded her so much of Teddy at that moment!

Parker came up beside them. "I'll take you fishing," he said.

"Really?" Gus's eyes lit up. "But we have to take Jem, too."

"Jem?"

Meg nudged him in the ribs and pointed to the dog.

Parker nodded. "Sure, sure. Jem can come, too."

"Good. I named him after Huck Finn's friend, but since he's a dog not a boy, it's spelled J-E-M." Gus whistled and the dog trotted over. He halted in front of the three of them, cocked his goofy-looking head to one side, then shook his body as if his life depended upon it.

A spray of water descended upon them. Parker pulled her back but too late. Meg gazed down at her splattered dress.

But she wasn't looking at the splotches. All she could see was Parker's hand on her arm. He seemed to have forgotten he'd reached for her. It was sweet, the way he was so protective. Ted had never been like that, never opened the car door or leapt to her aid. She'd been so used to taking care of herself she hadn't noticed the lack of those courtesies.

Courtesies that Parker performed so well.

At that moment, he obviously realized his hand still linked him to her. "Sorry," he said under his breath, and dropped her arm.

"That's okay," she said, wishing he hadn't acted like he was letting go of a fish he'd yanked by mistake out of the river.

"Let's get back to the house," he said. "We can change and figure out what to do about Jem."

She nodded and began to walk toward the car.

Gus ran ahead of them, his lean-to where he'd fallen asleep earlier and been hidden from them, along with a salvaged piece of tin, abandoned at the water's edge. The dog nipped at his heels, barking his half howl, half yip.

Parker's shoes made squishing sounds with every step and water dripped from his pants. Even in his ramshackle state, he appealed to her. If his hair looked good when it was dry and combed, it looked just as sexy wet, especially the way it curled on the back of his neck and around his ears.

"It seems as if I find myself thanking you yet again," Parker said as they climbed back up the bank behind the boy and the dog.

"It's nothing, really," she said.

"No?" He smiled down at her. The smile turned the light back on in his eyes and he no longer seemed so stern. "Do you have any idea how many women would have complained about treading up the levee in a dress and heels? Or how many women couldn't have gotten themselves ready to bolt out the door in hot pursuit of Gus?"

"You must hang out with all the wrong people," she said.

"I think I told you about that shortcoming of mine last night," he said, any vestige of a smile disappearing from his face.

They'd reached the car, which relieved Meg of any intelligent response to Parker's reference to the prior evening. She sincerely hoped he wouldn't bring it up again.

She'd missed her plane to Las Vegas. She would have to live through at least another day in proximity to Parker.

Proximity that was torture to her.

"You brought the Porsche," Gus cried. "Cool. I bet Jem's never ridden in a Porsche before."

Parker looked in horror from the muddy dog

to the car. "What makes you think he's going to ride in one today?"

Gus stared at him open-mouthed. "You said I could keep him!"

Meg bit back a laugh at Parker's look of consternation.

"It's a two-seater, Gus," Parker said, reasonably enough.

"Oh." The boy peered in the car window, then turned, a triumphant smile on his dirty face. "Meg and I can take the streetcar and Jem can ride with you, because everyone knows dogs can't ride on the streetcar."

"I've never ridden the streetcar before," Meg said.

"Where did you grow up?" Gus stared at her the way she and Parker had eyed the dog on first sight. "Well, don't worry, I'll show you how it's done," Gus said.

"Hey, wait a minute," Parker said.

Jem rolled over on his back and pawed the air towards Parker.

Parker frowned.

Meg waited for Parker to refuse to take the dog. She couldn't blame him; the car was spotless and obviously one of Parker's prized possessions. The dog was filthy.

Instead, Parker said, "Do you have a dollar, Gus?"

He nodded.

Parker pulled a bill from his money clip and handed it to Meg. "You need exact change for

the streetcar," he said, then walked to the trunk
of his car. He pulled a towel from a gym bag.
"Let's get this circus on the road."

"You're pretty cool, Uncle Parker," Gus said.
He patted Jem on the head. "Do whatever Parker tells you or he may turn you over to the
dog catcher."

The dog bounced upright and licked Gus on
the hand.

With a reluctant glance at the dog, Parker
opened his passenger door, spread the towel
and, as if born to ride in an expensive sports
car, the dog leapt in.

Parker shut the door. Jem smeared his
tongue against the window. Parker shook his
head. "I'll drive over to the streetcar stop and
wait with you."

"We're not babies," Gus said. "I came all the
way out here by myself."

"Yes, and that's something we're going to
talk about when we get back to the house,"
Parker said in a grim voice.

Gus clouded over. "You can't tell me what
to do. You're not my dad."

Parker opened his mouth and closed it,
clearly at a loss as to how to answer that
charge. After a long moment, he glanced over
at Meg, the plea for help clear in his eyes.

Meg looked from man to boy. They could
easily have been father and son; Gus had Parker's darker coloring rather than Jules's light
brown hair and blue eyes. The Ponthier stamp

rested on the child's features as clearly as on
his uncle's. Neither one of them would give in
easily to any battle.

The family resemblance prompted her answer. "You're a Ponthier, right, Gus?"

He nodded proudly, not surprising given the
egotism of this family, a family that cast him
off to a military-style school and ingrained in
him the liturgy of tradition.

"And Parker is a Ponthier."

He nodded again.

"So he may not be your dad, but he can certainly teach you how a Ponthier is expected to
behave."

Gus grinned. "Guess you got me there."

"And Ponthiers do not run out of the house
at dawn and scare their family sick," Parker
said, his voice stern but with an undercurrent
of tenderness coming through.

"You mean you missed me?"

The wistfulness got to Meg. "Of course we
missed you," she said, "but you don't have to
run off to get us to feel that way."

Gus stubbed at the ground with his squishy
hiking shoe.

Meg reached out a hand to his shoulder but
he shrugged her off.

"Let's go," Parker said and walked around
to the driver's side. "Gus, you take care of
Meg."

The boy saluted and pointed toward the
road in front of them.

Meg walked beside him, stepping gingerly over the large rocks of the parking area beside the train tracks that ran between the road and the levee bank. She wondered at Gus's reluctance to be touched. Was it because she was an outsider? Or because he'd been foisted off on strangers for so long while his own mother paid attention to her own spoiled priorities?

All three of her children were huggers, not surprising since she'd cuddled them since their first day on earth. But now that she thought back over it, they hadn't been as cuddly with their father.

"Hey, how come you didn't give me the what-for?"

They'd stopped at the street waiting for the traffic to clear so they could cross to the grassy strip where the streetcar tracks ran when Gus asked his question.

"Parker is your uncle," she said.

"Well, you're my new mom."

She stared down at him, at his bedraggled t-shirt and baggy shorts, the socks wet and gray above his hightop shoes. His dark blue eyes, so much like Parker's, met hers and she had to glance away.

"Oh, I get it," Gus said disgust heavy in his voice. "You're going away like all the rest of them."

Guilt hit home. Yet she wasn't truly guilty. What did she owe this child? She'd made a deal with Jules, for better or for worse, and she had her own family at home waiting for her, expecting her, needing her. Yet she'd grown up an orphan and knew the pain of not belonging. Gus wasn't technically an orphan, but after reading his mother's carelessly written note on the floral arrangement, Meg had concluded he might as well be.

Gus's mouth twisted. He kicked at the metal track but said nothing.

A horn sounded. Parker pulled up alongside them at the curb. Jem pushed his shaggy body against Parker and yelped out the window.

Parker worked the dog back to its side of the car.

Gus laughed.

Meg marveled at the difference when the child laughed. All traces of his scowling anger disappeared, giving her hope he would heal from the sorrows of his young years. She heard a rumble behind them and turned to see the streetcar approaching. As it ground to a screechy halt, she said softly to Gus, "I'm not going to be like the others."

"Yeah, well prove it and then I'll believe you," he said, before he jumped onto the streetcar and slid his dollar into the fare box. She followed his example and they climbed into a seat.

Parker waved from the car and drove off, Jem's head hanging out the side, his tongue tasting the breeze.

Meg waved back, wondering if Parker knew

what a hero he had proven himself to be.

Gus had half turned from her, his face pointing out the window. As the car racketed homeward, she could think of only one solution to Gus's situation. And to achieve it, Grandfather Ponthier would have to take her side.

"Get back, you smelly excuse for an animal," Parker said, lowering the dog's still-damp backside to the towel-draped seat.

Jem yelped and cocked his head. The upright ear dipped.

"And don't touch the dash, or you'll wish the dog catcher had found you."

Jem whimpered and stuck his head out the window that Parker had lowered after watching the dog swipe his tongue across it a few times.

On his left, the streetcar had just passed. Gus half hung out the window, a none-too-happy look on his face. Poor kid. If the dog cheered him up, it was worth transporting it and facing Teensy. He'd wanted to call a cab for the animal but somehow he knew that would have cost him a great deal of stature in his nephew's eyes.

And in Meg's.

Though the latter shouldn't matter to him at all. His gut tightened as he pictured her lying beneath him the night before. Soft and willing and tender. She'd given him the only moments of ease from his grief he'd yet to know.

He liked her.

He wanted her.

But he didn't trust her.

As soon as he cleaned himself up, he was heading to his office. If it meant calling in a team of investigators, he was going to learn every detail he could about Meg "Was-her-last-name-really-Ponthier?"

Before she wormed her way any further under his skin, before he wanted her even more, he had to know the facts. And if his instincts were right on, there was a lot about herself she hadn't been telling him.

He wanted the truth and he wanted it now.

Sixteen

That evening, Meg shifted from foot to foot, watching Grandfather Ponthier watch her the way Garfield eyed his favorite mousehole.

"So, I ask you again, if the woman you left in charge of your children has no idea you married my grandson, what other details are you not sharing?"

Meg tried to produce a smile but it died before her lips could move. Grandfather beat the fingers of his mobile arm on the padded leather rest of the wheelchair.

"She's—um—only the babysitter."

"Is that so?" He glared at her. "Mrs. Fenniston and I enjoyed quite a cozy chat. It took me awhile to figure out when she referred to you as a 'struggling young widow doing your best with three lively ones' that she was referring to your first widowed state, not to your loss of Jules."

Meg sat down. Maybe if she felt less like a

kid called on the carpet she could think more
clearly.

"And she said you'd come to New Orleans
on a *job*."

Mrs. Fenniston did love to talk. Meg considered a full confession. He'd be pretty mad and
rave about the Ponthier honor but maybe he'd
keep it their secret, the way he hadn't mentioned her three children to anyone. Or not yet
anyway. That way Parker wouldn't have to
know what she'd done.

But what about the family vote? What did
she owe Jules? If she confessed, they'd block
her from voting, but that might even be for the
best. Miserable, Meg sank her shoulders
against the back of the couch and clasped her
hands together.

"Not to speak ill of the dead," Grandfather
went on, "but I guess I could see how you'd
call marrying Jules a job."

She nodded. Maybe he was coming around.

"You would've had your hands full if he
hadn't gotten himself killed, you know. Between my son and that half-wit he married,
Jules never stood much of a chance."

"Parker is different," Meg blurted out, forgetting it was Jules she was supposed to be in
love with.

"True," his grandfather said, "and the reason for that is because Jules got all his parents'
warped attention." He cleared his throat and
glared at her again. "At least you've got

enough sense to see the difference between the two of them. I still don't understand why you married Jules in such a hurry. The two of you obviously had nothing in common. If you've got any sense at all, now that you're here, you'll cozy up to Parker." His eyes gleamed and a smile played at his lips.

Crazy old fox, Meg thought. Was he trying to trick her to see what she'd say? Test her? Was he warning her away?

Meg kept her expression as neutral as possible, trying not to think of what might have happened last night if she hadn't mentioned the stock shares while wrapped in Parker's arms.

"I'm through with matrimony," Meg said.

"Well, if you change your mind, you might want to think about my other grandson." He gazed at her, a speculative gleam in his eyes. "And I wouldn't say that to just any outsider."

"Thank you," she said, touched by what was for him a compliment.

Just then Gus bounded into the room. "Teensy says she's going to send Jem to the SPCA!" He ran over to Meg. "You can't let her get rid of my dog. I even gave him a bath."

The object of the turmoil dashed in, followed by Teensy brandishing a violin bow.

"I will not stand for this—this creature in my house."

Gus lunged for the dog and wrapped his

skinny arms around him. The dog licked the boy's face.

Teensy waved the bow. Dressed in a sapphire-blue suit, her feet ensconced in black pumps topped by neat velvet bows, she looked incongruous chasing the dog.

Grandfather said in a mild voice, "Now, Teensy, I think as long as there's breath in my body this pile of bricks is technically my house."

She fluttered her hands. "You can't mean to allow him to let this beast run free. Think of the priceless antiques, the Aubussons, the floors."

"Think of the child," Grandfather said.

Gus planted his hands on his hips and stuck his nose in the air.

"Ever hear of a gracious winner, Gus?" Meg asked quietly.

He shook his head.

"I think it would be nice of you to thank your grandfather and work out a plan for which rooms of the house Jem may visit."

"Why should I do that?" He set his jaw.

"Because that's what your Uncle Parker would say any Ponthier would do."

Grandfather barked a laugh. "She's got you there, boy."

"Thank you, Margaret," Teensy said. "Keep the dog out of the Great Parlor and the front sunroom. He's allowed only up the stairs and into your room. No one else's."

"What about Parker's?" Gus asked, stroking the dog's droopy ear.

"I don't think your uncle wants anything to do with that mongrel," Teensy said.

"Oh, yeah? Well, then why'd he let him ride in his Porsche?"

Teensy blanched and Grandfather chuckled.

Gus, looking pleased with himself, said, "Come on Jem, let's go outside."

After the boy and his newfound pal left, Meg said to Teensy, "Perhaps you can arrange for obedience lessons."

She nodded faintly, closed her eyes, and rubbed her forehead over the bridge of her nose, as if the idea were too much for her to deal with.

"Yes, and we'll send the kids to lessons, too," Grandfather said.

"Kids?" Teensy's eyes fluttered open. Then she turned to Meg with a look of joy on her face. "Are you expecting another grandchild?"

Meg could have oozed through the floor from the awkwardness of Teensy's question and the sadness she felt at the eager anticipation on the woman's face. There was no way she was pregnant by Jules. "No, I'm not."

"Then why did he say kids?" She looked puzzled and Meg couldn't blame her. Guiltily, she thought of the evening before with Parker and how close she'd come to giving herself to the son she hadn't married.

"You did say kids plural?"

Meg looked over at Grandfather Ponthier,
who was sitting there with a very smug expression on his face.

The door to the sunroom swung open and
Horton appeared. Before he could say any-
thing, three children rushed past him. "Mom!
Mommy! Mother!"

Meg's jaw dropped. She looked from Teddy,
Ellen, and Samantha back to Grandfather. Then
Mrs. Fenniston entered, elegant as always in a
dark blue suit with pearl buttons.

Meg smiled at her friend and held out her
arms and all three of her children raced into
them.

Samantha's voice drowned out the others as
she said, "Mommy, we flew on a plane and we
were the only ones on it!"

Meg's gaze flew to Grandfather Ponthier,
who was watching the scene with satisfaction
on his face. He must have chartered a plane for
them. And Meg had been worried about how
to replace her single ticket home from the flight
she'd missed that morning.

Teensy dropped her violin bow. It landed
with a clatter on the floor. She fanned herself
with one hand and said, "Horton, go tell Dr.
Prejean I must see him now."

Predictably, Ellen pulled away first from the
family reunion. "Mom, you don't have to
squeeze the oxygen out of our lungs."

"Sorry, sweetie," Meg said. Samantha clung
to her leg when Teddy stepped back to survey

this new territory. "Mrs. Fenniston, how can I ever thank you?"

The silver-haired woman bustled over, looking every inch a cross between Princess Margaret and Angela Lansbury on "Murder She Wrote." "Don't mention it. I've always been curious about New Orleans," she said, taking in the gracious room. She breathed deeply and added, "My, I do believe I smell roses. And in December, too."

Teensy quit fluttering her hands. "They're from our hothouse."

Mrs. Fenniston smiled at her. "Delightful. Now, Meg, don't worry about thanking me for anything. I've never had the opportunity to visit New Orleans before. The colonel's travels never brought us here. Too much of a navy town, I suppose."

Grandfather rustled in his wheelchair. "So who do we have here?"

Meg rose, Samantha still attached to her leg. "Mrs. Fenniston, meet Grandfather and Teensy Ponthier. And this is Ellen and Teddy and Samantha."

The kids said hello politely enough, relieving Meg of any embarrassment over their manners.

Grandfather nodded and gestured with his right hand at his wheelchair. Meg sensed his keen frustration at his disability. "Forgive me for not rising, Mrs. Fenniston," he said, sounding positively friendly.

Teensy produced a smile, a frigid gesture

that evoked little sense of the famed southern hospitality. "Are all these children yours, Meg?"

The three kids stared at her. "Of course we are," Ellen said. "Can't you tell we look alike?"

Teensy glanced at all of them, then shrugged. Obviously, if they weren't offspring of hers, they held no interest. Which wasn't surprising, given that she scarcely paid attention to Gus, her own flesh-and-blood grandson.

Teddy had been staring hard at Grandfather Ponthier. Finally he walked over and said, "Are you my grandfather, too?"

Mrs. Fenniston put her arm around him. "Now, Teddy, you've already met your grandfather."

"Only one. Kids are supposed to have two."

"Well, then, I'll be the other one," Grandfather Ponthier pronounced. "That is, if you'd like me to be."

Meg had never heard him take such pains to be gentle. What had gotten into him?

She could tell Teddy was considering the offer by the way he tipped his head to the side. He always did that when he thought hard. "That would be good because it would mean my mom's not an orphan anymore."

Meg was touched. "That's very thoughtful, Teddy."

Gus burst through the doorway and charged straight at Teddy. "Well, you can't have him. He's *my* great-grandfather!" He snatched the violin bow off the floor and flourished it at Teddy's chest. "On guard!"

Never one to run from a challenge, Teddy knocked the bow aside and the two boys lunged and rolled together on the floor.

Dr. Prejean walked in. "What is the meaning of exposing Teensy to such violence?" He addressed his question to the room at large; everyone ignored him.

As long as they did no damage, Meg didn't see any harm in letting the two boys get acquainted. Ellen, however, evidently had other ideas. She pushed her twin aside and jumped on top of skin-and-bones Gus, straddling his chest.

Gus stared at her. "Hey, you're a girl. Get off me."

Jem came bounding into the room, yelping, and made a beeline for the downed Gus.

"Haven't you ever heard of sharing?" Ellen ignored the dog and glared at Gus.

Meg caught Teddy by the arm to keep him from escalating the fight.

Gus said, "Ponthiers don't share."

"Oh, yeah?" Ellen grabbed his hair and thumped his head against the floor. "Maybe you will after I knock some sense into your thick skull."

"Ellen, that's enough," Meg said.

Ellen let go of his hair but didn't move from her position of dominance.

Grandfather wheeled his chair over beside

the kids and grabbed Jem by the scruff of his neck, holding him off. "I like a show of spirit but enough's enough. You're all Ponthiers now, so get up and act like it."

Ellen climbed off Gus, who leapt up. Hands on her hips, she said, "I'll have you know I'm a McKenzie, not a Ponthier."

Grandfather beetled his brows. "McKenzie? Which husband was that?"

"My maiden name," Meg supplied. Three months after Ted's death, about the time they'd been forced to move from their family home, Ellen had informed her she was renouncing her father's name in favor of Meg's, even though her daughter knew McKenzie had been the name of the foster parents Meg had lost when she was ten, not her birth name.

"Well, you've got some tough females in that clan," Grandfather said, but he followed his stern words with a chuckle.

Teddy approached Ellen. "I didn't need your help."

She shrugged. "We're twins. It's genetically encoded in me to react that way."

Teensy looked up from the shelter of Dr. Prejean's arm. "How old is that child?"

"Ten," Ellen said. "I guess you're wondering about my vocabulary. It's quite advanced for a child my age. That's because my mom teaches us."

Meg knew at a glance Teensy and Dr. Prejean found it hard to believe the interloping outsider from Vegas with a GED had instilled those traits in her offspring. She let it drop. She'd had enough turmoil for the day. It was late, though as late as it was, there'd been no sign of Parker returning to the house. Even with all the commotion and the reunion with her children, she still felt his absence. Without Parker, the house felt empty.

"Bedtime," she said.

As expected, all the kids groaned.

"Not for me," Gus said, freeing Jem from Grandfather's clutches.

"Why not you?" Teddy asked, obviously still spoiling for a fight.

"I go to bed when *I* say."

Teddy looked at Meg. He was holding back a yawn but interested in her answer to Gus's independent stance.

Meg smoothed Samantha's wild curls and wondered how to respond. Finally she decided a roundabout approach would work the best. "Let's go see what bedtime snack Horton can find for us."

"Who's Horton?" Samantha asked.

"A nice man who knows where the milk and cookies are hidden." Meg began moving toward the door, Samantha in tow. Ellen and Teddy fell into step.

"You go ahead," Grandfather said. "I'll entertain Mrs. Fenniston." Turning his chair towards Mrs. Fenniston, he said in his nicest voice, "May I offer you a glass of sherry?"

Meg smothered a smile. "Want a snack, Gus?"

He shrugged and muttered something that sounded like milk and cookies are for babies. But after they left the room, he trailed behind them, Jem his faithful shadow.

With Horton's help, Meg got the kids fed and bathed and made sleeping arrangements. Samantha and Ellen she put in the room on the other side of Parker's, though she knew Samantha would insist on sleeping with her, which meant Ellen would probably join them.

Horton offered to make up the spare maid's room on the ground floor for Teddy when Gus surprised them all by offering Teddy the other bed in his room.

When all was set, the twins and Samantha tumbled onto Meg's big bed, ready for their good night pillow talk. Samantha still clung more than usual, which caused Meg an extra dose of guilt for having left her children for as long as she had. She reminded herself to thank Grandfather first thing the next morning for bringing them to her.

Even though they'd all soon be winging their way back to Las Vegas.

Meg sat on the bed, Samantha's curly head lodged on her lap, her daughter's small hand resting in hers on the pillow Meg had placed in the center of the bed. Teddy leaned against the headboard, only his foot grazing the pillow. Since Ted's death, her son had joined in a little less easily than he had in the past. Ellen stretched out lengthwise on the bed, her eyes half-closed, her head lying on the pillow.

"Pillow talk time," Meg said in a soothing voice. "And I want to say first how very thankful I am to have you all with me again."

"Don't ever go away again," Ellen said, her eyes now wide open and fierce. "It's scary when you leave us."

Meg bent over and kissed her cheek. "I'm sorry, sweetie. Sometimes I have to do things that are complicated but I try to do everything I can that's best for all of us."

Ellen sighed. "I just wish we can all stay together."

Teddy said, "And I wish just once you'd let me fight my own fight."

Ellen sat up.

Meg interrupted. "Hey, guys, this is pillow talk. Peace and quiet, okay?"

Ellen lay back down. "I wouldn't jump in if I didn't love you, squirt."

Teddy made a face. "Who is that other kid?"

"He's the son of one of Grandfather's grandsons. And his father just passed away."

"Like Daddy?" Teddy sounded very somber.

Meg nodded.

"Oh," Teddy said.

A rustling noise sounded in the doorway. Meg glanced over to see Jem's nose poking through from the hallway. Where Jem went, Gus was not far behind. She thought of calling out and asking him to join them, but she sensed Gus needed his distance. He'd suffered many wounds and losses; when he was ready, he would join them.

"Mommy?"

"Yes, Samantha?"

"My wish for my dreams is that you find us another daddy and that you never go away ever again."

Meg smiled, but she knew sorrow showed on her face. "Let's go to bed, little ones," she said, and rose and led them to their rooms.

Tucking herself under her covers, she wondered once again where Parker was, what he was doing, on what pillow he would lay his head that night. She sighed and tossed and turned.

Then she heard the patter of feet and Samantha and Ellen, as she'd predicted, slipped into bed with her. What surprised her, though, was when she woke the next morning, she found Gus, his head pillowed on Jem's body, asleep on the rug on the floor near the foot of her bed.

Locked in his office downtown the next day, Parker paced the floor, trying to absorb his shock.

Jules had revoked his prior will after his divorce from CeCe, and hadn't signed the new one before he left for Vegas. Which meant he'd

died intestate and his property passed to his
wife and son.

And he'd filed no prenuptial agreement with
his lawyers.

Perhaps Meg had a copy.

Surely Jules hadn't married without ensuring that she signed one. After learning that the
marriage had indeed been validly registered in
Las Vegas, Parker had set about reassuring
himself Jules had protected the Ponthier's business interests.

But it looked as if he'd done exactly the opposite.

Or put more bluntly, tried to line up his own.

It wasn't like him not to insist on a prenuptial. He'd drafted it, then had his lawyers pore
over it when he'd married Marianne and then
CeCe. Maybe he'd taken a copy of that all-
important document that prevented a widowed or divorced spouse from having any say
over Ponthier family shares to Las Vegas with
him.

Without a prenuptial, Meg could outvote
Parker.

Damn his brother, Parker thought, then
pushed the reaction guiltily from his mind.
Their entire lives his brother had messed up
and Parker had had to straighten things out.

Even after death, that pattern continued.

He crossed his office once more, pausing in
front of the floor-to-ceiling windows that over-
looked the downtown business district. In the

near distance he could see the Greater New Orleans bridge reaching like a silver arm across
the Mississippi.

Impossible to think that only yesterday Gus
had fallen into those same muddy waters, waters that looked clear and peaceful from this
distance, an image Parker knew was false.

He'd stayed away from Ponthier Place last
night and all day, lest he be tempted into any
more foolish behavior should he chance across
Meg dressed in that strangely appealing t-shirt.
He'd returned to his comfortable home along
Bayou St. John but instead of the peace he usually found there, he felt alone in a way he never
had before.

All day he'd worked at a furious pace, catching up on business as well as fielding the news
from Jules's lawyers and checking with the investigator in Las Vegas.

As he'd gone through the day, he kept thinking of Meg. She was no longer his sister-in-law;
she was his uninvited and unwanted business
partner.

That thought made him groan. He couldn't
work with the woman; he couldn't stand being
in the same room with her. She made him feel
like a randy eighteen-year-old at the same time
she made him feel like a stuffy and predictable
snob. How she managed to elicit such oppos-
ing reactions, he had no idea.

He told himself he had to understand her in
order to work with her. He told himself he had

to spend more time with her to understand just what game she and Jules had been playing. He told himself his interest in her was based purely on protecting the Ponthier business position.

Simply business.

Seventeen

By the time he'd parked his Porsche in the carriage house, covered it, and dashed through the rain towards the house, Parker had forced himself to admit he was more interested in Meg than business required. He also told himself that until he'd seen her prenuptial he shouldn't jump to conclusions on her standing within the Ponthier family corporation.

Jules may have been a fool in many ways, but he'd been a lawyer who'd never yet let his heart run away with his pocketbook, not even in his disastrous first two marriages.

Guilt nipped at him for thinking poorly of his brother, but somehow the level wasn't as high as it might have been. Death did not sainthood impose, Parker reasoned as he strode to the house.

Lights glowed throughout the massive structure. For some reason, the house looked friendlier, more cheerful this evening than Parker remembered it looking in a long, long time.

It was late, after nine o'clock. Parker decided
to stop in the kitchen first and see what left-
overs the cook might spare him. Slipping in
through the back sunroom door, Parker heard
music blasting from farther to the front. It certainly wasn't Teensy's Tchaikovsky or one of
his grandfather's operas. He paused, and made
out an old Rolling Stones song.

Meg?

His appetite for food forgotten, Parker
headed toward the source of the music.

The doors to the library stood open; the
Stones blasted from the music system in his office. Surprised at the intrusion into what Parker
considered both a personal and professional
refuge within the house, Parker reserved judg-
ment as he walked into the room.

The Stones weren't the only invasion.

Chairs had been moved around, lined up in
front of his desk. Draped over the chairs were
blankets and sheets. Beneath the sheets he saw
movement, heard voices and giggles, and sure
enough, beating against the side of one of the
blankets was what had to be Jem's tail.

Parker sat his briefcase on the floor.

"Shh," he heard, "the sheik is coming!"

"He's no sheik," a girl said, "I thought we
were playing dancing school."

"Are not." That was definitely Gus's voice.

"Are too."

"Why don't you two grow up?" Another
boy's voice entered the fray. "We already did

scissors, rock, and paper and now we're playing war."

"Pow! You're dead and now I'm the sheik!"

The blankets moved roughly. A chair upended and smacked the side of Parker's desk. He winced just as Jem yelped.

"What's—" His words were cut off as a small child with curly brown hair crawled from beneath the edges of the blankets.

She sat back and regarded Parker with large, dark eyes that looked oddly familiar. She said, "I'm not supposed to talk to you because I don't know you."

"I see." Parker realized he must be intimidating to the little girl. He lowered himself to his knees and sat back. "Well, I wouldn't want you to do anything you're not supposed to do, but do you think you could tell me your name?"

She shook her head vigorously. Her curls danced.

The rough and tumble under the blankets came to an abrupt halt. Three sets of hands reached out and pulled the girl back under the blankets.

Then after muffled discussion, Gus stuck his head out. "Uncle Parker, what's hanging?"

Parker rose and turned down the volume on the Stones. "Maybe I should ask you that question?"

Gus shrugged, only his head showing. Jem pushed his nose out near the floor and whined.

"I take it you're having some friends over to play?" That would explain the well-lit house. Teensy must be entertaining the other children's parents, though it wasn't like her to include youngsters along with any invitation.

"Sort of."

"Did you have to play in my study?"

"Ellen said you had the best stuff for making our tent."

Parker nodded. "Ellen must be a very discriminating tent builder."

"She's okay." He added, "For a girl."

Parker wondered whose family had come to call. "Where does Ellen go to school?"

"I don't think she does. Her mom teaches her, though."

"Her mom must be pretty smart."

Gus snorted. "She thinks so."

Parker wondered if the antecedent for that pronoun was Ellen or the mother.

"Just a minute." Gus disappeared under the covers.

Parker listened to the whispered conference, but couldn't make out the words. He loosened his tie, stripped off his jacket, and surveyed the mess of his retreat. Gus and his pals had enjoyed a picnic in front of the fire. A bowl of popcorn, several half empty glasses of milk, and a saliva-drenched dog bone lay atop yet another sheet. Well, at least they'd had the good manners to cover the Aubusson rug with a protective layer.

Gus stuck his head back out. "You want to join us? We're playing sheik."

"Sheik?"

"You know, it's make-believe." Gus stared at him. "Didn't you ever play make-believe?"

Parker stared back at his nephew. Certainly he'd never had the nerve to upend the furniture in Teensy's perfectly mannered household. He found it hard to believe Gus, schooled in as rigid a manner as Parker had been, had thought of such a thing and wondered again whose kids were hidden beneath that tent.

Well, one way to find out was to join them.

Don't be silly, Parker. You've got work to do. You can't go crawling around on the floor under a pretend bedouin tent.

Gus whispered something over his shoulder and turned back to Parker, disappointment clear. "Ellen said you wouldn't do it."

"Oh, Ellen did, did she?"

Gus nodded. "She said dads never want to play make-believe. She said they're always too busy working."

Parker unfastened his cuffs, tossed the gold links on top of his desk, and got down on his hands and knees. "What do girls know, anyway?" Gus opened the tent and Parker crawled inside.

As he did, he remembered where he'd seen those huge, dark eyes before. But before he could ponder the coincidence, a beam of light from a flashlight blinded him.

"Show the captive to the seat of truth," the girl commanded.

Thankfully the flashlight bounced in another direction. Gus patted a cushion Parker recognized from the loveseat. Playing along, he moved on hands and knees over to the cushion, then sat on it crosslegged. The tent rose barely above the height of the two wing chairs that formed its main supports.

Shadows danced from the bobbing flashlight. Parker made out a girl and a boy about Gus's size, Gus, the dark-eyed Orphan Annie who'd stuck her head out, and Jem, of course.

The older of the two girls clapped her hands. She wore a towel over her head as did the other boy. Gus had one draped around his shoulders. "Give our guest some dates grown in our oasis," she commanded.

The other boy formed a machine gun with his arms and hands. "Rat-a-tat-tat-tat! We're playing war and we don't feed the dead."

The girl yanked on his towel. "It's no wonder you always get an F in cooperation. Gus, will you do it, please?"   .

To Parker's amazement his nephew smiled and lifted a heavy silver tray Parker recognized as one of Teensy's treasured wine bottle coasters. It was empty but he carried it over to Parker solemnly. "Dates from our desert oasis," he said. Then under his breath, he added, "Come on, it's a game."

Parker nodded. "Thank you to my gracious

hosts," he said and pretended to select a date. He nibbled on air, licked his fingers, and said, "Most delicious."

From the thankful smile Gus flashed, Parker figured he hadn't caused him to lose too much face. Emboldened, he said, "My princess sheik, what oasis are these from?"

The girl "tasted" one of the dates. "Las Vegas. Where all the best things are from."

Parker choked. He glanced from the older girl to the younger waif. Same eyes, same curly hair, same . . .

The curtained doorway to the tent parted. Meg's head poked through. "Bedtime in five minutes."

"But, Mom, we just captured our first prisoner," the boy said.

"And we haven't played dancing school yet," Ellen said.

"All right," she said, not glancing all the way into the tent. "Finish boiling your captive in hot oil. You can play dancing school tomorrow."

"That's rather inhospitable treatment for a desert visitor," Parker said.

Meg swiveled her head back into the tent. Parker! Sure enough, he sat crosslegged on a cushion. "Oh, my," she said, rocking back on her heels. "I didn't see you."

"She probably thought we had an imaginary captive," Teddy supplied helpfully.

On her hands and knees, her head sticking

through the doorway of the tent, Meg said, "What are *you* doing in here?"

"I was invited—er—captured."

"You didn't have to play along."

His eyes met hers. "I know," he said quietly, "but I wanted to."

Samantha wiggled over. "We got you, too," she said. "Now you have to sit on the seat."

"Great idea," Gus said. "Onto the seat of— what's it called, Ellen?"

"Seat of truth," her daughter pronounced.

Meg hesitated. She could round them up for bed, or she could let them have fun a little bit longer. But sitting next to Parker on that cushion, the same cushion if she was right, where she'd lain beneath him two nights ago was the last thing she wanted to do.

"March, lady," Gus said, "or we will boil you in hot oil."

She sighed. She deserved that one, having given them the idea. On her hands and knees she crawled over and took her place on the cushion beside Parker. She tried to arrange her legs so as not to graze his thigh, but within the tight quarters, she failed. Heat from the brush of his thigh against hers traveled up her leg, fanning the flame that had burned within her since their ill-fated tumble on the loveseat. Try as she might, she hadn't been able to extinguish the slow burning of desire he'd ignited within her.

The cuffs of his shirt had been turned back,

and his hands rested gracefully on his knees. Staring hard at those hands, she could feel him in her mind touching her the way he had the other night. She would have given herself to him then. Meg swallowed and trying not to think of what might have been, kept her eyes fastened on those hands.

The sight of him playing with the children amazed and pleased her. Parker Ponthier was a man to be reckoned with. If she weren't careful, and given the chance, she'd yield to him again.

Teddy grabbed Ellen and Gus by the shoulders. They held another conference punctuated by giggles.

While they planned what to do next, Meg couldn't help but glance up at Parker. He was smiling softly. "So you like this make-believe?" he asked.

"I usually play along."

"Hmmm." His hands, which had been hugging his knees, drifted downward to the cushion. One just brushed the side of her leg as it settled innocently enough against the cushion. "If my imagination led me to believe that these three charming playmates of Gus belong to you, would it be leading me to guess the truth?"

"Well, now that you mention it—"

"Quiet!" Ellen waved the flashlight. "The desert sheik has reached her decision."

"I still don't agree that you get to be the

sheik," Gus said. "Girls can't be sheiks."

"But I'm the oldest. And I'm a princess sheik."

"By two minutes," Teddy said.

"And three days," Gus added.

"I said quiet."

Meg tried to read Parker's expression but he sat there, inscrutable. Now that he knew she had three lively children, she'd not have to worry about another pass from him. Even if he did decide to forgive her deception, what man in his right mind would take on a household of masters of commotion? Yet here he was playing with them in their tent. Her heart filled with a hope she had no right to feel. As Ellen commanded quiet yet again from Gus and Jem, who'd started yelping, Meg also wondered, on a more pragmatic note, when her child had grown so bossy.

"You two shall be married and banished on a desert honeymoon," the princess sheik pronounced, then ruined her dramatic effect with a long, pealing giggle.

"Rather extreme sentence, isn't it?" Parker said, but in a mild voice.

Jem yelped even louder.

"You've got at least one dissenter," Meg pointed out.

"What's a dissenter?" Gus asked.

"Someone who disagrees with a decision," Ellen said.

Meg caught an appreciative look in Parker's eye as he glanced at her.

She wondered what she'd done to earn that look of approval. Well, approval or no approval, there'd be no mock wedding. "Time's up for tonight, kidlets," she said, moving off the cushion.

"But we haven't carried out our sentence," Gus said.

"There's always tomorrow."

"Ah, saved by the clock," Parker said.

Gus blocked the doorway. "If there's always tomorrow, does that mean we can play again tomorrow?"

Meg hesitated, looking towards Parker. No doubt he'd stumbled across the crew on his way in search of peace and quiet in the library, peace and quiet so he could concentrate on whatever work he'd carried from the office. Would he voluntarily play again?

"My fate is in your hands, oh sheik," he said. He looked at Gus when he spoke, but Meg could have sworn he brushed his hand against hers. But when she took a quick peek downwards, his hand rested on his knee as before.

"Okay," Gus said, "but don't try to escape or I'll hunt you down on my desert camel."

Parker managed to look suitably impressed by the threat. Meg suppressed a smile and said, "Say hello to Mr. Ponthier." Teddy, Ellen and Samantha introduced themselves, Samantha peeking shyly up at him. In response, he said,

"Call me Parker, please," then winked at Meg.

Meg didn't miss the wink or the friendly response, but she kept her voice businesslike. "Let's get this cleaned up for tonight. You can make another tent tomorrow. In another room." She headed for the tent's exit.

"Oh, that won't be necessary," Parker said, crawling behind her. "I like the tent; it adds a nice touch."

In her surprise, Meg stopped short. Parker bumped into her, and Ellen and Gus did the same. Ellen and Gus started a tickle fight and for one wild moment, Meg thought of doing the same with Parker. Then reason recaptured her mind. "Everybody out. Now."

Parker picked up his pace when Meg's voice took on that firm, no-nonsense tone. He moved along with the kids as they followed her out of the tent, collected the picnic remains, and trooped to the kitchen where Meg directed them in cleaning up their mess.

Nibbling on some of the leftover popcorn, Parker forgot about his earlier hunger. Now the only thing he wanted to do was watch Meg in action. But after she put the kids to bed, he wanted some answers.

Truthfully, he wanted some action. He'd wanted her earlier and he wanted her still. When she'd settled beside him in the tent, just the subtle brush of her leg against his heated him beyond bearing, it was all he could do to concentrate on the game playing.

The game he wanted to play had nothing to do with children. Meg's offspring, to be sure, were an unexpected complication, but nothing he couldn't handle. For Meg, he could manage a lot.

He hadn't even known she'd had children. She'd mentioned another deceased husband. The children must be from that marriage. He couldn't believe otherwise. Despite her hasty nuptials with Jules, she didn't seem the type of woman to bear children out of wedlock. That all three of the kids had the same father he had to believe; their coloring mimicked hers, but the family resemblance was strong in ways that didn't match Meg's looks. For instance, all the kids were tall, even the youngest, and Meg barely topped Parker's chest.

Parker's musings were interrupted by Gus, noisily balking at being required to wash his milk glass. "The maid does that," he said, indignant.

"Did the maid drink out of it?" Meg asked without emphasizing the question too strongly. She was busy guiding Teddy away from the cookie jar.

"That's a stupid question," Gus said.

"And that's a stupid answer," Meg responded. "Now, rinse your glass, then put it in the dishwasher."

Parker waited for the refrain he expected to hear: Ponthiers don't do dishes. But instead, Gus joined the others at the sink.

Would miracles never cease? Parker tried to catch Meg's eye but she was having none of that. He pulled a glass from a cupboard, crossed to one of the two refrigerators, and poured himself a glass of milk. Unbidden, the image of Meg clutching her mug of warm milk to her breasts filled his mind. He sucked in a breath and chugged down the milk.

Maybe she'd notice him if he washed his glass, too. Parker joined the kids at the sink, but they'd all finished. Gus looked at him as if he wasn't quite sure what to make of his uncle rinsing his glass. Parker gave him an encouraging smile.

Meg said, "Okay, everybody upstairs, brush your teeth, and I'll meet you in my room."

Gus hung back. Jem, caught between loyalty to his savior and the other kids' racing out the door, dashed out, then returned to lick Gus's hand.

Meg walked over to him. "You, too, Gus," she said softly.

"I still don't hold with that sissy stuff."

"That's okay, but you can listen if you'd like."

Gus shrugged. He'd pulled his pocketknife from the deep trousers of his baggy shorts. Snapping it open, he said, "What if I made a dream wish. Would it work for me?"

Meg seemed to consider her answer. As she did, Parker admitted to himself he wanted to wish for Meg in his life—and that he was willing to make that dream come true. He nodded at his nephew just as Meg said, "Let's try it."

Gus bobbed his head, then loped out the door, Jem tagging behind.

"Whatever you just did," Parker said, "was smart. And wise."

"Really?" She looked at him, as cool as the proverbial cucumber. "I do find it's never wise to make promises to a child one isn't sure will be kept."

Parker regarded her. Wow, but she was mad at him. Had he been that insufferable the other night? Or was she just being prickly to keep him from asking her where the kids had materialized from?

Before he could ask any of his questions, she sashayed from the room.

He took his time following her. First he dropped by the Great Parlor. To his surprise, he found Grandfather still up, sitting beside a fire playing chess with a woman Parker had never seen before. A huge gray cat, most definitely a stranger to Ponthier Place, was curled on Grandfather's lap.

When Parker stuck his head in, Grandfather rumbled, "Come in and meet Mrs. Fenniston but don't disturb my concentration. The woman's hell on wheels with her rooks."

Parker looked with interest at the dainty silver-haired woman seated opposite his grandfather. He'd never heard such a compliment from the old man. For years his grandfather had told him he couldn't wield a pawn properly, let alone a bishop or a rook.

He nodded. "Pleased to meet you. I'm Parker Ponthier."

The woman smiled. "Mrs. Fenniston. Delighted to meet you. I'm making my first visit to your city and your grandfather is making me feel so at home."

Parker wasn't sure what to say in response to that. Being browbeaten over a chess game wasn't Parker's idea of seeing his beloved city. But now that he thought about it, Meg had scarcely seen any of the city he called home. He'd have to remedy that. Maybe that would soften her up. Not that he was trying to soften her up, he corrected himself. But if he had to conduct business with the woman, he should get to know her better.

"Did you meet the children?" Mrs. Fenniston asked, one fingertip stroking the white bishop.

Grandfather glared at the board. Parker figured he either disliked the subject of the little hooligans or Mrs. Fenniston had just figured out how to best him on the chessboard.

Parker nodded.

"They are exceptional," she said. "And sweet Meg has done such a marvelous job with them. And under such difficult circumstances."

"Her husband," Parker asked, unable to control his curiosity. "When did he . . ."

"Pass on?" Mrs. Fenniston whisked her

bishop diagonally across the board. "Check," she said.

The look on his grandfather's face was priceless.

"More than a year ago. And such troubles she's faced with never a whimper." Mrs. Fenniston sighed. "It's made me happy to be able to help her. Especially since my dear husband's been gone more than a year now."

"A year, is it?" Grandfather shot the question out.

Parker smiled. He'd learned what he wanted to know. Apparently so had his grandfather. "I'll let you two finish your game," he said. "Nice to meet you."

Mrs. Fenniston smiled at Parker. "There, Mr. Ponthier, look what I've done to your queen," she was saying, as Parker backed from the room.

The door to Meg's room stood ajar, almost as if she knew he wouldn't be able to resist sharing their bedtime pillow talk.

Which Parker found himself powerless to do, even though he remained in the hall, just outside, listening. And as he listened, he remembered how good he'd felt sitting beside her on Gus's bed as she explained pillow talk to him. He'd wanted to kiss her then and he wanted to kiss her now.

He heard the gentle thump of Jem's tail against the floor. Farther away, but quite distinguishable, he made out the voices of Meg and the children.

"What are your dream wishes, Samantha?"

He could picture her smoothing the little girl's mass of curls as she asked the question.

"A dress-up Barbie and a new daddy," she said.

There was no immediate response, then Parker heard Meg say, "We'll see what we can do about the Barbie. How about we start with making a new outfit for the one you brought with you?"

"Okay," murmured a sleepy-sounding Samantha.

Parker had to hand it to Meg. She'd neatly sidestepped the second request.

"And you, Teddy?"

"Tomorrow we get to play war."

"Hah," Ellen said. "Boys are so stupid."

"Hey, speak for yourself," Gus piped up.

"Shh," Meg said. "This is pillow talk. It's okay to ask for what you want, because knowing what you want in life is the first step to achieving it."

"You're sure smart," Ellen said.

"Thank you, sweetie. Gus, do you want to share?"

A long silence followed. Parker held his breath, wondering whether his nephew would join in. Hell, he wanted to join in. He wanted to curl up on the bed beside Meg and her children and wrap his arms around her loving body and whisper just what he wished he could have.

But he, Parker Ponthier, was a grownup.

Pillow talk was for kids.

"Nah," Gus said at last. "Fairy tales are just as bogus as Santa Claus. And most mothers."

Parker sucked in a sharp breath, his heart breaking for Gus. Marianne was such a bitch. It was just like her to dally in Switzerland when Gus was home suffering. He leaned forward, wondering what in the world Meg would say to Gus's comment.

Before Meg spoke, he heard the younger girl say in a sleepy voice, "You can share our Mom. She's not bogus."

"That's very sweet, Samantha," Meg said. "Teddy? Ellen?"

"As long as we get to play war tomorrow."

"That makes you sort of my brother," the older girl said. "Which is okay as long as you do what I say."

Parker thought he heard Meg sigh.

"Forget that!" Gus said.

"Yeah," Teddy said. "But now at least it's two against two for awhile."

A round of high-fiving took place, punctuated by Jem's high-pitched yelps.

A few minutes later, Meg appeared in the doorway, an arm around Teddy. Gus hung to the side, but he looked much less withdrawn than he had the past few days. Meg saw Parker and glanced at him, confusion on her face.

"I confess," Parker said. "I was eavesdropping. Want some help?"

"I don't—" She glanced at Gus. "Sure. Tuck the boys in for me, will you?"

Just like that, he found himself walking them across the hall. He watched as they climbed into the twin beds in Gus's room, then he moved over beside Gus's bed, unsure of what to do next. He had no idea how to tuck a child in.

He saw Meg had joined him on the opposite side of Teddy's bed. She leaned over and kissed him on the cheek. "Sleep tight and don't—"

"—let the bed bugs bite," Teddy finished for her. "I love you, Mom," he said, then seemed to fall asleep immediately. Meg remained beside him, stroking his hair.

Gus looked up at him, all seriousness. "Do you believe in all that make-a-wish stuff?"

Parker glanced over at Meg. In the dim glow of the bedside lamp, she shimmered between shadow and light.

"Well, do you?"

Parker smiled at Gus and nodded. "Dreams do come true. Wishes do get answered. And sometimes even the frog turns into a prince."

He looked down at Gus, who was watching him as if he wanted to believe in what Parker said. Stooping, Parker brushed his lips across his nephew's forehead. "Goodnight," he said.

Gus smiled. "Thanks, Uncle Parker."

Meg walked over and blew a goodnight kiss to Gus. Then she moved quietly from the room. Parker followed, admiring her quiet dignity.

"No wonder you've known how to deal with Gus."

She gazed back, still not saying anything.

Parker wanted to take her in his arms and beg her forgiveness. He couldn't quite figure out why, because only two nights ago he'd thought she was the one who owed him a huge apology.

But tonight was different. "Come downstairs with me?"

She started to shake her head. He sensed she was going to flee from him.

So he said the word a Ponthier rarely uttered. "Please?"

Eighteen

If Parker only knew what that word coming from his lips meant to her. Almost shyly, she smiled at him, then reminded herself she had too much pride to swoon into his arms at the slightest softening of his stance towards her. But for a man who'd just had three young children foisted on him, he was asking awfully nicely.

Reason and common sense told her to say goodnight and tuck herself in.

Desire and the beckoning of temptation urged her to match his steps as he moved down the hallway and towards the staircase.

Desire and temptation won.

Halfway downstairs, he said, "Did you meet Grandfather's new chess partner?"

"You mean Mrs. Fenniston." Meg was surprised he hadn't yet asked her about the children. "She's my friend from Las Vegas who was staying with my children."

He looked at her with curiosity. They were

crossing the foyer and heading back to the library. "Did my brother know?"

"About my children?"

He nodded.

So did Meg. The less said the better.

"Jules must have been a changed man." He said it softly, with a corresponding softening of the normally solemn lines around his mouth.

He paused at the doorway to the library. Meg preceded him. "They do make a rumpus, don't they?" The usually pristine room was a shambles. But with the severe order disturbed, it looked much more comfortable and welcoming.

Meg followed Parker as he crossed to one of the two loveseats in front of the fire. The cushions from the one they'd shared the other evening lay on the floor inside the children's tent. She observed how naturally they moved together. They might be any couple relaxing after settling the children to sleep for the night.

A wave of emotion overcame her. Ted had worked so many late hours she'd been the one to put the kids to bed, the one who'd created their pillow talk tradition. Tonight with Parker had given her a glimpse of an impossible dream.

Meg forced herself to look across the room to the computer atop the large desk. Parker was just as much a workaholic as Ted. He couldn't have come back to the house much before nine, if that early. He'd been kind to join in tonight, but she knew better than to build any castles in the clouds.

She settled on the far end of the loveseat and tucked her feet under her. Mrs. Fenniston, bless her heart, had brought some of Meg's clothes, including her favorite purple tights and over-sized Goofy t-shirt. The look was quite at odds with the loveseat's silk tapestry pulled tight against the ornate carving, but Meg felt safe in her comfortable at-home wear.

Parker sat on one of the two cushions of the loveseat. Giving his cuffs another turn and not quite looking at her, he said, "I've learned a lot from you tonight."

"You have?" His comment surprised Meg. She kept waiting for him to quiz her more on the kids and her plans. He didn't strike her as one to leave other people's business alone, not when it overlapped with his. He was, after all, a Ponthier.

He turned toward her, one arm sliding against the back of the loveseat. Meg caught her breath, the intimacy of the other night crowding into her mind. She yearned to lean over and accept his embrace, but pride held her back. Rejection hurt. Badly.

Parker lay his hand behind her shoulder without touching her. He'd sensed her stiffen slightly and knew she wasn't ready for his touch. He'd been such a jerk the other night he couldn't blame her. The same way he couldn't blame Jules for falling for a woman this sweet and innocent. So different from any other woman he'd ever known.

"I've learned why you've been so good with Gus. I should have guessed you had children. No one else would have known how to handle him."

"That's not necessarily logical," Meg said, twirling a finger around a long lock of her hair. He wondered if she had any idea what that gesture did to him.

"No?" He murmured the question, not wanting to argue logic. He'd far rather slide his arm down the loveseat and around her shoulders. But he bided his time. "Evidently his mother doesn't know how to handle him."

"True," Parker said. "Well, I guess I should know good parenting isn't genetic and doesn't arrive along with the child." He managed to keep any residual harshness from his voice; he'd long ago given up on Teensy.

What concerned him now was the shadow that crossed Meg's face. Parker knew he'd stirred some very deep wounds. Leaning forward, he caught her free hand in his. "Did I say the wrong thing?"

"It's okay," she said, but to his relief, she didn't withdraw her hand. "Being an orphan, I guess I can't help but react to that statement. I've dealt with the issue but still sometimes I wonder why my parents gave me up. But there are many, many men and women who should never be parents. So, no, it's not something that comes along with the baby."

He stroked her hand. "I'm sorry for that pain, but you are a wonderful mother."

"Thank you," she said, tugging gently at her hand.

"Do you want me to let go?"

She raised her eyes to his. In her frank way, she watched him as she obviously considered the question. Then, a gentle smile curving her mouth, she said, "No, not really."

He turned her hand over and traced the long line curving from her wrist towards her index finger. "You also taught me about make-believe tonight."

"I did?"

Parker lifted her hand and brushed his lips across the tips of her fingers. She quivered in response. He dropped his other arm around her shoulders and eased her closer. She was skittish and unpredictable and the last thing he wanted to do was scare her off tonight.

"Am I imagining that you're about to kiss me?" She whispered the words and turned her face upwards as she spoke.

"That part"—Parker said as he lowered his face to hers—"would not be make-believe."

Her kiss was sweeter than any he could imagine. Sweet but with that innocent hesitation he found so appealing. But as he traced the line of her lips with his tongue and pulled her more tightly to him, her hesitation disappeared.

Her lips parted and he forced himself to claim her mouth oh-so-slowly. Their tongues danced and he heard her sigh. Parker cupped the back of her head with one hand and rode the kiss until the strength of his passionate reaction to her forced him to stop. If he didn't pull away he'd take her right there on the loveseat with the door wide open.

When he released her mouth, she gazed up at him, eyes dark and wondering. "Oh, my," she said. "Are you sure that wasn't make-believe?"

He shook his head. Taking her hand again, he said in a low voice, "Do you mind if I close that door one more time?"

She licked her lips. Obviously she understood what he was really asking. Would she take this chance to excuse herself? Remind him that he was the one who'd pushed her aside when they'd been this close once before? Hell, he ought to be the one reminding himself of all the reasons he should flee the room, but right now, watching her eyes glowing with passion and her lips rosy and moist from his kiss, reason was the last thing on his mind.

And reason sure wasn't ruling his body. He shifted, knowing full well his arousal had to be more than evident, as he awaited her response.

Instead of answering with a yes or no, she got up from the loveseat, moving almost in slow motion. Without a word, she crossed to the door.

Parker could have kicked himself.

Then she shut it and turned the key.

Meg faced Parker, her back to the door, hands by her side. She didn't think of herself as impulsive. But when she wanted something, she wasn't one to hide from the desire. Not too many people she knew would have taken Jules up on his offer.

Of course, she couldn't imagine any woman turning Parker down.

He walked toward her now, his eyes fixed on hers. He needed, Meg realized with a sudden insight, reassurance. Parker wanted her to want him.

That thought made her almost dizzy. She opened her arms and he pulled her into his embrace.

"There's just something about you," he said between kisses, "that is special."

Meg kissed him, savoring the feel of his arms around hers, the hint of a beard but nothing close to icky stubble on his face, the faintest hint of that same cologne she'd liked so much the other night.

"Forgive me if this isn't right," he went on, "but I want you."

She nodded, her head moving against his chest. He was waltzing them slowly toward the middle of the large room. Beside the children's tent of blankets and chairs, he paused.

"I could use another lesson in make-believe," he said.

A gust of wind and rain hit the windows lining the far side of the room. Meg savored how protected she felt within Parker's arms. Maybe she'd addled her brain because she should be feeling anxious and nervous and worrying about what he'd think of her in the morning.

He kissed her neck, trailing his lips to the point where the skin was blocked by the cotton of her t-shirt. Reaching down, he worked her shirt up over her legs, past her hips, to her waist. Meg caught her breath. "The way make-believe works," she said, "is you use parts of reality and blend them with what you want to happen in your mind."

"I see," Parker said as he lifted her shirt from her shoulders and let it fall to the floor. Then he knelt in front of her.

Meg's tummy fluttered as he kissed her belly button. Then, as he shimmied her tights from her legs, more than her tummy danced. She hadn't been naked with a man in so long. And she hadn't been naked with a man other than Ted ever.

She clutched his head and eased her shoes off as his hands skimmed her ankles.

Parker leaned back and gazed up and down at her body. All she had on was her bra and panties. Thankful she hadn't worn her old scrubbies, Meg watched nervously as he studied her.

"You are so beautiful," he said, a look almost of awe on his face.

Meg laughed a half-laugh. "Now I know you're already into make-believe. I'm far from beautiful."

"Oh, no," Parker said. "I don't think you give yourself nearly enough credit." He traced a finger up the inside of one leg, starting at the ankle and winding his way slowly past her strong calf, circling the back of her knee until she gasped, then moving up her inner thigh. "Beautiful."

"I've had three children and with each one my hips grew about a mile."

Parker leaned towards her and kissed the side of each hip. "Perfect."

She sighed. "Maybe I should play make-believe more often."

Parker rose. He held out his hand and she took it.

"Come with me," he said, and led her to a massive mirror that dominated the wall behind Parker's desk.

"When Teensy put this up," Parker said, stopping behind her so that her back was to him, her body facing the mirror, "I objected."

"But now," he said as he tipped her face up to meet her reflection in the mirror, "I'm very, very thankful."

Meg barely recognized the woman in the

mirror. She wore only a bra and panties and leaned back against the most handsome man she'd ever met. Parker's expression was serious as he watched her study herself.

He kissed her shoulder. "Mmm, delicious," he said. He cupped her breasts gently. "Perfect," he said.

Meg wriggled against him, the touch of his hands on her breasts loosing an explosive desire within her. She started to turn, instinctively seeking his embrace.

Parker held her gently enough, but she could tell he wasn't letting her move from her position in front of the mirror.

One hand moved lower, the other remained on her breast, heating it through the lace of her bra. "My hips are too wide," she said though her heart wasn't in her objections anymore. "And my breasts sag."

"Let me be the judge of that," he murmured. He dipped a finger beneath the line of her panty. His hips pushed forward and she felt his arousal pressing against her buttocks as he circled his fingers around her pubic mound.

She thought she'd scream from his teasing touch. Instead, she answered his need with a slow circular motion of her hips against his. He withdrew his hand from her panties and moved it behind her back.

She felt her bra loosen as he slipped the clasp in the back. Meg nuzzled her head back on his chest, unconsciously rubbing herself up and down against his body. Her eyes must have closed because she heard him whisper, "Open your eyes, Meg."

When she did, she found herself watching Parker ease the straps of her bra over her shoulders. He had one arm around her waist. The tops of her breasts were revealed, then as he slipped the bra lower and let it fall off her arms to the floor, she heard him catch his breath.

"Tell me that's not a beautiful sight," he said, his voice almost a growl.

Meg ran her tongue over her lips. They felt full and pouty, and she experienced a sexual power she'd never known possible.

She'd never once looked at herself full-length naked in the presence of a man. Plenty of times she'd done so alone, always critically, inspecting for flaws, for stretchmarks that never disappeared, for a belly that wouldn't quite flatten.

When he gathered her breasts in his hands, the heat of his touch was almost more than she could bear. He leaned over her shoulder and circled one swollen nipple with his tongue. As he did, she reached up and filled her hands with his hair, drawing him down to her. His tongue flicked and danced and teased and she cried out.

He freed one hand and yanked at his belt buckle. This time when Meg turned to face him he didn't try to stop her. She unfastened the buttons of his shirt as he kicked off his shoes and stripped his pants and briefs from his legs.

She tried to keep her eyes on his broad chest and strong arms, or at least on the narrow hips and long legs that belied that this man spent so many hours behind a desk. He had to spend just as many working out.

But try as she would, her gaze drifted lower. Oh, he wanted her, all right. Feeling suddenly shy, Meg whispered, "Did I do that to you?"

Parker smiled and opened his arms. She moved into them and they stood. He turned them slightly towards the mirror. "Oh, yes," he said, his body burning as he pressed her closer. "You did that to me."

"Good," she said, and kissed first one nipple, then the other.

Parker groaned and took care of the only garment she still wore by dropping to his knees and skimming her panties down her legs. She stepped free of them and he said, "You know how you said make-believe comes from using parts of reality?"

"Mmmm."

"Well, I think I felt some rain drops just a minute ago."

"You did? Where?" Meg seemed unwilling to tear her attention from the sweet torture she was inflicting on his chest.

He laughed softly. "Make-believe, remember?"

"Oh, right." She glanced around. "If we're going to be caught in a rainstorm, maybe we'd better find shelter."

"Exactly what I was thinking," Parker said. He pointed to the children's tent. "I think I see a nice warm, dry place right over there."

He took her hand and naked, they crossed the room toward the tent. Meg looked so alive and so young Parker's heart twisted. Moving as one, they dropped to their hands and knees and crawled inside the tent and onto the love-seat cushions.

"What a lovely shelter," Meg said.

"And there's some light, too," Parker said, his hand closing around the flashlight and flicking it on. Its beam danced against the low overhang of one of Teensy's cashmere blankets, filling the tent with flickering shadows. "The better to see you with," he said, lowering himself beside her on the cushions.

Outside the storm gathered strength, rattling the windows with gusts of wind and water. Safe and warm inside their shelter, Meg in his arms, Parker could have cared less if it rained for forty days and forty nights.

He kissed her breasts. She sighed and lifted her arms over her head. While he tasted her, he eased one hand up to touch her between her legs. She was wet and hot and, unable to restrain himself, he slipped one finger inside. She gasped and arched against his touch.

"It's been so long," she murmured.

That statement didn't make too much sense to Parker, but he was beyond reason. His mind had given up control to his body. He lowered his mouth to where he stroked her with his finger.

"Sweet, sweet, Meg," he said, then tasted her.

"Oh my," Meg said breathily, her hips lifting to him.

He caught them up with his hands and drove his tongue deeper, then pulled back, flicking so lightly around her outer lips and inner thighs that she panted. He loved the way she wanted more and he dipped his tongue to give her what she sought.

Tonight, he wanted to give her everything.

Meg gave herself up to the sensations Parker was creating within her body. With every stroke of his tongue, she spiraled higher. In the shifting shadow light, through eyes half-closed from ecstasy, she watched Parker.

She could see only part of his face, but as she gazed and gave herself up to passion, he glanced up. He smiled with his eyes.

That moment of connection pushed Meg over the edge. The sweet swirling sensations within her caught her up and she cried out softly as her body accepted the invitation to surrender to Parker's incredible touch.

"Oh my," she said, laughing softly. "That was so perfect."

Parker kissed her inner thigh, then moved to

her other leg. He was grinning. "I think you liked it."

"Liked it?" Meg smiled and lifted her arms. "Oh, Parker, I—"

"Good," he said, fitting himself above her, smiling down at her, then easing himself inside where she still throbbed and trembled from the joyous release he'd given her. He began to move, slowly at first, then with growing intensity. "Good," he said, "because tonight you're mine."

Meg met his every thrust with a hunger she hadn't known she possessed. When Parker reached beneath her and drew her buttocks up, claiming her even more deeply, she went wild. She must have called out his name, over and over again, and as she gave herself up to the rhythm, she felt the surge and shudder of his release.

"Oh, Parker," she said, clutching his hair and holding him tight, her arms and knees wrapped around him as if she'd never let go. "It has never been like this for me."

After a very long moment, he stirred and lifted his head. His eyes were still smiling, and so was his mouth. He traced the line of her throat down to the hollow between her breasts. A trickle of perspiration dotted her body there. He dipped his finger, then licked and tasted it.

"I'm glad, and if this is make-believe," he said, "I never want to return to reality."

Nineteen

The problem with reality, Meg thought the next morning, was that it didn't go away. Not even after nights like last night.

Especially not after nights as magical as that.

She and Parker had fallen asleep curled in one another's arms. Sometime before dawn, she'd awakened and slipped from the tent. She hated to leave him there, but she had to get back upstairs before the children woke up. She'd found her clothing, dressed, and tiptoed upstairs.

She'd spent the next two hours daydreaming, reliving every moment with Parker.

Then Samantha woke up cranky. And Ellen woke up, talkative as ever. It didn't take long for Teddy, with Gus hanging back only slightly, to appear in the doorway.

While the kids got dressed and brushed their teeth, Meg listened to the convoluted dream Ellen was describing, and kept one ear open for any indication Parker might be coming their way.

Maybe she should have awakened him before she crept out of the room, but he'd been sleeping so soundly.

And, too, she'd been slightly embarrassed. She'd given herself to him so freely, so easily, that she began to worry what he might think of her in the clear light of the next day. Once she shuffled the kids into the kitchen, she planned to peek into the library. It was better to face him without the children as witnesses.

He wasn't in the library. The tent was there, exactly as she'd left it in the wee hours of the morning. Meg glanced in the mirror and found herself drawn towards it.

She gazed at her image, now fully clothed, of course, and wondered how she could be the same woman who'd stood so openly and freely naked with Parker's arms around her. Had she left Parker sleeping because of the children or because she was afraid—afraid of what he'd awakened within her?

He'd given her a taste of paradise and the punishment for her deal with Jules was knowing Parker lived in this world and not being able to have him in her life.

If she told him the truth about her arrangement with Jules, she knew he'd be repulsed. Three days for thirty thousand dollars sounded so mercenary. He'd take her for a fortune hunter.

They were both too proud for that.

"Looking for me?"

Meg lifted her eyes and saw him in the mirror. Images of the evening before filled her mind. Parker advanced, and the way he gazed at her told her that despite her leggings and tunic, he was seeing her naked once again.

He hadn't shaved, and his hair was tousled. With the way she'd run her fingers through it during their lovemaking, that was no surprise. He wore a t-shirt and running sweats.

She thought he'd never looked more gorgeous, except maybe last night when he'd stripped off his clothes and stood before her in front of the mirror, fully aroused.

She swallowed and tried to find her tongue. "I-uh . . ." but for once she was speechless. Slowly she turned to face Parker, looking shyly up at him. "You're not upset I disappeared during the night, are you?"

He shook his head and took her hands in his. "You're too good of a parent to let your children catch you playing the game we were playing."

Relief flooded through her. He understood. She smiled at him and he leaned to kiss her.

"Whoa!" Gus's voice ricochetted around the room.

Meg and Parker jumped back, guilty as a couple of junior high kids.

Gus looked from Parker to Meg, then nodded, as if satisfied by what he'd seen. "Ellen says she can beat me at FragZone and I say she can't. Can we use your computer to settle this?"

"It's okay with me," Parker said, looking over at Meg.

Meg nodded. She hoped Parker and the kids had forgotten the sentence they'd threatened to carry out in their sheik game. The computer challenge would divert them nicely. "After you've played for half an hour," she said, "we'll do lessons."

Ellen groaned. Gus made a face. The two of them settled behind Parker's desk. Teddy wandered in, leading Jem. "Jem wants to go for a walk. May I take him?"

"Sure," Gus said, intent on the screen.

"Samantha and I will come too," Meg said.

Horton appeared in the doorway, Meg's youngest dancing around his feet. "Horton Who!" she cried, then collapsed into giggles. Suddenly she stopped. Gazing up at Parker, she regarded him, intent and serious, then ran back to Horton.

Parker rubbed his jaw. "I think I'd better excuse myself and go shave. I'm scaring Samantha." He smiled at Meg, a smile that promised he'd return. Then he left the room.

Despite the combined commotion of the children and the dog, the room suddenly felt empty.

Horton patted Samantha, who'd clamped herself on his leg, on the head. "Would you care for some breakfast, Miz Meg?"

"I don't think I could eat a thing," she said, quite truthfully.

Horton smiled, in a quietly wise way that reminded her of pictures of the sphinx. Meg colored, wondering if this ageless retainer knew all the secrets of the household.

From behind the computer monitor, Ellen called out, "Breakfast is the most important meal of the day."

Shaking her head, Meg followed Horton from the room, Samantha, Teddy, and Jem in their wake.

They were halfway across the central foyer when Jem halted. His tail rose, and he strained forward, sniffing the air and growling.

"Oh, no," Teddy said, "it's Agamemnon!"

Meg couldn't believe it. "Mrs. Fenniston brought the cat?"

A streak of silvery gray fur slashed in front of their eyes. Jem bolted, his leash trailing, toward the smaller of the two parlors.

"We had to, Mom," Teddy said. "He's never been boarded and the girl who keeps him was out of town. And Mrs. Fenniston said we had to leave in a hurry."

Meg heard a crash of wood on wood and covered her ears. Then she remembered she was in charge of this traveling circus and sprang into action. "Go get that dog!"

Teddy moved almost as fast as Jem had. Meg followed and found Jem in the front parlor whimpering in frustration. He'd knocked over a small table but the weight of the marble top had trapped the end of his leash.

Agamemnon sat just out of range, licking his front paw and applying it to his face, all the while keeping a close eye on the dog.

"Breakfast later," Meg called and set the table upright, then she herded Teddy, Samantha, and the dog to the side door.

Parker told himself to leave the house by the seldom-used front door. The more he saw of Meg the more he wanted. And he had no business craving time alone with his brother's widow.

Besides, he had a ton of work waiting for him at the office. There were the lawyers to deal with, and it was December, which meant the sugar cane fields were in the final stages of harvesting. Plus the international conglomerate that had been dangling after their commercial real estate holdings, the company Jules had been courting, had asked if Parker could meet with them that afternoon.

He showered and began to shave. He felt better than he had in days—no, months. The only problem was his body ached for more.

More Meg.

He didn't like to think that she'd been married to Jules even for a day, but whatever her reasons for that decision had been, he could not believe his brother had possessed her heart.

No woman whose affections lay elsewhere could have given herself as generously and lovingly as Meg had done last night.

He pictured her in front of the mirror when he'd slipped off her bra and freed her breasts. She'd been so open and vulnerable, a goddess he wanted to suckle and fill with his seed.

Parker dropped his razor. It clattered around the porcelain sink and rattled to a halt atop the stopper.

He hadn't used protection.

"Son of a bitch," he said to his reflection. He, Parker A. Ponthier, had never once slept with a woman without taking care of contraception.

He glared down into the sink, gripping the edges. A cloud formed in his mind and he tried to force it away. She had to have had sex with Jules less than a week ago. Surely she was on the pill. But that didn't cover health measures.

He reached for the razor and finished his chin, inflicting two deep gashes on himself in the process. He couldn't bear to think of her with anyone else. He'd have to discuss the issue, though. Which meant he should remain at the house and wait for an appropriate moment. He could ask her for a copy of the prenuptial agreement at the same time.

Damn. What had he been thinking?

He rinsed his razor and faced himself once more in the mirror.

He hadn't been thinking at all.

He'd let feelings guide his actions, something Parker Ponthier never did.

And it had felt so very, very good.

After walking Jem and downing a muffin, Meg had managed to settle Ellen, Teddy, and Gus in a circle around Parker's desk. She led them through a geography lesson. Over a year ago, she'd set up a web site for the kids' lessons and homework and linked it to some great educational resources. Thanks to the marvels of technology, Ellen and Teddy wouldn't be too far behind when they returned home.

Samantha, miracle of miracles, was playing fairly quietly with the one Barbie and Ken doll Mrs. Fenniston had permitted her to pack. She'd pulled the remaining cushions off the loveseat. Ken "lived" on one; Cheerleader Barbie on the other.

Meg knew the instant Parker walked into the room. She glanced across the monitor, a shy smile on her lips.

He was dressed for business in a dark charcoal suit. Despite the ease with which he wore his professional attire, he didn't look nearly as relaxed as he had earlier in his grubbies. He just stood there, looking as if he wanted to say something but unsure of the territory.

Which was silly as they were in his library. "I'm afraid we've invaded your world completely now," Meg said, wondering if the mess had started to bother him.

"No problem," he said. "I have to go to the office downtown anyway."

"Okay." What she wanted to say was don't go. Strip off that expensive jacket, roll up your sleeves, and name the capital of Botswana.

He started to turn away.

Samantha picked up her Ken doll. Speaking to the doll, she said, "Do you think Parker will play with us?"

Parker hesitated.

Would he ignore Samantha and keep going?

Carrying her dolls, Samantha walked over to Parker and tugged on the tail of his jacket.

He slowly faced her. "Me? You want me to play?"

Samantha nodded. "I'm the littlest and I don't go to school yet so there's no one to play with me. But you're not busy."

The funniest expression crossed his face. Meg almost laughed. The comment that Parker, consumed with running the Ponthier empire, wasn't busy couldn't sit too well with him.

"Mom, click the mouse!" Ellen's impatient voice cut across whatever Parker said to Samantha.

When Meg looked back, Samantha was leading Parker by the hand towards the loveseat cushions. As if he'd read her mind, Parker shrugged off his suit coat, dropped it on the base of the loveseat, and sat crosslegged on the floor beside Samantha.

"I'll play for a few minutes, but I'm afraid you'll have to tell me what to do."

Meg smiled. That was the only way Samantha played.

Thirty minutes later, having asked Barbie out on a date, picked her up in his make-believe Ferrari fashioned from one of his shoes, taken her to dinner at a restaurant located on the terrace that opened off the library's french doors, then delivered her back to her "house" and kissed her goodnight, all as instructed by Samantha, Parker was both oddly disappointed and relieved to be rescued by Meg calling time on their activity.

He leaned back against the loveseat and smiled up at her. "What's next, teach?"

Meg glanced toward the window. "It's a beautiful day so I think we should pack up and go on a picnic. But you said you had to go to the office."

"Picnics are for sissies," Gus said.

"Ken and Barbie want to go," Samantha said.

"Dads always have to go to the office," Ellen said.

"Parker's not a dad," Gus said, "He's my uncle."

"How about a trip to Sugar Bridge?" Parker couldn't believe he'd asked the question. He had to be out of his mind. Sugar Bridge was almost two hours' drive time from New Orleans and he actually did have work to do.

"What's Sugar Bridge?" Ellen asked.

"It's where the Ponthiers grow sugar cane," Gus said. "I've only been there once and believe me, there was nothing to do."

Gus's words decided the issue for Parker. Nothing to do at Sugar Bridge? Why, it was one of his favorite escapes from town. It would be just like Marianne and Jules to have taken Gus there all dressed up, ordered him to sit on the porch and not make a mess.

"The sugar cane harvest is almost done but there's one field left to cut. Put on some old clothes and I'll show you how much there is to do at Sugar Bridge."

Meg's surprised expression held an appreciative smile. She probably thought he'd never walked barefoot or dressed down in his life. Two points that were pretty much true, except for the times Grandfather had let him spend summers at Sugar Bridge. Away from Teensy and his father, he'd roamed, explored, swam, fished, and rode.

"Kids?" Meg looked from Ellen to Teddy to Samantha.

"Sounds kind of hokey to me," Ellen said, one eye on Gus.

That was evidently all it took for her brother to say, "Best plan I've heard all day. Let's get Jem and go!"

"Jem's my dog," Gus said. "If I say he goes,

he goes. And if I say he doesn't, he doesn't."

"Oh, yeah?" Teddy doubled up his fists.

"Last one ready to leave is a rotten egg," Meg said. "And Jem goes only if Parker says it's okay for him to go in the car."

"Car? Hmm, we'll need a bus, but don't worry, I'll find one." Parker mentally counted heads. For this group, they'd need a van. Thankfully, Horton drove one. He'd go arrange to borrow it, change clothes, and call the office.

That conglomerate would have to wait another day to talk to him. He was leading a field trip to Sugar Bridge.

Twenty

Sugar Bridge had been in the Ponthier family since the days the family had settled in Louisiana in the late 1700's. The upriver plantation had served as home and production facility; the original Ponthier city home had naturally been in the French Quarter. It had been burned down twice and rebuilt, until the Ponthiers made the move to the Garden District, then on to Uptown in Grandfather's father's day.

Meg learned all this history from Parker as they drove out of the city, following the Mississippi River. Family tradition alone, though, didn't explain the almost boyish excitement in his voice as he described the country home.

When they approached the house from the river side, Meg immediately understood Parker's fondness.

A lane of massive oaks, trunks swayed this way and that as if giving testimony to a century of storms, led through a grassy park to a two-story house. Meg caught a glance of pink or maybe rose through the trees.

Parker drove past the front and turned onto a gravel side road. As they approached the house from the side, Meg saw it was painted a shade of pink that shimmered from rose to pale raspberry depending on how the light touched it through the trees.

"How beautiful," she said.

Parker nodded. He stopped the van next to a small pickup.

"Does someone live here?" Meg asked as the kids tumbled out.

"Right now only the caretaker." With a rueful smile, he said, "In my dreams I'd live here, but it's so far from town and I'm always—"

"—so busy," Meg finished Parker's sentence along with him. It was a darn good thing she had to go back to Las Vegas. Here she was, falling for another workaholic. Hadn't she learned her lesson?

Halfway out of her seat, Meg stopped. Panic clutched at her like a spider web that, no matter how she pulled at it, wouldn't let go. Falling for Parker? No. No. No.

"No," she whispered, setting her feet on the gravel drive and staring at her Reeboks as if they could save her. It was one thing to give in to a night of passion, of lovemaking sweeter than she'd ever known. It was quite another to fall in love.

Parker held out his hand. "Coming?"

She lifted her head slowly. His hair, usually so neatly combed, had ruffled in the breeze. In contrast to his usual suits, he wore a Tulane sweatshirt, faded jeans, and trail boots. The expression in his eyes was warm and gentle and full of anticipation for the day.

"Yes," she said, knowing that as soon as possible, she would have to leave.

Rather than dampen her spirits, that thought motivated her day. Determined to savor every last minute of her time with Parker, she accepted his outstretched hand as she climbed from the van.

Jem danced around, yelping delightedly. A rooster pecked at the edge of the gravel and Jem took off after it. So did the boys and Ellen.

Samantha clung to her Ken and Barbie, a speculative look on her face as she skipped alongside Parker.

"You've got a new playmate," Meg said.

Parker smiled. "And if we were Ken and Barbie, I'd know exactly what to do on a date." He winked. "Maybe we'll get to practice soon."

She colored and pointed up the brick pathway that led to the house. "Time for a tour?"

"Think we should let them run off some of that energy first?"

"Right! Whatever am I saying?" Parker at least was thinking logically. For her part, Meg was wishing she was still holding Parker's hand, but she didn't want to confuse the children by doing so in front of them.

Thankfully, they'd accepted her presence and their visit without much questioning. As cozy as Mrs. Fenniston and Grandfather had been, Meg suspected the children had decided they were old friends, which explained their stay with the Ponthiers.

"Remember the day Gus ran away?"

Meg nodded. While she'd been lost in her thoughts, they'd walked towards one of several side buildings. Parker opened the door to the low-ceilinged rambling structure.

"I thought we'd take everybody fishing."

Fishing. Meg pictured squirming worms but if it meant she'd be plastered to Parker's side, she'd squelch her queasiness. "I've never done that before," she said, "but I love to try new things."

Gus came barreling over, his sweatshirt and baggy shorts flapping. "I don't remember that rooster from last time."

Parker turned back from his search within the building, three fishing rods in his hands. "That rooster probably wasn't allowed indoors," he said.

Gus made a face of disgust. "Yeah, and when I came here I had to sit on that damn"— he spotted the rods, and a smile creased his face—"darn porch."

Parker handed a rod to Gus. "No porch-sitting today," he said. "I'll go find Mr. Solomon—he's the caretaker—and get the rest of the things we need."

"Are we going out on the river?" Gus asked.

"Better than the river," Parker said. "We're going to my super secret fishing hole on Sugar Bayou. That's the stream that runs through the back of the land." And to Meg so only she heard he said, "An excellent spot for skinny dipping in the summer."

Her heart skipped at the image. Dappled sunlight reflecting on water that rippled and danced where she and Parker, deliciously naked, cavorted in the water before retiring to the bank to—Meg jerked her mind away from the thought.

Next summer she'd be back in Las Vegas, alternating between sweltering out of doors and freezing in the air-conditioned civilization fashioned out of the desert.

Fortunately she was distracted by the need to gather supplies, haul the ice chest Horton had packed out of the van, load everyone with gear, and march away from the house. Between her and Parker, they shared the load of the ice chest and trooped past a weathered semi-decayed structure that Parker identified as the remains of the earliest sugar mill on the plantation.

Jem ran ahead yelping and running back as if to announce he'd cleared the way for them. Soon they reached the banks of a narrow stream at a curve where it widened and rippled over a cache of huge boulders piled at the bend.

"Jules and I pulled those rocks out of the middle of the stream so we could dive. Every summer we'd clear them again."

Parker gazed in silence for a moment, then he lowered the cooler to the ground. "I'm glad we came here."

"Clearing the rocks was one goal you and your brother agreed on."

He gave her a swift look. "That's exactly what I was thinking and it made me feel a lot better."

For the next hour Parker showed them the art and craft of fishing. To her relief, he used oddly shaped, brightly colored plastic lures rather than slimy worms. Gus, Ellen, and Teddy each wielded a rod with Parker moving among them along the edge of the stream.

Meg was more than happy to lean against a boulder with her youngest and play Ken on a picnic date with Barbie. Gus kept jerking on his pole and crying, "I got a bite! I got a bite!" He'd yank his line out of the water to find it dangling only the lure.

Teddy sat quietly, lost in his thoughts. Meg sometimes worried that Ted's death had scarred him in a way she wouldn't be able to help him heal. He'd been quieter than normal, acting older than his ten years. Meg was sure her husband had never taken Teddy fishing given they lived in the desert and she couldn't remember any day trips to Lake Mead. Teddy had been his father's companion to basketball and baseball games.

It made Meg feel both sad and happy to see how easily her son took to Parker, patiently accepting instructions and then casting his line as if he'd been sitting beside a Louisiana stream for the ten years of his life.

Ellen's approach had a lot more in common with Gus's.

Meg watched Parker with a full heart as he worked with the kids. Her mind told her she hadn't known Parker long enough to have fallen in love with him.

But her heart answered otherwise.

After Barbie and Ken's end-of-date kiss, Samantha fell asleep with her head in Meg's lap, arms curled around her dolls. Meg stroked her hair lightly. Parker helped Gus cast his line yet again, then turned to her. "Sure you don't want to take a turn?"

She shook her head, too content to move. Or, as content as she could be knowing she would be heading back to Las Vegas with a hole in her heart bigger than Ponthier Place.

"What's next?" It was Ellen who asked the question. "This is getting bor—"

Her question ended in mid-sentence. "Hey!" She grabbed at her pole, which had jerked from her hands. She missed it and the pole skidded towards the stream.

With a shout, Gus threw himself on the pole

and clung to it. Parker grabbed Gus's original pole. "Easy, easy. Hang tight. Bring it up. Okay, now wind it in. Slowly. Nice and easy. That's it." The line broke the plane of the water and a flash of silver danced on the end of the line.

No matter what, Gus wasn't letting go. His face a study in determination, he fought the fish as it flung itself to and fro.

Ellen, standing now, was watching, her eyes fixed on the flapping fish.

Samantha woke with a start. Another commotion sounded and as Parker was helping Gus dump his prize into the bucket Mr. Solomon had provided, Teddy in much quieter fashion reeled in a fish, too.

Meg thought it likely Ellen would insist on sitting on the edge of the bank the rest of the day and night if it took that long for her to reel in her own fish, but she complained not at all when Parker said they needed to have their picnic and think about heading back.

And later, as they hiked back to the house, her usually tough no-nonsense daughter took her hand and whispered, "I'm glad I didn't catch a fish because I felt sorry for it. It was so pretty and it was fighting for its life but it lost."

Having sympathized with the fish, too, Meg gave her a hug, preparing to find words of comfort. But as soon as her daughter had pronounced her sentiments, she dashed off in pursuit of Gus and Teddy.

Parker smiled as Meg's daughter raced to catch up with the boys. Their start back to the house had been delayed by Gus and Teddy negotiating over who got to lug the bucket containing their catch. Gus had claimed precedence as he'd not only caught the first fish, but had saved Ellen from losing hers. Teddy refused to relinquish the honor, insisting reasonably enough that they had each caught one fish, therefore they could both carry the bucket.

Gus had finally settled by offering to let Teddy play with his prized pocketknife for the next hour if he let Gus have the sole privilege.

Parker enjoyed the exchange. Gus had mellowed so much in just the short time he'd been away from St. Suplicius.

Thanks to Meg.

He smiled at her over the ice chest they carried between them. During their picnic and walk back, the sun had dipped farther toward the west than he liked. He wished he could raise his arms and hold it back, delaying their return to New Orleans, to his life of putting duty before pleasure.

He still had to ask her about birth control and apologize for his rash behavior. He couldn't say he regretted the moment but his irresponsibility rankled with him. Well, he wouldn't be caught with his pants down again. Even today he'd come prepared. Just in case. *Okay, Parker, admit it, you want her. And bad.* He glanced back at Meg. She'd been awfully quiet all afternoon. "Penny for your thoughts."

A flash of her usual spirit crossed her face. "Does anyone really say that?"

He nodded, what he knew must be a goofy grin on his face.

"Okay, then," she said, "I'm just absorbing the moment. What's it like here in the summer?"

Had she been thinking about his skinny-dipping comment? He hoped so. "I wish I could say it's equally beautiful in the middle of July but actually it's hot and humid and the air is abuzz with mosquitoes."

She looked surprised. "But you said you loved coming here in the summer."

"The bad stuff fades in your memory, doesn't it?" He grinned. "What's a ten-year-old care about a few dozen insect bites? Imagine Gus and Teddy. If they're that happy with one fish apiece, they'd go nuts over a basketful."

She laughed. "Do you still spend summers here?"

"Only a few days here and there. But now I plan to spend a lot more time."

"Now?"

"Sure. I can't let Gus and Teddy grow up without bucketsful of fish."

"Teddy?"

Her voice carried an edge to it. He'd gone and done it again. Organizing her life like a bossy Ponthier. "I mean, if you'd want me to invite Teddy, I'd bring him, too."

"Oh." Either his answer or the question or both made her sad. He felt the weight of her sorrow. Her step slowed.

He matched his pace to hers. Before he could say anything else, Ellen and Samantha ran back to them. "What's next?" Ellen asked, clearly expecting to be entertained further.

"Sugarcane harvesting," Parker said. "Most of it's finished by now but there's still a field left to be cut."

"Oh." She considered for a moment as they walked. "That's okay," she said, "as long as it doesn't flop when it's cut."

"Absolutely no flopping," Parker said seriously.

They'd reached the edge of the back garden. Parker spotted Mr. Solomon next to his pickup truck and waved him over. He introduced Meg and the children. Samantha held up Barbie and Ken to be introduced, too.

Mr. Solomon's sun-lined face crinkled even more around his eyes. He had at least a dozen grandchildren. "Mr. Ken and Miss Barbie, too. Well, now, I'm honored to meet you both."

Samantha glowed. Parker assumed most adults ignored her penchant for treating her dolls like friends in tow. He pretty much had until Meg taught him about make-believe.

Make-believe.

"Meg, would it be all right with you—if Mr.

Solomon had time, that is—if he showed the kids the sugarcane harvesting while I give you a tour of the house?" He held his breath, willing none of the children to proclaim they'd rather see the house than a bunch of plants.

Meg gazed back at Parker. He read her message. She wanted to say yes. She wanted to be alone with him as badly as he wanted her in his arms again.

"Mr. Solomon's a very careful driver and most strict chaperone," he said.

The older man nodded. "That is true." He scratched at a piece of lint on his spotless overalls. "Father of five and grandfather of eleven," he added, throwing a thoughtful and speculative look in Parker's direction.

A look Parker didn't miss. He'd introduced her only as Meg, omitting a last name. Earlier when Parker had collected the paraphernalia to go along with the fishing rods, the caretaker had expressed his sympathy for Jules's death. Either news of his marriage hadn't reached Sugar Bridge or Solomon, who'd had little use for Jules in recent years, paid it little heed.

"The crew's in the field about five miles down the road," Solomon added.

"Say, yes, Mom." Ellen had one hand on the handle of Solomon's pickup.

Meg raised her brows. She didn't have to say a word; her forbidding expression said it all.

Parker felt like glaring at the girl himself. He didn't want the private tour he had planned for

Meg spoiled, but he did understand the need for discipline.

Teddy kicked Ellen. "Can't you ever remember to say please? Don't spoil it for the rest of us."

"I'm sorry, Mom. *Please* may we go? I'm sure it's much more educational than catching fish."

Gus made a face. "Girls."

"You'll behave and do as Mr. Solomon says?"

They all nodded. Even Jem barked, which made Parker smile.

Meg turned to him. "Could he take the van so they don't have to ride in the back of the pickup?"

Groans issued from the kids.

"Anything you say," Parker responded, winking at Solomon.

The smile she gave him made him glad he could indeed give her whatever she desired. He tossed the keys to Solomon, thanked him, and listened as Meg reminded the kids to behave.

They piled into the van and drove off, the bucket of fish forgotten. Parker collected it as he and Meg walked toward the house. He'd dump ice over the fish. To Meg he said, "They'll be fine with Solomon."

"Did he raise you here the way Horton raised you in New Orleans?"

Parker nodded. "Pretty much. Teensy hated it out here—almost as much as my father did.

Grandfather would stay when he could but he was usually busy."

"Working?"

He nodded and as they were headed to the house via the brick pathways and shrubbery separating the outbuildings from the main house, he changed the subject. "That back building is the original kitchen. It was set well away from the house for fire prevention and cooling purposes."

"Makes me appreciate my microwave," Meg said. "They had to carry the food all this way?"

"The house dates from 1837. In the antebellum or pre–Civil War days, slaves would have done that. Afterwards"—he shrugged—"for a few years there was scarcely enough food to worry about whether it was hot or cold. When fortunes picked up again, so did technology."

He thought she was looking at him a little strangely and understood why when she said, "It's odd to hear someone say slaves so matter of factly."

"It was just that—a fact of life, a reality of the labor system of the old south. Though in 1809 transporting slaves into Louisiana from other countries was made illegal."

"That long before the civil war?"

"Well, they could still be bought and sold across state lines."

"Oh." She looked around, taking in her surroundings. "That certainly seems a long time ago."

"A different world, to be sure, but I do think we're a product of our history, the sum total of our family traditions."

Meg was silent.

He could have slapped himself for his thoughtlessness. What a thing to say to a woman who knew nothing about her parentage let alone the almost two hundred years of tradition he represented. "I'm sorry," he said. "What a klutz I am."

"No, it's okay," she said, lifting her eyes to his. "It's just such a different world view. It's actually fascinating, but it does make me feel as if somehow I've been traveling through life missing something powerful and elemental."

They stopped at the back of the breezeway beneath the second-floor balconies, which were supported by columns arranged around the entire first floor level of the house.

"And," Meg went on, "I think I'm a little envious, too."

He sat the bucket of fish down. "Remember what Samantha offered Gus the other night?"

Her eyes widened. She nodded.

"Same offer. I'll share my heritage." As he said the words, he wasn't sure himself what he meant. The words were ambiguous. Just how much was he willing to share?

His words might be ambiguous, but his feelings were not.

He leaned closer, tipping her lips to meet his kiss.

After a long, sweet plundering kiss, he lifted his head. He could have sworn he detected a glimmer of moisture in her eyes before she pulled his mouth back to hers.

When she finally broke free of the hungry kiss she whispered, "Is there a Mrs. Solomon loitering about the house?"

He shook his head.

"Good," she said, wrapping her arms around his waist.

"Let me throw some ice on these fish," he said, cursing his own sense of responsibility. But he wasn't going to be the one to tell Gus his catch had spoiled.

"Hurry," she said, in a throaty voice he scarcely recognized as Meg's, "or you'll have to ice me down, too."

Twenty-one

Ice me down? Where had that brazen comment come from? Meg had amazed herself. But she wanted to experience loving Parker again before she walked out of his life. Now that she'd been offered the opportunity she was going to—as Ellen would say—go for it.

Yet she stood rooted to the porch. Parker had left the door open when he whisked inside for the ice. Rather than follow him, she asked herself if she weren't having some sort of mid-life crisis about a decade early.

The Meg she knew, the woman who packed lunches and oversaw homework and mediated quarrels and wore five-year old dresses so the kids could have new shoes, wasn't the woman poised on the back terrace of a Louisiana plantation house.

A woman about to make love for the second time to a man she'd known less than a week.

Parker reappeared carrying two fancy ice buckets. He tossed the contents over the fish, set the containers down, and held out his hands to her. "Now," he said, "we can concentrate on us."

Us.

What a sweet-sounding word. Meg smiled and, raising one of his hands to her lips, kissed the line of his knuckles. For today she'd indulge. For today she'd swap make-believe for reality.

Hand in hand they crossed through a cheery kitchen, a walk-through pantry, and into a long hallway as wide as any of the rooms at Ponthier Place. The ceilings stretched way above her head and the chandeliers that hung down were ornamented by decorative plasterwork.

They traversed the length of the hall, passing two different arrangements of a table and two chairs. Each table held a beautiful display of fresh flowers.

"What beautiful bouquets. Are you sure there's no Mrs. Solomon?"

Parker dropped her hand and put his arm around her, pulling her close. "Now that's a sexist assumption."

"Oh." Meg considered that. "You are right."

"Solomon's the green thumb. There's a greenhouse that he rules over."

Meg leaned over and breathed in the scent of the roses. "So good. So alive," she said.

"You like roses?"

She nodded, stepping back from the table.

"Especially pink and yellow. Not red, though. Red are so self-important."

Parker laughed. "Then no red roses for you." He pulled two of the yellow roses from the vase. "If I were still ten, Solomon would have my hide for this, but I think he'll forgive me this time."

Rather than handing them to her, he carried them in his hand. Almost to the front door, he stopped and turned Meg to face a mirror twice as large as the one in the library at Ponthier Place.

She immediately blushed.

Parker whispered, "No need to feel self-conscious. You are the most perfect woman I've ever known."

Meg shook her head. "Oh, no. You've got that all wrong." Even make-believe couldn't go that far.

Parker stroked the soft petals of a rose against her cheek.

Meg felt the touch on her body as she watched him performing the gentle action in the mirror. The combined effect heightened her already yearning senses. She started to twist around, her need to press full length against his body driving her.

"No hurry," Parker said, reaching for the top button of her long-sleeved shirt, then trailing the rose down the side of her neck.

"But I feel like hurrying," Meg said, surprising herself at her own bluntness.

Parker grinned. "Good, but you don't need to. I told Solomon not to come back for at least an hour." He slipped the second button free. "Now let me show you another room."

Giving in to his game of slow seduction, Meg gazed at him in the mirror. She savored the hungry look in his darkened eyes. He wanted her as much as she wanted him. Reaching her hands behind her, still watching him in the mirror, she ran her hands down the front of his thighs, then slowly worked them up just until her fingers rested out of reach of his arousal.

She circled her derriere against him and whispered, "Two can tease, you know."

He caught her and turned her, pressing her against him exactly the way she wanted him to. He possessed her mouth with his and this time she let her hands rise to cradle him. Even through the fabric of his jeans she felt the heat of him.

Freeing her mouth, she knelt and pressed her lips against the bulge in his jeans.

He groaned. Or moaned. Or called her name. She wasn't sure which, but she knew she reveled in his reaction. She wanted to give him everything today, hold nothing of herself back.

"Meg," he finally said, "I think we ought to do the rest of the tour later."

"What happened to nice and slow?" She asked, her eyes opened wide, batting her lashes to play with him.

"Can't do it," he said. He tugged gently on

her shoulders and she eased her body back to a standing position, kissing his abdomen and chest as he lifted her.

A wide staircase rose from the central hall. Parker steered her towards it, an arm around her holding her close. He'd managed not to drop the roses, Meg noticed.

"The master bedroom is downstairs, as it was in plantation days," Parker said as they mounted the stairs. "Typically there were bedrooms for the younger children, and when the boys reached about age twelve they slept in an outside house called the *garconnierre*."

"To keep them out of mischief?"

He grinned. "Or so they could get away with it without disturbing the rest of the house?"

"Maybe we should go there," Meg murmured.

"Too far away." He caught her even closer. They'd reached the top floor. "In modern times we've converted some rooms to guest rooms. I'll show you my favorite."

His favorite was a spacious room with tall windows that opened like doors onto the upper balcony that ran the length of the house. They paused in front of the windows overlooking the lane of spreading oaks.

"That's the Mississippi you see beyond the trees," Parker said, returning to where he'd left off on the buttons of her shirt.

"So beautiful," Meg murmured.

"So beautiful," Parker echoed, tugging her

shirt free of the waistband of her jeans and sliding it from her body.

"I don't know about that," Meg said. Even in the fading December sunlight, this room was much more well-lit than the darkened library where they'd made love the other evening. Plus when things had gotten really intimate they'd been under the covers of the children's tent with only the bobbing shadows of the flashlight.

Parker lay the roses on a table and held her lightly by the shoulders. "Meg, you are one beautiful woman. I think maybe you don't give yourself enough credit."

"No?" She knew she sounded hopeful. She wanted to believe him because he made her feel so beautiful.

"No." Parker brushed a kiss across her lips. "The other night you taught me about make-believe. Today I'm offering to teach you just how beautiful you are."

She considered his offer. It was no more preposterous than the fact that the two of them were about to bare their bodies to one another and share the most intimate gifts two people could give to one another. "For today," she said.

"I'll take what I can get," Parker said, stripping off his sweatshirt and wondering what had happened to the arrogant man who could have his way with any woman of his acquaintance. Here he was, practically begging Meg to let him prove to her how beautiful a woman she was.

The women he was used to accepted their beauty as a given, his appreciation as their due. God, but she had turned his world upside down.

He smiled at her and reached for the buckle of her belt. With Meg, he liked his world so much better.

She guided his hands, then placed both their hands on his belt. Easing it free, she tugged at the zipper of his jeans. She knelt and untied his shoes. He kicked them off and she did the same with hers. Then together, they both stripped free of their jeans and underwear.

Naked, standing together in front of the broad windows, they gazed at one another. "You are the most generous-hearted woman I know," Parker said. He picked up one of the roses and offered it to her.

The other he carried as he led her across the room to the four poster bed.

Meg watched as Parker pulled back the yellow and white coverlet. Her earlier boldness had almost deserted her when they'd stood naked in front of one another but Parker's admiring gaze had bolstered her confidence.

Parker plucked several petals from the rose he held and scattered them over the sheets. "A bed fit for a beautiful princess," he said, "a beautiful princess who taught me the value of make-believe."

Meg slipped onto the bed, half-sitting, half-lying against the mound of pillows. Parker sat on the edge of the bed facing her. He trailed the rose over her lips, then said, "The way you smile along with life is a beautiful thing."

Running the silky petals up to her forehead, he said, "And your mind, so lively and sharp, makes you even more beautiful."

"Keep going like this and you'll embarrass me," Meg said.

He shook his head. "I promised to teach you how beautiful you are."

She felt the touch of the rose on her earlobe and breathed in the scent. "You listen to people. And you don't just listen with your ears"—he lifted the rose and placed it over her heart—"you listen from here."

Meg held out her arms to Parker. "Shh, you're making me feel all funny inside, telling me these things."

"Funny good or funny bad?"

"Oh, good."

He smiled and circled the rose around her pubic hair. "And your sensuality, Meg, is unmatched."

"It is?" She wanted to believe him but she'd always thought of herself as one who held back from expressing the full strength of her desires. Or perhaps she'd just never been with the right man before.

He kissed the spot where the rose had touched and she sighed and dropped back more fully against the pillows, her legs parting and opening her body to Parker's exploration.

But after that one kiss, he lifted his head. "No more till we talk about something," he said.

"Talk?" she murmured the word. She didn't want to talk, she just wanted him to keep touching her in that way he had, that way that turned her insides to jelly.

"I have to apologize for my behavior the other night."

That got her attention, but it didn't make any sense. "But you're here with me again today."

"Oh, yes." Parker glanced away, then back. "What I'm apologizing for is completely ignoring protection. That is something I've never done in my life." He swallowed. In a most serious voice, he said, "And I want you to know that if you get pregnant, I'll be fully responsible."

"Thank you, Parker," she said. She was touched but the same concern hadn't entered her mind. "I never even thought about that. It took me six years to get pregnant with Samantha and that was with really, really working on it. And she's five, so I pretty much never think about contraception."

"So you're not on the pill or using anything else?"

"No."

Parker looked even more serious. "Well, there are health reasons to think about, too."

"As long as you're healthy, we're okay. I mean, I'm practically a virgin."

"What do you mean?"

"Why, Ted's been dead for over a year and before that we . . ." She trailed off. "Well, there was never anyone else before Ted."

He rose up on one elbow. Staring at her, he said slowly, "Aren't you forgetting someone?"

Meg realized what she hadn't said. She played with her fingers, then said, "Jules and I never had sex."

"You don't have to say that just to protect my feelings," Parker said in a rough voice.

"It's the truth."

Parker listened to the quiet dignity of her voice. She lay there naked before him, telling him she'd never had sex with her second husband. With what he knew about his brother, Parker found it hard to believe. Yet he was glad. His relief overwhelmed his sense that there was more to the story than she was revealing.

He touched her abdomen, then moved his hand slowly up to her breasts. He circled her nipples with his thumb, then leaned over and sucked first one, then the other. His need for her grew with every demanding movement of his mouth on her breast. With his other hand he parted her legs, running his hand along her thighs, then dipping two fingers inside her to explore the heat of her inner lips. His fingers came away slick and wet.

He raised his mouth from her breast. She'd thrown her head back against the pillows. Her lips were parted and her breath came quickly.

"Thank you for giving yourself to me," he said. To himself he added, "And thank you for not doing so to my brother, for whatever horn-brained reason."

She must have interpreted his expression because she said softly, "Only you, Parker."

When he heard her say those words, he wanted to plunge inside her, claim her in the most primal way. But he hadn't yet pulled on the damn condom and he most certainly wasn't making the same mistake twice.

Meg lifted her head, then almost in slow motion moved so that instead of him lying above and beside her, she knelt in front of him. "Lie back," she said.

He did as she asked. She moved between his legs and dipped her head. Kissing one leg slowly from ankle to calf to knee to the thigh, she said, "I've thought of a way to thank you for making me feel so beautiful."

"You don't have to thank me," Parker said softly. "You're giving me more pleasure than I deserve."

She smiled, glanced up at him, then took him in her mouth.

Parker exhaled sharply and closed his eyes. But only for a moment. He gazed at the beautiful sight of Meg's dark hair spread over his groin, her lips hot and tight around his arousal.

She swallowed him more deeply. With one hand he lifted her hair to one side, the better to watch her pleasuring him.

But as she moved her mouth, then started a delicious dance with her tongue, he moaned, closed his eyes again, and let his body move with the rhythms she was orchestrating.

He knew he couldn't hold out much longer. "Meg, Meg," he said, touching her hair. "You'd better stop."

She lifted her head. "Do you want me to?"

"No. Yes." Parker groaned, then opened his arms. "Come here, I want to be inside you."

She wiggled onto his chest, then leaned over the edge of the bed to reach the condom he'd left there at the start of their discussion.

She slipped to his side. He took it from her, ripped it open, and jammed it on.

He wanted her now.

But he could wait a little longer.

Rather than entering her at once, which he was sure she expected, he circled her right earlobe with his tongue. "You know the saying that what's sauce for the goose is sauce for the gander?"

"Yes."

"Well, it works both ways." And before she could ask him what he meant, he'd slipped between her legs and lowered his head to taste her.

"Oooh, Parker," she breathed. "That is so, so exquisite."

She clearly had never had enough good loving. He mouthed, then sucked, then slowed his tongue so that he was scarcely touching her. She writhed against him and clutched at his hair. Her legs came around his neck, drawing his head even closer to her inner lips.

He licked faster, feeling her pleasure mount. She panted and cried out and tensed. He slowed his tongue against the tiny nub, letting the sensations build until they overcame her. Still clasping his hair, she pulsed against his mouth and cried out. He lapped and held her as she reveled in the release.

And only then did he enter her, claiming her once more as his. And only his.

Twenty-two

Even Jem slept as Parker rounded the bend from Carrollton and turned onto St. Charles Avenue. After describing the harvesting they'd watched with Mr. Solomon in great detail, with Ellen in particular claiming sugarcane farming superior to fishing, the kids had requested a stop at McDonald's.

Afterwards they'd fallen asleep, with Meg drifting off about half an hour later. Behind the wheel, Parker didn't feel at all sleepy. He felt more alert and yet also more at peace than he ever remembered being.

And ironically enough, confirmed bachelor that he'd become, he felt like a family man. His ex-fiancee Renee, and about a dozen other women Parker could call to mind, would swear that Parker A. Ponthier would never spend a weekday ferrying four children, a mongrel dog, and a mother to and from a day in the country.

A most beautiful day in the country.

He glanced over at Meg, who stirred and slowly opened her eyes. With a start, he realized this life could be his. It didn't have to be a pleasure adopted only for the moment.

The vision both pleased and frightened him. He gripped the wheel. The voice of caution reminded him he barely knew the woman seated beside him and that her marriage to Jules was an unsolved mystery. He must have frowned because she asked softly, "Are you tired?"

"Far from it," he said.

"Thanks for doing all the driving." She stretched and yawned. "What a delicious nap. Oh, look at the lights!"

The Christmas display featuring animals fashioned from white lights illuminated the entrance to Audubon Park and Zoo on their right; on their left the front of Tulane University twinkled and glowed with the traditional white lights found all along St. Charles Avenue.

When he saw the delight on Meg's face, he pulled the van over in front of the outlines of elephants featured in the park display. "Teensy does Ponthier Place, too," he said, "but the decorator is behind schedule."

Meg woke the kids. Samantha blinked then cried, "Did I sleep until Christmas?"

Meg reassured her she hadn't missed Santa Claus. Even Gus said, "Yeah, they're kind of nice, if you like that sort of thing."

For Gus that was high praise. Parker pulled

back into the line of cars crawling along St. Charles Avenue and smiled as Meg and the kids ogled over the Christmas lights on all the avenue's finest homes.

Parker had driven the street so many times, over so many years, he was ashamed to admit it, but he rarely slowed to admire the beauty of the scene. Driving the avenue, as Meg had just said, was like being part of a 3-D Christmas card.

They reached the block before Ponthier Place. Parker was glad to see the display at the house was illuminated at last. Teensy must have had the decorator working double time while they'd spent the day in the country.

White lights sparkled in the trees around the expanse of grounds. Traditional green garlands laced with more white lights hung from the wrought iron fence that marched the full way around the block. On the front terrace a wire and light design of a sleigh pulled by reindeer vied for superiority with the decorations put up by the Audubon Zoo's designers.

"Wow," Ellen said. "Your house is the best of all. I'm glad we're staying here. Christmas will be so much neater with all these lights."

"Yeah, and Santa can't miss us cause his sleigh is already here," Samantha added.

Meg's heart caught in her throat. How was she going to explain to the children they were headed back to Las Vegas? She'd been worried about bringing them to New Orleans, and might not have done so if Grandfather hadn't taken matters into his own hands. And now she had to worry about wresting them away.

She should have left immediately after the funeral. Before she'd ever made love to Parker the first time. Before the children had been brought here, now to be disappointed in their return.

Life at Ponthier Place was make-believe. Their real world existed in Las Vegas, in the half of Mrs. Fenniston's house she'd been so sweet to rent to Meg.

When Parker came around to open her door, Meg tried to shake off the cloud that had descended on her spirits. But she couldn't quite meet his gaze.

"You must be tired," he said. "Go on in and I'll get the kids."

How she loved hearing those words from Parker's lips. But she had to stop her silly daydreaming. She'd married this man's brother for money with the understanding that she'd help him sell Ponthier Enterprises away from Parker's control.

No man could forgive such treason.

She pulled her hand free from Parker's. "That's okay. I don't need any help." Then she turned her back and opened the van's sliding passenger door.

She knew even without glancing at his face she'd hurt him. After everything they'd shared that afternoon, her behavior was a slap in the face. Maybe that was for the best; he wouldn't mind when she slipped away and let him return to his previous well-structured existence.

A Mercedes-Benz sat in the drive in front of the van. Hauling a sleepy Samantha from her seat, Meg hoped she didn't have to face any guests. The kids were covered in grime, and she and Parker didn't look much more presentable.

They were all trooping through the foyer en route to the kitchen to clean the fish, when Teensy appeared with her arm around a much younger woman.

A woman, Meg realized, who looked far too much like Gus not to be related. Not to be his mother.

"There's your baby," Teensy said.

An older man, silver-haired and dressed in an expensively tailored suit, joined the two women.

"Marianne," Parker said. "This is a surprise."

Gus hadn't said a word. He stood clutching the bucket with the two fish, a glare in his eyes as he summed up the man who'd just taken his mother's hand.

"Meg, Marianne, Gus's mother," Parker said.

"How do you do?" Marianne gave her a formal nod, the corners of her lips scarcely moving. "Teensy told me who you are. My condolences on the loss of Jules. May I present my fiance Cleveland Morrisette.''

He and Parker shook hands. Meg nodded, her hand in Samantha's.

"You didn't have to get a new husband on my account," Gus said.

"Mind your mouth, Auguste," Marianne said in a waspish voice. "And come give your mother a kiss."

Gus didn't budge.

She shrugged and looked up at Cleveland as if to say, see what I mean? He's impossible. "Go clean up and put some decent clothes on. You look like a ragamuffin. We're late for dinner."

"I already ate." Gus's tone warned he was ready to do battle.

"Then go change your clothes and thank Mrs. Ponthier for taking care of you. You're coming with me tonight. You've been a burden here long enough."

"Oh, he's no burden," Meg said before she could stop herself. It was really none of her business but her heart went out to Gus. There wasn't one drop of affection in Marianne's behavior towards her son.

"I'm sure that's sweet of you but if you knew my little boy the way I know him—well he's the spitting image of his father and that ought to tell *you* something."

Meg was overcome by a strong urge to scratch the woman's eyes until they bled.

"Go to hell," Gus said, and turned and ran from the room, Jem at his heels.

Marianne sighed. Cleveland remained impassive. Teensy fluttered her hands.

Ellen ran after Gus.

"What did I tell you?" Marianne said. "Just like his father. Look, he already has a girl-friend."

Meg refused to dignify that comment by responding. Instead she followed Ellen and Gus.

An hour later, an inconsolable and furious Gus was led away by Marianne and her fiance. His mother refused even to consider letting him bring Jem. Only after Parker swore on his honor to keep Jem safe with him would Gus allow himself to be dragged away.

Flashes from the miserable years following the death of her foster parents swam in Meg's mind. The McKenzies had been her family for more than six years when they were killed in an auto accident. The social worker had collected her on the day she was supposed to be celebrating her tenth birthday, and Meg's world had gone downhill quickly after that. Her spirits drooped even more with the memory, and it made her feel even worse when she reflected that, with Gus gone with his mother, there was no need for her to remain in New Orleans.

That night's pillow talk consisted of the same wish for everyone—to have Gus back with them. Jem lay on the floor beside the bed, cocking his head every time a floorboard creaked.

Meg didn't know where Parker had gone, but as coldly as she'd treated him earlier, she couldn't blame him for not seeking her out.

When she walked Teddy across the hall to his bed, she found Parker sitting on Gus's bed, his face a study in concentration. He smiled at Meg and Teddy and rose.

"Do you think you can rescue Gus?" Teddy looked up at him, faith in his eyes.

Parker patted Teddy on the shoulder. "I'm working on it."

"Great!" Teddy jumped into bed, his trust in Parker's ability evident as he settled happily under his covers. Not ten minutes earlier he'd been moping despite Meg's every attempt to comfort him.

Jem appeared in the doorway, his lopsided ears looking even more off-balance than usual. He whined. Teddy called him. Jem jumped on top of Gus's bed, where he wasn't permitted, and settled his nose on his paws with a heavy sigh.

And not one of them had the heart to chase him off the bed. Meg kissed Teddy goodnight and Parker gave Jem a gentle pat on his lopsided ear. Then Meg and Parker left the room together.

In the hallway, Parker smiled and took her hand. "This is starting to feel familiar," he said.

She nodded, a lump in her throat, and extracted her hand from his. "Do you think Marianne will send Gus back to that awful school?"

"It depends."

"On?"

"On whether Cleveland Morrisette is willing to foot the bill. Jules paid for it before."

"And Marianne doesn't have her own income?"

He shrugged. "Enough for most people but her lifestyle is extravagant. To the max, as Gus would say."

She'd seldom heard such a critical tone to his voice.

"Unfortunately," Parker continued, "Cleveland is more than able to afford St. Suplicius and there's no way he'll want Gus underfoot." Parker frowned. "If necessary, Grandfather will sue for custody."

"A court would grant it to a great-grandparent over a mother?" Meg knew she sounded disbelieving.

"Don't underestimate Grandfather," Parker said in a dry voice. "He has a way of getting what he wants."

Meg thought of how he'd rounded up Mrs. Fenniston and her children, zipping them from Nevada to New Orleans in a private plane and wondered how she'd convince him to send them all back the same way.

"Let's go downstairs," Parker said.

She hesitated.

Standing so close to her, yet feeling as if she

were holding him at a great distance, Parker saw her hesitation and couldn't understand why she'd retreated from him. He thought of the one word that had worked the other evening and said in a low voice, "Please?"

Still she hesitated. Then in a troubled voice she said, "Oh, Parker, I shouldn't."

"And why shouldn't you?" At least her feet moved forward even as she sought to justify her reluctance.

"It's been a long day and I'm sure you have work to do and—"

"—and I've moved too far too fast and you need me to back off before I frighten you away?" He put an arm around her as they descended the stairs. She stiffened slightly but did lay her head briefly against his arm. "Just tell me, sweet Meg," he said, "and I'll slow down."

The side door opened before Meg answered him. Mrs. Fenniston walked in followed by Grandfather. They wore evening clothes and were talking animatedly, with Grandfather humming a few bars of music to punctuate his conversation.

Parker thought he'd never seen his grandfather looking so happy. Just then Mrs. Fenniston broke off their discussion and with a glance towards the bottom of the stairs, said, "Meg, Parker, hello. We've just been enjoying the most scintillating evening of chamber music."

Grandfather waggled his right hand. "Hor-

ton said you spent the day at Sugar Bridge. I
suppose those kids are sleeping soundly tonight."

"Gus caught his first fish," Parker said.
"Why don't we go into the library? There's
something I need to tell you."

"Good idea," Grandfather said, a satisfied
smile on his face. "We have a bit of news ourselves, don't we, Elizabeth?"

Mrs. Fenniston smiled, then looked at Meg,
as if to check her reaction at Grandfather's use
of her first name.

Someone had dismantled the tent and re-
stored the room to the ordered arrangement it
had enjoyed before the advent of four imagi-
native children.

Parker took in the difference, not as pleased
as he expected to be. He'd rather enjoyed the
jumble of blankets and cushions, once he'd gotten used to it, and missed the physical re-
minder of the place he'd first made love to
Meg.

Playing host, he poured cognac for everyone.
They settled on and beside the loveseats. The
remnants of a fire burned in the grate, reduced
almost to the glow of embers as the last log
scattered into a few smoldering fragments.

Grandfather lifted his snifter towards Mrs.
Fenniston. "I want you to be the first to know
I've asked Elizabeth to do me the honor of becoming my wife. And"—he said with a proud
smile—"she's accepted."

Parker choked on his brandy. Fire burned in his throat but he forced a quick recovery, grateful that Meg was responding much more properly.

"Now I know you're thinking this is way too fast," Grandfather said, "and I know I'll get no end of grief from Mathilde and goodness knows who else, but I have only this to say." He took a deep breath and smiled at Mrs. Fenniston. "We know life is short but what we don't know is just how short. And I'm not one to lose a good thing. A woman who can beat me at chess and loves chamber music—why, I'd be a fool to let her out of my sight. Especially at my age," he added.

Mrs. Fenniston lay one hand on Grandfather's right arm, giving him a gentle caress. "I never thought I'd marry again," she said, "but Augie's changed my mind. I do hope, Meg, you'll be able to manage without me back in Las Vegas. That does concern me."

Parker stiffened at her words. Had Meg planned her return and not told him?

Evidently so, because she said, "You musn't worry about us. I'd never stand in the way of your happiness, and yes, your happiness shows!" She moved over and hugged Mrs. Fenniston first, then Grandfather, before sitting back down on the facing loveseat.

"Oh, thank you, dear. And I want you to take over the whole house, and never mind about any of the rent."

"I couldn't do that," Meg said.

"I insist."

Meg nodded but she looked as if she'd preferred to continue arguing the point. Parker assumed she would, later. But he could scarcely be concerned about such a minor issue when all he could register was that she was planning to leave New Orleans. And soon, or so it seemed.

"Now, what's your news?" Grandfather asked his question with a wink. "Maybe it will make all this talk of Las Vegas beside the point."

Meg colored.

Parker shook his head. "I'm afraid it's about Gus. Marianne returned, engaged to Cleveland Morrisette, by the way, and swept him off with her."

Grandfather snorted. "That old so and so. He's twice her age. At least." He thumped his empty glass on the arm of his chair. "Jules sure had bad taste in wives—until you, that is, Meg."

Still looking unhappy and withdrawn, she nodded.

"I didn't interfere while Jules was alive, but now that he's dead and buried, that puts a whole new light on things," Grandfather said. "Come see me in the morning, Parker, and we'll decide what to do about Gus. That woman's a bad influence and I'll be damned if I'll let her ruin the boy." He shot a glance at

Meg. "Especially when he was starting to straighten out."

Parker nodded.

Grandfather put his glass down on the side table. "It's late and I'm tired, so I'll say good night. Confound that darn useless woman," he muttered as he and Mrs. Fenniston left the room.

Parker carried the empty crystal across to the bar. When he returned to Meg, he sat on the loveseat that faced her, rather than taking his seat beside her.

She looked over at him, that same distant expression on her face. "I'm very happy for your grandfather and Mrs. Fenniston," she said.

He nodded. He wished he could say the same for the two of them. "Like I said, Grandfather does have a way of getting what he wants."

"And knowing what that is," Meg murmured.

Parker heard her comment but he didn't know how to respond. Wasn't it obvious to her that he wanted her? "So you're planning your return to Las Vegas?"

Her hands clasped between her knees, she nodded.

"When?"

"Soon." Meg looked over at the fire. "The children need to get back into school. And it's almost Christmas and I haven't done a thing."

"I see." He thought of pointing out the kids

had already said how much fun Christmas in New Orleans would be.

"Would it matter to you if I asked you not to go?"

Her eyes definitely brightened, which gave Parker hope. But then she said, "Why?"

"Why what?" Man, this was hard. He should have sat next to her, taken her in his arms, swept her up the stairs to bed, then asked her to stay. He started to run a finger around his collar then remembered he was wearing his Tulane sweatshirt.

"Why should I stay in New Orleans?"

Because you've brought light into my life. Because I can't live without you. Because I need you. The true reasons screamed out in Parker's mind but as he stared at Meg, he found he couldn't say them. What if he'd been wrong and she was only indulging in a fling to while away the time? What did he really know about her?

He drummed on his knee, realizing as he did that he was unconsciously imitating his grandfather in an agitated state, and finally said, "The kids will love Christmas here. They haven't been to the zoo or City Park. And neither have you. And there's a lot of work to be done settling Jules's estate. You'll need financial and legal advice . . ." he trailed off.

That first day when he'd met Meg in Jules's suite, she'd reacted strongly to his arrogant assumption that she had been bought and paid for by Jules for the pleasure of the evening. But he'd never seen her eyes with such fury or the skin above her lips turn white.

She rose. Her hands in the pockets of her jeans, she said, "Thank you, Parker. The next time we take a family vacation maybe we'll consider New Orleans. But for now we're going home."

He'd blown it. Parker stared at her stiff back as she walked toward the fireplace. Maybe there was still a chance. Maybe if he said forget all those reasons. Stay because I want to get to know you better, to make love to you, to share life with you.

Meg swung around, her back to the fireplace, her hands now clasped behind her back. She gazed at Parker, realizing she'd most definitely reaped what she had sown. She hadn't been honest with Parker from the beginning. If only she had, perhaps they might have had a chance. Perhaps she could even now be whispering to him, safe within his arms, I want to stay because I want to be with you.

Tell him the truth. You have to go home anyway; it's clear he doesn't feel for you the way you feel for him.

He was about to speak when she said, "Parker, there's something I want you to do for me and there's something I have to tell you."

He rose from the loveseat and crossed to stand in front of her. "Tell me," he said, anticipation in his voice.

Meg heard that note with dread. He wasn't going to like anything she had to say. She took a deep breath, then said, "First I'd like your help in setting up a trust. Anything I inherit from having married Jules should be put in trust for Gus."

"Everything?"

"Every penny."

"You're talking about a lot of money."

She shrugged. "All of it. And I'll sign whatever is necessary to give you control of my shares in the company."

"What's this about?" No eager anticipation in his voice now. "Washing your hands of the Ponthiers?"

Meg forced herself to meet his gaze. "You said earlier you couldn't understand why I married Jules. I'm about to tell you and it's not pretty."

"Let's hear it."

"Jules offered me thirty thousand dollars to marry him for three days and vote my shares along with him in favor of the buyout."

Parker eyes narrowed. "My brother really did that?"

She nodded. The details weren't necessary; she'd hurt him enough.

Parker stepped back. Almost to himself he said, "He told me he'd do whatever it took and I even wondered when you showed up, but—" He rounded on her. "You made me forget all about those crazy ideas. Oh, yeah, you and your lying body. You drove every suspicion from my mind."

"What we did together had nothing to do with this."

He laughed. "Do you expect me to believe that? Believe a woman who would do such a thing?" He rubbed a hand between his eyes. "God, you and Jules. Two of a kind."

"It wasn't like that, Parker. I only did it for the money."

"Money!" Parker paced to the loveseat then turned back. He advanced on her, standing so close she could see his chest rising and falling. He raised one hand and clamped it on the mantel. "Thirty thousand dollars?" He took her chin in his hand and lifted her face up to his. "And what else did Jules get for that money?"

"What do you mean?"

His mouth twisted. "I'm talking about sex. My brother would have gotten his money's worth from you."

"I told you before I did not have sex with Jules." Meg tried to keep the quaver from her voice but failed.

"Oh, right. Why not tell me another lie?" He let go of her chin and jammed both his hands in the pockets of his jeans. "Dammit, I knew you were too good to be true."

Meg caught her breath. "Please, Parker, I know what I did was wrong, but I had my reasons. I didn't want to tell you but I thought it was the right thing to do."

"The right thing to do?" He glared. "It's a strange time to be thinking of that. I could have lost what I've worked for my entire life, what's been in my family for generations. I'm glad you did tell me, just so I know what kind of person I'm dealing with."

"I'm sorry, Parker." It was all she knew to say. Of course he was upset; he had every right to be. Only, she wished he could separate out what the two of them had shared. "What I did with Jules, it had nothing to do with you and me."

He laughed and said, "Oh, no? You'd married one Ponthier for money. Why not sample the other one? Trade more sex for money?"

Meg saw red. She hadn't done any of what she'd done to hurt anyone. "If you had ever once in your life been faced with a child crying because his shoes are too tight and you don't have the money to buy new ones, you might look at life a whole lot differently than you do! I did what I did for my children, and for that, I'll never apologize."

Fists clenched at her sides, ice in her voice, she said, "And that sex the other day? Don't mention it; that was on the house."

And before he could see the tears welling in her eyes, she rushed from the room.

Twenty-three

Things could be worse, Parker reasoned, slumped in his desk chair in his downtown office. He could have slit his throat shaving after his sleepless night. But since he hadn't done that, he had to face what he'd done to Meg the night before. Over and over in his fingers he turned the miniature Barbie doll shoe he'd found in some papers he'd taken from the library after Meg stalked out.

Stalked, Parker thought with a knife to the gut, didn't do justice to her furious exit.

And after a sleepless night of recrimination and reflection, a night in which he'd spent his fury against both Meg and his brother, he couldn't blame Meg for being so furious with him.

He'd said some terrible, horrible, nasty things to her.

Yet it wasn't Meg who'd wronged him—it was Jules. And he'd ravaged her when his anger should have been directed solely at his brother.

Within minutes after Meg had cleared the stairs, Parker had snatched some papers from the library desk, stuffed them in his briefcase, and torn from Ponthier Place in his Porsche. He'd battled the urge to floor the accelerator, gripping the wheel as he drove blindly, unaware of any destination.

He ended up at the lakefront past the University of New Orleans. Towards his right he made out the purposeful lights of the Lakefront Airport and the party-oriented ones of the casino boat docked just beyond.

He walked along the breakfront dividing the waters of Lake Pontchartrain from the shore, absorbing the extent to which his brother had gone to sell out Ponthier Enterprises from under Parker. Jules saw only the money to be gained. But for Parker, the family business was the focus of his life. Sadly, he reflected that he and Jules had been just as divided as if a wall, like the solid rock wall beside him, had marched between them all their lives.

For whatever reason, their mother's world began and ended with Jules. He was inclined to think that the seeds of that distinction lay in the shrouded history of his parent's marriage. But as he listened to the lapping of the lake waters along the shore, and stood staring up at the night sky lightened by the life of the city, he knew he would never know the reason. Even if he asked his mother, she would have no answer for him.

Perhaps she and his father were still in love when Jules was conceived and born. By the time Parker came along three years later, life with the young Ponthiers probably hadn't been as rosy. Parker's father had been notorious for his womanizing.

No matter the reason, Teensy had cosseted and preferred Jules and blamed and distanced Parker. His father, whether to his credit or not, had ignored them equally.

And now Jules lay rotting in the family mausoleum at Metairie Cemetery and he, Parker, very much alive, was actively screwing up what he sensed was his one chance at happiness in his life.

Parker stopped and gazed out across the lake. Lights from the Causeway bridge led out over the dark waters in the distance. If he could find his way to forgive Jules for engineering the buy out and involving Meg in it, perhaps he too could find his way back through the night.

He turned and began walking towards his car. He'd struggled with his brother's troubled self for years; given a choice Jules would take the easy out every time. When the multi-million-dollar buyout offer had come along, Jules had seen only the immediate profits he would reap. He cared nothing for tradition or building a better company over the long term.

So Jules had schemed and he'd hired Meg to help him.

Why Meg? What about Meg had prompted Jules to think she'd entertain his offer? That question gnawed at him. Had Jules seen Meg with her children? He replayed what she'd said about doing anything for her children, and thought it was possible. Jules had a way of seeking a person's weaknesses and using them to achieve his own ends.

Even as Parker had experienced the darkness that dwelled within his brother, he'd seen the light that sparkled in Meg's eyes, a brightness that reflected a pure heart and a generous spirit. He still found it hard to accept that she'd agreed to go along with Jules, but he did believe, now that he'd calmed down and processed the shock of the planned betrayal, that the blame lay squarely with Jules.

Parker had driven home, calmer and exhausted, yet still unable to sleep, unable to answer the question, "Could he trust Meg?"

Again the next morning he fingered the tiny toy shoe. He'd still been too upset with Meg to show up at Ponthier Place to meet with his grandfather to discuss Gus's future as they'd agreed last night. His grandfather had phoned the office earlier and Parker had told his secretary to tell him he was too busy to make it to Ponthier Place.

He felt guilty about his cowardly action, especially as he thought of Gus being torn from the friendships he'd made with Teddy, Ellen, and Samantha. Marianne might be Gus's mother, but she was not a friend to her son.

The intercom buzzed, jerking him from his thoughts. Before he could answer, the double doors of his office swung open. His grandfather rolled in, his eyebrows meeting over the bridge of his nose. "A fine thing when I have to come down here to meet with my own grandson." He drummed the fingers of his right hand on his knee.

Parker's assistant had followed in the wake of the wheelchair. "May I get you some coffee, Mr. Ponthier?"

"Never mind the frills," Grandfather answered. "We've got business to attend to."

She backed out, too professional to ogle, but Parker knew she had to be curious. Grandfather Ponthier hadn't been to the Central Business District offices of Ponthier Enterprises in over a year, since the day he'd settled his shares of Ponthier Enterprises equally on Jules and Parker.

The doors swung shut.

Grandfather advanced on Parker's desk. "Is there some good reason you didn't come to the house? You don't look so occupied you couldn't get away from here."

"Well, I am." Parker heard the obstinate note in his voice and regretted it immediately. He

had no reason to be disrespectful to his grandfather.

"No need to be rude. You know it won't faze
me." He relaxed his fierce frown slightly.
"Now did you and Meg have a fight?"

"How did you know?"

He snorted. "You didn't show your face at
the house, you look like you've been up all
night—and for no good reason—and you're
not smiling. Besides, Meg was drooping so low
this morning, it only takes a half wit to put that
two and two together."

Parker smiled despite himself, though he
hated to hear Meg described as drooping, especially when he knew his own harsh words
had caused her low spirits. "Okay, we had a
fight."

"Good."

"Good? How can you say that?" Parker
pushed back from his desk but remained
seated. He hated towering over his grandfather, a man he'd looked up to all his life. Which
was silly, because even confined to the wheelchair, his grandfather dominated any situation.

"If you can fight, you can love. There's kindling for emotion there. Works both ways. If
you love, you'll fight some, too." Grandfather
glanced out the windows at the view of the
Mississippi River. After a long moment, he
said, "I've known you all your life Parker, and
with not one woman you've ever dated—the
ones you brought around to the house at

least—have I ever seen you be any more than surface polite. And that Renee, the one you were going to marry, you would have been miserable with her. Too much pretending to be polite but nothing substantial underneath."

Parker gazed at his grandfather, absorbing his words. It was true that he'd already clashed with Meg twice in the short time he'd known her. And grandfather was right; Parker never fought with anyone else.

And, Parker remembered with a smile, those two clashes had been balanced by the two times they'd made love, both times high points in his life.

Parker tried to push those memories to the back of his mind as he picked his way through his thoughts, intent on sparing Grandfather the knowledge of what Jules had schemed to do. "I can't tell you what she did that set me off. But it was something I have trouble understanding any woman or man doing. Yet she's this wonderful person—or so she seems. So who is she? I keep asking myself if I can trust her."

"Did she explain why she did whatever it was she did that upset you?"

"No—" Parker heard the denial cross his lips and corrected himself. "Well, she did, but I have to confess I wasn't listening very closely. She did say something about needing money pretty badly."

Grandfather nodded. "You know, when I

was born, the Ponthiers were at pretty low tide. You don't know what it's like to go without, but until I was almost fifteen, my dad and grandpa struggled, still trying to build back the family fortunes. Then the sugar business revitalized and they rode the stock market up and had the good sense to get out ahead of the crash. When others were selling, they were able to buy. But before that, life wasn't so sweet."

Parker followed his grandfather's story, knowing he wouldn't talk so long without a point. It wasn't his nature.

"Mrs. Fenniston has shared with me some of what Meg has gone through—how her worthless husband died and left her holding a bag with no sides, top, or bottom to it. So if she did anything to earn money to keep her family together and fed, I'd think long and hard before I condemned her for it."

"Even—" Parker stopped. He wanted the secret of Jules's final betrayal to remain buried.

"Even if it had something to do with Jules?"

Parker stared. Did he know? "What do you mean?"

Grandfather shrugged. "Women have married for money before. He was a good-looking guy, probably flashing a wad of bills around in Vegas. Maybe she saw a good thing and played her cards to cash in."

Parker shook his head. "Then why ask me to set up a trust in favor of Gus with anything she inherits from Jules?"

Grandfather drummed on his knee. "She's giving away the gains so what's not to trust?" He smiled at his own pun, then serious once more said, "I don't think it's Meg you're worried about trusting. I think it's your own heart you're afraid of."

Parker digested his grandfather's words.

"Don't think about it too long," Grandfather said, "Life is short."

Parker gave him a wry smile. "Thanks for listening and for your advice. Now what do we do about Gus?"

"Custody. You and Meg can watch him."

"Right." Parker frowned. "I know nothing about children and Meg is going back—"

The intercom buzzed. Parker pressed the speaker.

"I'm sorry, Parker," his assistant said, "but that's your nephew on line one and he said it was urgent."

Parker grabbed the phone.

Farther uptown, at the Audubon Zoological Gardens, Meg pointed out the white alligator lifting its head from behind a fallen log. "Look, kids, there it is."

"That's not an alligator," Samantha said. "Alligators are green. Everybody knows that."

"Shows what you know," Ellen said. "This is an albino alligator. Guess you didn't learn too much in kindergarten, did you, dummy?"

Meg snapped her head around. "Ellen Mar-

garet Cooper, you mind your tongue. There is
no reason to speak to your sister that way."

Ellen's eyes widened and to Meg's dismay,
her tough-as-nails daughter burst into tears.

Samantha promptly did the same, wailing,
"I'm not a dummy, I'm just little!"

Teddy covered his ears. "Girls," he said, his
voice an echo of Gus's. Ellen cried even harder.

A young couple, arm in arm with eyes only
for one another, moved away with an annoyed
look back at the crying children.

"Sweetie, I didn't mean to make you cry,"
Meg said to Ellen, "but it's important to speak
to your sister in a caring and respectful way,
the way you like others to speak to you."

"Why does that matter when the world is
coming to an end?" Ellen dashed her eyes and
glared at Meg.

Meg put her arms around Ellen and Samantha. "Are you sad you're going home? Is that
why you feel the world's ending?"

Ellen kicked at the ground and nodded. Samantha copied her sister's actions.

"Don't you want to go home? You can see
your friends and sleep in your own beds and—"
She stopped, at a loss to find treats that compared with white alligators and sugarcane harvesting and a new friend named Gus.
Determined to make an effort to raise their spirits, she said, "I'll take you to see the white tigers
again when we get home."

"Everyone's seen those," Ellen said in disgust.

Teddy had uncovered his ears when the girls stopped crying. He walked back to them, a hopeful look in his too-sad eyes. "Hey, Mom, I've been thinking. Nothing's been the same since Dad died, so why not stay here and maybe Parker could be our dad?"

Dismayed at the eager looks on the girls' faces, Meg tightened her arms around her daughters. "It's not really that simple."

"Have you asked him?" Ellen demanded.

"Of course not. Listen, kidlets, becoming someone's dad means becoming someone's husband, too, and Parker and I are not—"

"How do you know if you haven't asked him?" Ellen stuck to her argument. "You always tell us, 'You never know the answer until you ask.'"

Hearing her daughter imitate her own voice so perfectly, Meg had to smother a smile. As she thought of how best to respond, a herd of men and women sporting name tags of a tour group surged around the white alligators. Meg drew her children away and said firmly, "Remember how I've taught you that some things are for adults to decide and others are for children?"

They nodded.

"Well, daddy and husband questions are for adults." And those questions are too complicated for this particular adult, Meg thought.

"Now let's go see the komodo dragon."

"Let's not," Ellen said.

"Good idea," Teddy said. "Who cares about some stupid dragon."

Then Samantha piped in with, "Let's go home. I miss Jem."

Meg studied her suddenly mutinous children. "Yesterday you said you wanted to see the dragon."

"That was yesterday," Ellen said.

"Before Gus had to go away," Teddy added.

"It wouldn't be right without him." Ellen and Teddy spoke in unison.

Accepting defeat, Meg nodded. She'd been the one trying to avoid Ponthier Place, hoping to slip out of town without bumping into Parker. Well, if he turned up there, she'd be polite, yet cool. And she'd salvage her pride by not letting him see how much she wanted him to forgive her and ask her to stay. "Okay," Meg said, "let's start hiking."

The childrens' spirits picked up a little as they walked the mile or so across Audubon Park on their way to the streetcar.

It was Meg who grew more sad as she waited by the yellow streetcar stop marker. Memories of Parker cartwheeled through her mind. She didn't want to leave, but she couldn't stay. Not with the way things were.

She hid a shiver, continuing to put on a brave face for her children. Red-eyed from crying herself to sleep after Parker's angry reaction, she'd met with Grandfather Ponthier early that morning and asked if he would send them home that evening in the Ponthier plane.

As sharp as he was, Meg could tell he figured out she and Parker had had a disagreement. He didn't try to persuade her to stay, though, which tormented Meg. Had Parker said something to him about Jules's plan? Or maybe Parker slept with every woman he said hello to and Grandfather knew better than to expect his grandson to be wanting Meg to stick around in New Orleans. The city held plenty of women who'd fall for a Ponthier.

No matter what direction her imagination traveled, the road was bleak. She'd thanked Grandfather Ponthier and retreated to her room. She had promised the kids one last day of sightseeing but not told anyone at the house her plans for the day or when they would return. Only Grandfather and she knew the time they had to be at the small lakefront airport where the jet was hangared.

"Mom! Come on." Meg felt a tug on her elbow and realized Samantha was pulling her towards the open doors of the streetcar. From their vantage point on the steps of the car, her other two children regarded her as if she'd lost her marbles. She heard Ellen whisper to Teddy, "I bet she's thinking about your idea."

In the driveway at Ponthier Place, Parker got back into his car and slammed the door. Horton had no idea where Meg and the kids had gone. Teensy had gone shopping, accompanied by Dr. Prejean. Mrs. Fenniston had gone to meet Grandfather downtown.

When he'd suggested Parker take Meg and the kids to Mississippi to collect Gus, Grandfather must have assumed Meg would still be at the house.

Grandfather's words about not understanding the desperation of having no money shamed him. He could hear Meg as clearly as if she were speaking. She'd said, "You don't know what it's like to hear your children cry when their shoes are too tight and you don't have the money to buy the new ones."

Yet he hadn't listened. His fury had filled his ears and his heart. And today he was ashamed of his selfish reaction. He'd thought only of himself. What a jerk. Meg hadn't done anything to him. Knowing Jules as he did, Parker could almost hear the way his brother would have described Parker and the evil that would be wrought if Meg didn't help him out.

She'd said it last night—she'd done what she'd done to help her family. Her first husband must have been a real loser to saddle sweet Meg with problems so massive she'd had to take such drastic measures.

Having reasoned out the situation, Parker was eager to beg her forgiveness for his harsh words of the evening before, and he was frustrated beyond belief when he couldn't find her.

"Dammit," he said, drumming on the wheel with one hand and rubbing his bleary eyes with the other.

A yelp sounded from the side of the house. Jem rounded it, loping towards the car. He skidded to a stop, sat back on his haunches, and cocked his head, dipping his droopy ear even farther.

"At least you're here," Parker said.

Jem yelped but refrained from jumping on the side of Parker's car, showing at least the possibility he remembered a few things Parker was trying to teach him.

Staring at the dog, Parker thought of the choked-back sobs in Gus's voice. He'd called from the infirmary phone, having presented himself there with a self-proclaimed stomachache and lain in wait until the nurse went outside to smoke her morning cigarette.

This he told Parker in between pleas for Parker and Meg to come get him out of prison. Marianne hadn't even kept him with her overnight; she and Cleveland had driven him straight to Mississippi, complaining of the cost to replace his missing school uniform. But, Gus added bitterly, he heard them discussing how they were going out gambling at one of the casinos there after they dumped him at the school.

Jem whined and Parker got out of the car. "Okay, dammit, you win." Parker walked around to the trunk, Jem dogging his heels, his tongue panting with anticipation. He found another gym towel, covered his leather seat, then stood back.

"Got that *deja vu* feeling?" Parker said to the mutt as he settled on the seat with a pleased sigh.

And he could have sworn as he slipped the car into gear, and said, "Let's go get Gus," that the dog actually smiled.

She might not be able to avoid Ponthier Place, Meg thought as she and the children climbed the broad steps leading to the side door, but she could hide out in her room. After all, she had to pack for all of them and that should keep her busy.

Ellen and Teddy barreled into the house as the door swung open. Horton smiled at the children and Meg and said, "Mrs. Fenniston was asking for you, Miz Meg. She and Mr. Ponthier are in the Great Parlor."

Meg's heart skittered. "Mr. Ponthier?"

As if he understood the question she was actually asking, and knowing Horton, he probably did, he said in a soft voice, "That would be Grandfather Ponthier."

"Oh, of course." Meg managed a smile.

"Would the children care for a snack?"

"Oh, yes," Samantha said, transferring her hand from her mother's to Horton's.

"Thanks," Meg said and crossed the elegant foyer towards the Great Parlor.

Mrs. Fenniston was just seating herself

across from Grandfather at the chess table. She waved Meg over, a happy smile on her face.

They exchanged greetings and Grandfather urged her to pull up a chair. Meg hesitated, not wanting to be caught downstairs in case Parker came by the house. But he gave her one of his bossy looks and she relented.

That's when she spotted the amazing emerald and diamond ring on Mrs. Fenniston's left hand. "Mrs. Fenniston!" Meg couldn't stop her exclamation. "What a fabulous ring."

Her friend blushed and smiled. "It is lovely, isn't it?" She glanced over at Grandfather, her admiration clear in her gaze. "Augie presented it to me this morning."

Grandfather fingered one of his pawns. "It's the Ponthier ring. Stays in the family. If you and Parker had come to terms first, it would've been yours." This time his glare was even fiercer.

"Oh, it looks much better on Mrs. Fenniston," Meg was relieved Grandfather had skipped over her marriage to Jules when referring to the ring but embarrassed that he was still trying to matchmake for her and Parker.

The doors to the terrace opened. Meg turned to see Teensy and Dr. Prejean walk in arm in arm, in what didn't look at all like a doctor-patient relationship. They strolled across the room and stopped beside the chess table.

Not letting go of Teensy, Prejean said, "Afternoon, everyone."

Teensy smiled and for the first time since Meg had been at Ponthier Place, she felt that Teensy actually felt happy as her lips curved upwards.

"Augie, I've got to hand it to you," Prejean said.

"Why's that?" Grandfather moved the pawn diagonally.

"Ooh, that's the Ponthier emerald!" Teensy patted Mrs. Fenniston on the hand. "Better you than me," she said.

Meg hid a smile.

"Teensy and I have some news for you," Prejean announced. "Augie, in acting as quickly as you have to declare yourself to Mrs. Fenniston, you've set an example to be admired. For many years I've cared for Teensy, properly as a doctor cares for a special patient. Well, during that time, I've grown to respect and admire—"

Grandfather said, "Are you trying to tell us that you're finally going to make an honest woman out of Teensy?"

Teensy lifted her eyes heavenward and clutched the doctor more tightly. "Dickie has made me the happiest woman in the world by asking me to become his wife."

Mrs. Fenniston rose and hugged both Teensy and Prejean. Even Grandfather extended his good hand for a shake. Meg, too, offered her congratulations, feeling hollow even as she said all the right things.

She knew she was being silly, but she felt like the only girl without a date at the homecoming dance. When Prejean called for a bottle of champagne to celebrate the occasion, Meg offered to tell Horton and used the excuse to slip out. Missing Parker more than she could describe, she made her way upstairs and refused to shed even a tear as she opened her suitcase.

Meg had her belongings ready to go and had started on Ellen's when Teddy raced into the bedroom. "Mom, you better come quick. Jem's missing."

Meg groaned. Of course she didn't want anything bad to happen to the dog, but how would she convince the children to leave if they were worried about Jem? It was tough enough for them to have seen Gus ripped away, obviously unhappily so. With a sigh, she headed downstairs to pour oil over the troubled waters.

It was a shame she had to leave, she thought, descending the staircase, her hand trailing down the polished banister. In the short time she'd been involved in the world of the Ponthiers, she'd come to feel remarkably at home. If only Parker could understand why she'd done what she'd done and let go of his anger perhaps she wouldn't have had to drag the kids—and herself—away so abruptly.

But after last night's tirade, no way was she

spending another twenty-four hours in New Orleans. Even if Parker forgave her, she wasn't sure she could do the same for him.

"Jem's been dognapped," Samantha said by way of greeting. She sat on the bottom step of the staircase playing with her dolls. "Just like the *101 Dalmatians*." But at least she calmly went on disrobing her Barbie.

Ellen and Teddy weren't taking the news nearly as calmly. Teddy was out on the porch, searching for tracks. Ellen had learned from Horton that Parker had been by the house earlier.

Meg snatched at that straw, at the same time grateful she'd spent the day out and about. She told the kids that Parker had probably taken Jem to the vet or the groomer.

"In his Porsche? Get real, Mom," Ellen said. "And it's been raining since we got back on the streetcar. Parker wouldn't let a dog with muddy paws in that car."

"Yeah, he loves that car," Teddy said.

Her children had been safely home in Las Vegas the day she and Parker had rescued Gus and Jem. Meg remembered Parker's initial opposition to bringing the dog home, especially in his beloved car. She pictured him rummaging in his trunk, then spreading a towel on the leather seat. It had been Parker who'd driven the muddy mongrel home in style.

She smiled softly at the memory. Parker was such a good man. She thought of him pulling

Gus and Jem from the water, remembered him patiently untangling the lines and recasting them for Gus and Ellen and Teddy, and pictured him scattering the bed at Sugar Bridge with rose petals before he made sweet love to her.

Yes, she could forgive Parker the things he'd said about her last night. He'd been hurt, but her love for him was greater than one night of wounded feelings could destroy.

Should she wait for him? Find him and talk to him? Ellen and Teddy ran outside to search around the house for Jem and Meg walked slowly back towards the staircase.

She paused to watch Samantha playing "date." Her daughter dipped Ken towards Barbie and said, "Would you like to go to the movies with me?" Samantha accepted for Barbie, then walked the two dolls hand in hand up one of the stairs.

Some things, Meg thought, followed a time-honored tradition. She'd never asked a boy or a man on a date and she didn't feel like she should start now. Parker had driven her away. If they were to be together, she needed him to want her badly enough that he would come after her. Even if that meant following her all the way to Las Vegas, Nevada.

Twenty-four

Cars stretched as far ahead as Parker could see. He'd been stalled on the I-10 bridge across Lake Pontchartrain for almost twenty minutes. Rain that had been only a light mist was building to a driving force that battered the windows and challenged the windshield wipers.

After assuring Parker in no uncertain terms he'd run away before he'd ever go back to that school, Gus had fallen into an exhausted sleep. Jem's scruffy head lay between Gus's bony knees. Every so often the dog opened one eye and checked on Parker but other than that seemed utterly content crowded into the floor space of the Porsche between Gus's legs and the door.

The traffic remained immobile. Parker tried once more to reach someone at Ponthier Place. Each time he'd called, the answering service had come on. He had a sick feeling in the pit of his stomach and the only thing that could cure it would be finding Meg still in New Orleans. Though if she had gone back to Las Vegas, Parker would be on the next flight out.

Once more, the recorded message filtered over the phone.

"Damn." Parker switched off his phone.

Gus stirred and so did his shadow. "Hey, what did you say?" His nephew didn't look at all sleepy as he stared at Parker.

"You're right, Gus, I didn't need to swear."

"Not unless I get to." He sounded hopeful.

Parker shook his head. He'd have to get used to watching his tongue around the kids. The kids. He gripped the wheel.

"What's wrong?"

"Must be an accident on the bridge."

"No, with you."

Parker reached over and brushed a hand over Gus's crew cut hair. He started to say "nothing" but Gus was too perceptive to buy that answer. "I wanted to talk to Meg and couldn't reach her over the phone."

"Hey, why didn't she come with you to get me like last time?"

"She and the kids had gone off to do something."

"What?"

Gus sure asked a lot of questions. Parker said, "I don't know. Maybe they went to the zoo." As soon as the words were out of his mouth, he could have kicked himself for not thinking of that idea sooner. He'd heard the kids asking about the zoo after they'd seen the lighted elephants at the edge of Audubon Park. That would explain them leaving Jem behind.

"I've never been to the zoo," Gus said, a wistful note in his voice.

If Parker could wrap his hands around Marianne's neck and squeeze hard, he would. Come to think of it, though, neither his father nor Teensy had taken him to the zoo as a child. He'd gone with his grandparents or Horton. "I'll take you," Parker said. "Before Christmas."

"With Teddy and Ellen and Samantha and Jem?"

What had Meg said about not promising something he couldn't deliver? Well, he had to deliver on this one, and not just for Gus's sake. He nodded. "We'll all go, except Jem."

The mutt raised his head and yelped.

"It's okay, we'll take you to the country and let you chase some roosters." Gus patted the dog's head. "Jem doesn't like to be left out."

Parker heard that message. Gus was the one who didn't like to be left out and he couldn't blame the child. "Your great-grandfather and I are going to work things out with your mother so that you can stay with us," he said. No matter what it cost, and Parker was realistic enough to know Marianne could be bought; Gus wasn't going back to her.

"Are you going to marry Meg?"

"What?"

Gus shrugged. "She is my stepmother. And

that way we'd be a family." Under his breath, he added, "And nobody would send four kids away to school."

"Don't worry about that miserable school," Parker said. "And whether or not I marry Meg depends on her. She may have plans to go back to Las Vegas." Plans he'd do whatever it took to change. Trust Gus to get right to the point. He was going to marry Meg—if she'd have him.

"Vegas," Gus said in a voice heavy with scorn. "Who would live there when they could live in New Orleans. You wouldn't believe all the things they don't have there. Ellen told me they don't have Mardi Gras, or streetcars, or a river. And she'd never even heard of *pain perdu*!"

Parker smiled. The sweet French bread dish was Gus's favorite breakfast item.

His car phone rang. Jem yelped.

Grandfather's voice boomed in his ear. "Everything okay with Gus?"

"He's here with me now."

"Good. At least that's under control. Now about Meg—"

"What about her?" Parker clenched the phone with his left hand. The traffic began to inch forward and he shifted gears with his right.

"She's leaving the Lakefront Airport at five o'clock on the company plane."

Only Gus's interested expression kept Parker's reaction under control. "You're helping her leave?"

"She's not gone yet, you young fool. I thought you'd find her at the house and the problem would have been solved hours ago."

Parker checked his watch. It was almost impossible for him to make it into New Orleans East before five o'clock. "I'll make it there," Parker said. "Thanks for calling."

Grandfather chuckled. "I'll be happy to give the bride away."

The line clicked dead and Parker lowered the phone.

He'd been a fool the other night. When Meg had asked him why he wanted her to stay, he'd rattled on like a tour guide. What difference did it make whether Meg saw Christmas in the Oaks at City Park or the antique shops on Royal Street? None of the safe answers he'd given had been answers from the heart.

He should have fallen on his knees and told her he loved her and couldn't live without her. Why hadn't he done that? Parker gunned the engine as the traffic began to flow.

He hadn't been ready to admit his feelings the other night. Perhaps the timing was for the best. And even though he still wanted to clear the air over the circumstances surrounding her marriage to his brother, Parker knew the details were just that. Details. Because what truly mattered were their feelings for one another.

*   *   *

The rain had slacked off a bit while Meg watched from the terminal window as a worker stowed their luggage in the small jet.

The kids whined and groused about being forced to leave without knowing Jem was safe. She couldn't blame them; she felt much the same. "Come on, let's go," she said, pointing them towards the door that led outside to where they would cross to the plane.

Ellen muttered under her breath, Teddy wore a distant look of unhappiness, and Samantha followed the other two in silence. Raindrops pelted them as they walked to the stairs pushed up to the side of the plane. Despite the wetness, not one of them picked up their pace.

Meg had just set one foot on the top step by the cabin door when Ellen said, "Why are we running away?"

She turned and looked at her daughter on the step below. "What did you say?"

Ellen planted her hands on her hips. "It feels like we're running away because Jem isn't safe and Parker wasn't here to say good-bye and Gus is . . ." Ellen clamped her lips together and Meg knew her daughter was battling both anger and sorrow.

She held out her arms but Ellen refused to accept the comfort. The plane's steward leaned out of the cabin door, a friendly smile on his face, "Ready, are we?"

Ready? Ready to run away, as Ellen suggested? Or ready to face Parker and gamble on sharing her feelings with him? Meg brushed the moisture from Ellen's face and said, "Wait here while I have a word with the pilot."

She turned and the steward followed her to the cockpit door. Meg knew they thought she was nuts when she told them they wouldn't be flying to Las Vegas, but she really didn't care.

Especially when she heard a shriek from outside the plane and Ellen cried out, "It's Gus!"

"And Jem," Samantha said.

Which meant . . .

Meg whirled around, then remembered her dignity. Slowly, she stepped into the doorway of the plane.

Parker, with Gus and Jem at his heels, raced through the small building that served as a terminal at Lakefront Airport. The people there knew him as a regular, a dignified executive who flew in and out on business on the Ponthier jet.

There was nothing dignified about the way he ran helter-skelter toward the tarmac. Right after Grandfather had called him, Parker's first instinct had been to pick up the phone again, call the airport, and instruct the pilot to delay takeoff. After all, the pilot worked more for him than for Grandfather.

But some instinct had warned him off that action. Meg would interpret it, fairly accurately, as an example of Ponthier power. He wanted her to stay, but he also wanted her to make that choice of her own free will. So, acting against the ingrained habits of his years of authority, he let matters take their own course.

He spotted the children first, on the steps to the plane, but rather than walking up, they were headed down.

And then he saw Meg, framed in the doorway of the plane's cabin. His heart caught and he started to call out to her. But no words came out of his throat.

Meg's kids shouted and ran down the stairs towards Gus and Jem.

Gus tugged on his jacket. "Jeez, Uncle Parker, don't let her get away."

Parker laughed. Rain sprinkled his face as he covered the yards to the plane, passing the happy huddle of four children and one dog.

"I knew you'd get him back," Teddy said.

The raindrops mingled with what seemed suspiciously like moisture in Parker's own eyes. At the foot of the steps, he paused and looked up. Meg hadn't moved from the doorway.

"Forgive me, Meg?"

She gazed down at him, her eyes larger and darker than ever. She lifted one foot; it hovered in the air between the doorway and the first step downward.

"Please?"

Meg moved out of the covering of the cabin.

"I was angry with Jules, not you. I said horrible things and I am so sorry."

Meg moved one step closer to him.

Hope driving him, Parker did the same, climbing the stairs till he stood just below her. "I should have listened to what you said about doing anything for your family." He pointed towards the children. They were all talking at once near the edge of the steps. With Jem's ecstatic yelping, his and Meg's words couldn't carry to the children.

"What changed your mind?" Her voice was low and serious.

"Grandfather kicked me in the butt," Parker said. "And I spent a long night thinking about my brother."

Meg nodded. "It's important to me that you understand, even though I know that's a lot to ask."

Parker gazed at her. He wanted more than anything to take that last step that separated them. But he needed to ask one more question; if he didn't, he knew he would always wonder.

"What is it, Parker?" Meg asked in a gentle voice.

"Why you?" He blurted it out. "Or do you know why Jules picked you? I mean, out of a million women in Las Vegas, what made him think you would do that job?"

Meg ran a hand over her damp hair. "I'm glad you asked, Parker. I would have told you last night but you lost your temper so fast."

He shook his head. "Sorry," he said, grinning ruefully. "Don't usually do that."

Meg smiled. "I don't usually marry for hire, either. Anyway, Jules told me why. He'd been watching me wait tables and he said I had the class to carry it off, but more importantly, he'd seen me show my children's pictures to this lady at the next table and tell her I was a widow." Meg sighed. "She was such a sweet lady, too, that I trusted her. And do you know she slipped off to the ladies room after four drinks and stiffed me for them. I had to pay for them out of my pocket and I was so upset that Jules asked me about it. So I blurted out more about myself than I would have under normal circumstances."

"So he picked you because he knew you'd do it for your kids."

Meg nodded.

"Maybe that makes my brother smarter than I was last night." Parker reached out a hand and clasped Meg's in his. "Now that we have all that straight, do you think we can get on to the important stuff?"

"Important stuff?" Meg murmured the words, her heart beating faster. She could barely believe Parker was one step away from her, standing in the light rain, gazing up at her with love in his eyes.

"Loving you," he said, and stepping up, took her in his arms. "Because I do love you."

"Oh, Parker," Meg said, holding him tight and snuggling against his chest, "I was so afraid it was only me."

He shook his head. "You are the woman of my dreams."

Meg raised her eyes and searched his face. "I've loved you since our first night together, since the moment in the mirror. But I was afraid that after what I'd done, you'd never accept my feelings."

He sketched the outline of her lips. "How can I be angry at either you or my brother when what he did brought us together?"

"I love you so much," she whispered, lifting her lips to his.

"Hey, if Meg's not going away, can we go to McDonald's?"

Gus's shouted question interrupted their kiss. Meg smiled and Parker said, "Let's get our family out of the rain."

Dear Reader,

Karen Ranney's love stories are so filled with passion and emotion, that once you open one of her Avon books I can't imagine you'll want to put it down. In next month's MY BELOVED, Karen spins an unforgettable love story between the convent-bred Juliana and Sebastian, a man haunted by the demons of his past. Wed when they were mere children, Sebastian refuses to share a bed with his wife. Can she break down the walls that keep them from surrendering to a passion neither can deny?

Readers of contemporary romance won't want to miss Patti Berg's delicious WIFE FOR A DAY. Samantha Jones needs money desperately, so when she meets millionaire Jack Remington she agrees to his wild proposal—pretend to be his fiancee for one night...no hanky-panky allowed. But when the night is over Samantha finds it nearly impossible to say goodbye...

THE MACKENZIES are one of Avon's most belöved series, and now Ana Leigh brings you another one of these wild-western men: JAKE. Jake Carrington is determined to win pert Beth MacKenzie any way he can...even luring her into marriage with a proposition she cannot refuse.

A dashing rogue, a young Duchess, and a Regency setting all add up to another fresh, exciting love story by Malia Martin, THE DUKE'S RETURN. Sara Whitney has no desire to marry again, especially not to rakish Trevor Phillips...but she has no choice but to surrender herself to him.

I know you're going to love each of these unforgettable Avon romances. And, until next month, I wish you happy reading!

Lucia Macro

Lucia Macro
Senior Editor

ael 0799

Compelling True Crime Thrillers
From Avon Books

FATAL PHOTOGRAPHS
by Jack R. Nerad
79770-4/ $6.99 US/ $8.99 Can

CLUB FED
**A TRUE STORY OF LIFE, LIES, AND CRIME
IN THE FEDERAL WITNESS PROTECTION PROGRAM**
by George E. Taylor Jr. with Clifford C. Linedecker
79569-8/ $6.99 US/ $8.99 Can

FATAL MATCH
INSIDE THE MIND OF KILLER MILLIONAIRE JOHN DU PONT
by Bill Ordine and Ralph Vigoda
79105-6/ $6.99 US/ $8.99 Can

SECRETS NEVER LIE
**THE DEATH OF SARA TOKARS-
A SOUTHERN TRAGEDY OF MONEY, MURDER,
AND INNOCENCE BETRAYED**
by Robin McDonald
77752-5/ $6.99 US/ $8.99 Can

THE GOODFELLA TAPES
by George Anastasia
79637-6/ $5.99 US/ $7.99 Can

SPEED KILLS
by Arthur Jay Harris
71932-0/ $5.99 US/ $7.99 Can